A DIFFERENT LIFE

NOW. ALWAYS. FOREVER.

A MARTINIERE MULTIVERSE NOVEL

JOYCE REYNOLDS-WARD

CHAPTER 1
AN UNREFUSEABLE OFFER
APRIL, 2030

Linda. Sorry I've been out of touch for so long. It's been— well, it's been one of those years. Too many different things happening to describe it all in email. It's been a while, it's my fault for dropping out of touch, and I'm sorry.

I also need to talk about your robotics tech application to the Martiniere Group's Los Angeles labs. It would be nice to take care of both catching up and—well—call me. As soon as you can.

This number is my direct, personal, and confidential contact. Call me with a good time to meet for lunch on Friday—I'll be in Corvallis then. Please.

Ruby Barkley Martiniere

Now *that* was one heck of an email for Linda Coates to open during lunch on a hectic Monday. A voice from the past. And that hint of an offer—well, that might just solve the emerging problem with brother-in-law Clyde Newsome about her lack of church attendance and her future after graduating from Oregon State.

Linda chewed on her lower lip as she reread it.

Ruby, of all people.

How long *had* it been since she last talked to Ruby?

A year since she'd *seen* Ruby in person. Specifically, that day when Justine Martiniere, now Ruby's sister-in-law, pulled Ruby out of Dr. Wareham's class, just before the campus had been evacuated. A knockout gas had been released nearby and Ruby was the target.

Linda and Ruby had talked several times a month on the phone since then, until—August?

Definitely not since college had started at the end of September. Ruby's sisters-in-law, Justine and Louisa, had shown up on campus. Linda expected to see Ruby in the senior year ag robotics classes.

Ruby had been excited about their senior year. Graduating in June. Her new life married to Gabriel Martiniere, and the opportunities it was bringing her.

But then Ruby wasn't in classes. Her old cell number no longer worked. Linda didn't know Louisa and Justine well enough to ask them about Ruby. Something had happened—but what?

Linda *did* know enough about powerful families like the Martinieres to keep her mouth shut and not rock the boat. One didn't question the richer-than-thou in this era of dictatorships and oligarchy. Especially since her brother-in-law was rising through the bureaucratic ranks of the Real Truther political party —no, Clyde and Sara were not who she wanted to think about now. The puzzle of Ruby was.

Ruby. After seven months of silence, then a contact out of the blue. Talking about a job application, no less.

The lack of contact was uncharacteristic for Ruby—she had been good at keeping in touch, even when she needed to be at the Double R Ranch with her sick grandmother.

Too many different things happening.

Well, that *would* sum up her friend's life over the past year, from earning a Martiniere Grant finalist position, to eloping with

Gabriel Martiniere himself, to—what?

Both Ruby and Gabriel had dropped out of sight in August.

Hmm. On a whim, Linda typed their names into her browser's search bar.

Nothing. No significant coverage about their activities since August—and since Gabriel was now heading up the Martiniere Group, the innovative agricultural technology company owned by the Martiniere family, there should be *something* in the media. Especially since both he and Ruby were supposedly working on significant climate change mitigation measures.

One way to find out. Linda punched in the number.

"Hello, Linda." Ruby yawned. "Sorry! It's evening here."

"Where are you?"

"Still in Paris—should have told you that in the email, I suppose."

"Paris? France?"

Another thing that didn't fit. Ruby's elderly grandparents lived on a ranch in Eastern Oregon. Ruby had agonized about going out on her own without being on the ranch to care for them; had been scheming means to build a rudimentary lab at the Double R so she could continue her microbiobot research while fulfilling family obligations. Funding that lab at the ranch had been one of Ruby's reasons for going after the Martiniere Grant—and led her into marrying Gabriel Martiniere.

"Uh-huh. I'm working with the Martiniere Group's European labs." Ruby sounded more awake now. "It's a long story. Can you meet for lunch on Friday? If you want to separate the employment interview portion from the catching up portion, I can schedule that before we go to lunch."

"You're in charge of scheduling the Group's interviews?" Had she missed something in the conversation?

This didn't make sense. Why would *Ruby* be involved in the Group's lab employment interviews? Yeah, she was Gabriel's wife, but marriage usually didn't confer that level of authority on a spouse. Even in a family-owned company, *especially* a multi-national conglomerate the size of the Martiniere Group.

"Yes. I'm doing the final lab hiring interviews in the US this week."

"Wow." So Ruby *was* working at that level. Good for her—but now Linda *really* wanted to know what was going on.

Ruby laughed. "That's one way to put it. When did we talk last?"

"Just before Justine's wedding in August."

Why doesn't Ruby remember that?

Silence. Then—"It *has* been a while. And there was so much I couldn't talk about then because of security. I want to tell you about it all, or at least as much as I can, but to do it properly calls for a long lunch. I'm really sorry about being out of touch for so long. Anyway. I have a proposal to discuss with you before we talk about that LA lab position. *Will* lunch on Friday work for you? And if our visit goes on long enough—we might end up doing dinner—that is, if you can stand being part of a Martiniere Grant function. I want to hear how you're doing. How things are going with Tony."

Linda snorted. "I can answer that one now. Tony and I broke up in November."

"Damn it, I'm sorry. He was good for you."

"I found out otherwise. And I'm good with everything happening over lunch. My last lab ends at eleven. Nothing else that day. Where shall we meet?"

"My last interview ends at eleven, in Old Betsy. Gabe's doing Martiniere Grant interviews there, along with me."

Linda laughed. Ruby still remembered their nickname for the main ag robotics hall, named after a properly obscure but well-off donor.

"Ag robotics offices?" she asked.

"Yes. I'm in the conference room while Gabe's in Green's office."

"Sounds like quite a production."

"It is, believe me." Ruby yawned again. "Sorry. Not that late, but it's been a busy day, what with physical therapy and all. Friday at eleven. Looking forward to seeing you."

"Looking forward to seeing you," Linda echoed.

She stared at the phone after Ruby hung up.

Physical therapy?

Just what on earth had Ruby been doing over the past seven months?

LINDA WAVED AT NAN, THE AGRICULTURAL ROBOTICS DEPARTMENT receptionist, as she headed toward the conference room. A blond man in a dark blue suit of a nicer quality than one might expect to see on someone in the reception area of agricultural college offices glanced up from his tablet as he sat on one of the reception area's couches.

His direct gaze made Linda's skin crawl—what was he doing here? Hopefully not bothering Nan.

"Ruby told me to expect you, Linda," Nan said as Linda blinked at the retina display to open the security gate that separated private offices from the outer area. "Her last interviewee just left."

"Then I'll go on back."

The man relaxed, and turned his attention back to his tablet.

Interesting.

Was he security of some sort? Gabriel Martiniere hadn't brought anyone like that when he interviewed Linda and Ruby for the Martiniere Grant last year. But Linda would be more than willing to bet this man was security. He looked and acted like the security her parents employed.

Curious.

Linda rounded the corner and halted. The lights in the hallway were dimmed—normal for a Friday. A couple stood silhouetted against the window at the end. The man had his arms around the woman, leaning his forehead against hers as they spoke, too soft for Linda to hear. He straightened up, sighed, and kissed her—and as she turned away from him, smiling, Linda *finally* recognized Ruby.

Long red hair pinned in a bun at the back of her neck, instead of the braid that Ruby had worn before. Elegant, flowing sleeveless sea-green tunic over softly-tailored, cream-colored wide-leg slacks, and flats instead of snap-button Western shirt, jeans, and cowboy boots. But the biggest change of all—Ruby was significantly thinner than she had been. Not that Ruby was a heavy woman before, but she was almost too damn thin now.

Ruby talked about physical therapy. Has she been sick?

Gabriel Martiniere—also much thinner than when Linda had met him last year—tangled his fingers with Ruby's and pulled her back for a second kiss, beaming.

This is private.

The creepy-crawlie sensation that she was *spying* made Linda ease around the corner and lean against the wall, careful to stay out of Nan's sight. She counted to five, then returned to the hallway. Ruby paused at the door to the conference room.

"Linda!" Her face lit up with a big smile.

"Ruby. It's good to see you." Linda fumbled for words, not knowing what else to say.

"Come on in. I need to get my stuff and—" Ruby grimaced and gestured at her knee. "I have to take care of this."

Linda followed Ruby into the conference room. Ruby sat, propped her left leg up on a chair, and pulled up her pant leg to reveal a brace on that knee.

"What's wrong?"

"Oh, I had a knee replacement that went bad," Ruby muttered, adjusting her brace. "It's kind of hard to fix a knee that's been shot to pieces with expanding bullets meant to wreck tissue. Fucking Philip Martiniere. If it were possible, I'd resurrect and kill him all over again."

"Wha-*what*?"

Killing? Ruby? No, that can't *be. Ruby isn't a killer.*

Is she?

How much had her friend changed since she married into the Martinieres?

Ruby sighed. "It's part of that long story." She slid the pant leg down and stood up, then gathered her tablet and papers, putting them into a Hermès handbag.

Hermès? Ruby never owned anything that expensive before—wait. She's married to a billionaire.

Another change, even more surprising. And for Ruby to be so casual about a Hermès bag—Linda's *mother* babied and prized the Hermès handbag she had received as a thirtieth anniversary present from Linda's father ten years ago, and the Coateses were comfortably rich.

This looked like Ruby's everyday handbag.

"Sounds like quite a tale," Linda said, reeling from all the changes she already saw in her friend. "So where are we going for lunch?"

"The Belvedere." Ruby named the most expensive restaurant in Corvallis.

"Ruby—" Linda calculated. Did she have enough in her account to pay for even a simple lunch at the Belvedere? Not really.

Ruby grabbed the cane leaning against the table. "On me. You bought lunch enough times when I was flat broke and living on ramen noodles. Time for me to start repaying you." She rolled her eyes. "Beyond what I owe you, it's a security issue. Our security staff like the Belvedere, and I'd just as soon not cause them a meltdown by going someplace they haven't already vetted. We won't be rushed through eating there. They'll let us stay the whole afternoon into dinner, if we want."

"If you say so," Linda said slowly.

Security. She *had* correctly identified the blond in the reception area.

So what the hell was going on?

Ruby paused. "A lot has changed, Linda. More than just marrying Gabe. But—as I said, that's a long story." She hobbled out of the room and down the hallway, Linda following in her wake.

The blond man rose as they entered the reception area. "Ready to leave, Ruby? Will Gabe also be going?"

"Gabe still has interviews," Ruby said. "If you could call a SUV up for us, that would be great." She gestured to Linda. "Linda, this is Lance Helgessen, the head of our personal security. Lance, this is my friend Linda Coates."

Helgessen nodded and bowed. "Pleased to meet you, Ms. Coates."

She bowed back. "The same, Mr. Helgessen."

"Wendy," Helgessen called. Another dark-blue-suited security person appeared, apparently seated out of sight behind Nan. "I'm escorting Ruby and Linda to the SUV. You're on primary now."

The woman nodded, took the tablet from Helgessen, and sat in his place.

Multiple security present. Very interesting.

Neither Linda nor Ruby talked as they took the elevator down to the main level. A black SUV idled in front of the building. Helgessen opened the back door, gave Linda a hand inside, steadied Ruby as she clambered in, then closed the door.

Ruby settled in her seat with a sigh. "There. I have to be careful about what I say in unsecured locations here in the US. We'll be able to talk freely at the Belvedere."

"Ruby, what the hell is going on? I didn't think the Martiniere Group was *this* secretive."

"It generally isn't," Ruby said slowly. "But Gabe and I were attacked in August, and damn near killed. While the people involved in *that* little endeavor are taken care of—mostly—the other piece is that I'm engaged in some top-secret research for the Group. Combine that with Gabe's position, my position, our money, our current physical condition, and—" she shrugged. "We're very vulnerable right now."

"I get it." Boy, did she ever. One of Linda's classmates in boarding school had come from similar circumstances, although Rafaela was also nobility. Of sorts. "But—you were nearly killed?" That would explain the lack of contact since then.

"We were attacked at the Double R." A grim tone tightened Ruby's voice. "Not unexpected—we had been warned, but thought we were safe enough riding horses within our security perimeter. Philip Martiniere—Gabe's biofather—and his Russian mafiya girlfriend jumped us. Still don't know how they got through the boundary sensors, because we had them cranked up to the highest levels. I got shot in the shoulder and the knee. Gabe in both arms and legs—we were wearing bulletproof safety vests and protective helmets, or it could have been worse. But he nearly bled out. I was told that he *did* die once, on the way to the hospital. Fortunately, the medics were able to resuscitate him. The aftereffects, however, have been hellish."

"My God, Ruby." Linda shook her head.

"Oh, it gets better. They had set a fire in the wheat field between us and the main ranch, and the wind was blowing it in our direction. I called for help, but it was touch and go. We suffered from smoke inhalation. Could have been much, much worse." Ruby bit her lip and stared toward the blacked-out window, away from Linda. "My memory is pretty fuzzy about details," she said finally, her voice wavering. "Including a lot of September into October."

Attacked. Nearly killed. *That* explained the lack of contact.

"Wow," Linda said. "I wondered what had happened when you didn't show up for classes, even though Justine and Louisa had. And—I didn't feel like it was my place to ask. I don't know them that well."

Ruby choked back a bitter laugh. "Coming back to Oregon State wasn't on the table, not at all. It took me until late September to heal enough for surgery. Gabe and I were in Los

Angeles, and—" she shook her head. "Surgery, physical therapy, and work. Half the time I felt like crap and didn't *want* to talk to anyone but Gabe, and the other half of the time I wasn't *allowed* to talk to anyone but Gabe. We've only resumed a public presence since February, in France, and we're still being cautious."

"I can understand that."

"Thank you. Others haven't been." Ruby leaned her head against the back of her seat. "It was corporate war. I hope to hell I never have to live through that experience again, though I probably will, because that's the nature of the beast now that I'm part of the Martiniere Group at the highest level. Gabe and I still need to keep a low profile for a while, because of—legalities."

Corporate war.

Linda had gone through a taste of organized corporate warfare during her last year in high school, right after such things became legal. But Dad had managed to keep the situation from getting *this* crazy, even after Grandma Jenni's murder.

She always wondered if there was more to her older sister Sara's sudden marriage to Clyde Newsome right after that. Why Dad was not objecting when Clyde fussed about Linda's post-college plans.

You know what the answer is. You just don't want to have to face it.

"That's a lot to have happen to you. Legalities?"

"More on that later. Tell me about Tony."

Linda shrugged. "What's to say? He got mad because I beat him out of the big biobot study project Dr. Green landed last fall. Then he "found Jesus"—" she inserted air quotes with her fingers. "—and started marching around like Mr. Macho Man. Hooked up with the church bros. Insisted that I needed to sign up for classes on feminine womanhood, because I clearly was in danger of hellfire due to being too independent."

Ruby's face twisted in a grimace. "Linda, I'm so sorry. Too damn easy for formerly nice guys to turn like that these days."

"You can say that again," Linda sighed. "Though, thinking

back, I see small indicators that suggest Tony was headed in that direction. He was far too friendly with my brother-in-law."

"Ew. Clyde. Tony and Clyde—yeah, like you said, after thinking about it, the hints are there." Ruby patted Linda's arm. "I'm still sorry to hear about Tony turning into—that."

"Thank you."

"I'm getting some exposure to the mindset myself. Not Gabe —some of the older Martiniere men are unhappy with his proposals. In the past, leadership in the Family and the Group has been passed on according to the old French Salic inheritance laws. Males only." She exhaled. "Part of my job is to bring strong women into the Group, and provide a buffer when Gabe gets criticized because he advances them."

"That sounds wonderful. I'm jealous."

"Gabe's committed to putting women in leadership positions. But getting there is part of the battle."

"It sounds like you have a pretty responsible role. Though weren't you already headed toward Group responsibilities once you two got married?"

"Oh yes. Gabe put me and his sisters on his advisory cabinet when he became the Martiniere—what they call the CEO of the Group, though it also extends to Family responsibilities. That had some effect on the hidebound elders." Ruby took a deep breath. "And then, at Christmas, Gabe announced that he was making my informal position as his research and development advisor a formal one. Did that ever cause an uproar."

The SUV stopped.

"I'll tell you more inside," Ruby said.

Another security staffer helped Ruby out of the SUV. She hobbled into the restaurant. The maître'd appeared and guided them to a private, windowless room that had a small table set for three, with two extra chairs. Ruby settled in one chair and pulled another one over to prop up her leg.

"Chardonnay all right?" she asked. "And a charcuterie board? We can nibble for a while, then decide if we want more."

"Works for me."

Ruby placed the order with their server. "Best that you sit to my right," she said. "Gabe will need room for his leg."

"So he's joining us?"

Ruby nodded. "I hope you don't mind. It'll be a while before he shows up. You and I should go ahead and eat. Gabe will order for himself. It's silly, but we just—" Her voice trailed away and she stared into the distance for a moment. Then she shivered and refocused. "Sorry. We get weird when we're separated for very long."

"I can imagine so, after the two of you nearly dying like that!"

Wrong. Linda *couldn't* imagine going through a comparable experience. Much less remaining as sane and steady as Ruby apparently was.

Ruby fumbled in her bag and brought out her tablet. "Anyway. Let's get the business over with."

"You said you had a position to discuss with me, besides the one I applied for." Linda's throat tightened. Was this one of those fabled moments when a friend would turn up with the perfect opening? Or a job leading to something big?

Network, always network, Dad always said, echoed by Mom. *Your connections are what get you places.*

And this was certainly one of the most unexpected connections. While Linda had met Ruby when they were competing against each other on their high school robotics teams, that acquaintance moved into a solid friendship once they encountered each other again during college. They were two bright women bonding protectively against the bias exhibited by their predominantly male counterparts. Their advisor, department head Dr. Asa Green, encouraged Linda and Ruby to work together.

All the same, if Linda could have picked anyone who was placed to give her an opening to a dream job—the last person would have been Ruby.

When she was in college, Ruby had worked two jobs to keep out of debt. And until Gabriel Martiniere came into Ruby's life, it had appeared that Ruby's path led straight back to the Eastern Oregon ranch she called home. In spite of her ambitious biobot plans. Her elderly grandparents needed her, and that need took priority over any career dreams Ruby had.

But now—

"Yes. I've told you a little bit about what I'm doing for the Martiniere Group. R & D heads report to me, and I report to Gabe. But there's more. That biobot I was working on last year? The foundation of my Martiniere Grant proposal? We're launching it. It's what I've been working on since last June, except for those months when I was recovering from the attack."

"That's—Ruby, that's fantastic. Especially since you had a five-year implementation timeline."

Ruby grinned. "I didn't account for marrying Gabe in those development calculations. It's amazing what can happen when the resources of a company like the Martiniere Group focus on a prototype."

"I bet."

Ruby leaned back in her chair, lacing her fingers together. "But. It's past time for me to hire an executive assistant. I've been putting it off. It's a touchy situation. I need someone close to me who knows ag robotics inside and out, because half the job requires someone who can work with me in the labs. Then, the more traditional EA piece is that my EA helps me with my role as Gabe's R&D advisor. She has to be someone to sort out the cranks and make sure that the people who need to talk to me in a timely manner get through. Someone who can look at lab reports and understand what they mean."

"You don't want to hire two people?"

"I'd much rather have one person and pay them the salary of two people. I really don't want to deal with more than one person who's going to be that close to me. Security reasons, and —honestly, after the last seven months, I want someone I can trust implicitly. Damn few people have the experience and ability to fit both roles." Her gaze fixed on Linda. "So. You fit. You're the first person I'm offering the position to."

"Ruby. Wow. Are you sure—don't you want someone with more—oh, I don't know, someone with more corporate experience?"

"Corporate experience isn't what I need. Someone who knows the biobots—someone who helped me brainstorm them—is."

"I'm flattered. So what's involved?"

"I need to have you sign a non-disclosure agreement before we talk further." Ruby pulled a stylus out of her bag and handed it to Linda.

"Not a problem." Linda signed the form on Ruby's tablet, checking off the box that sent a copy to her email.

"All right, then." Ruby opened an organizational chart. "This is how the labs are structured. The position will require travel. Part of what you'll be doing is to act as my eyes and ears. Gabe and I will try to be available as much as we can, but we can't be everywhere. Especially given our health. The following screens are the implementation schedule."

Linda flipped through them. "Tight deadlines."

"Necessary." Ruby's voice was cold and hard. She reached over, swiped that file away, opened up another. "This slide deck shows best and worst-case projections for grain production in marginal areas of Southwest Asia and North Africa, based on recent weather and drought modeling."

Linda gulped as she went through *these* screens. She looked up at Ruby.

Ruby nodded, her mouth set in a tight line. "The Group has access to the best projections, Linda. We don't have the luxury of a five-year implementation timeline. If we don't get those damn RubyBots in action within the next year—the potential exists for serious drought-related famine, worldwide. We may already be too late to stop it."

"Fuck," Linda whispered.

"And it spreads. Hell, every continent ends up being touched by this pattern. This region is just the first—but if we can turn it around there, then we can pull it off elsewhere. However. It's a big project, and I need someone trustworthy to help me manage it."

"You need someone with project management experience." Flattering, really, for Ruby to think that she could do this but—good Lord, Linda knew when she was going to be in over her head.

"I have those people. They'll report to you."

Ruby had an answer for everything, because she had already made plans and considered contingencies. *That* hadn't changed about her friend. Every instinct told Linda to run away, that this job was absolutely crazy and she would end up putting in huge, long hours, but….

On the other hand, this was *big*. A career-builder. And she would be working with Ruby. Her friend worked hard, but smart. No reason to think that would have changed, and since Ruby now had the money to back her ideas—

More than that. With the power of the Martiniere Group behind her, Linda could happily flip Clyde off, without putting Mom and Dad at risk.

Do it, she decided. *Once you know what you're getting paid.*

"All right. What are we talking for compensation? Where will I be based? You said there's travel—how does that work?"

"Base will be in Paris. France. Gabe's assistant Armand—another EA capable of multiple roles—will handle the visa technicalities, not that it will be a major issue, because the government there loves us right now."

"Wow." A good thing she kept her passport current. Part of an ongoing discipline since Grandma Jenni's death.

"You'll get a housing allowance, unless you want to stay at the Hôtel Martiniere—the family mansion in Paris, or in the chateau—The Residence—with me and Gabe. Then it becomes a furnishings allowance. Any residential option besides those two must be approved by security. Not to worry—both places are huge, and you'll have your privacy. Travel is by Martiniere corporate jet, our new hybrid solar fleet. Clothing allowance—we'll be doing enough entertaining that it's worthwhile, and there's peace of mind with security fabrics for everyday wear. Health coverage. Starting figure for this job is—"

Ruby named a six-figure amount that raised Linda's brows. "Wow."

"We're serious about attacking climate change solutions. I want someone I can trust by my side. And—this isn't a standard nine-to-five, forty hours a week position. Oh. This also includes security protection for your family, if they want it. Talk to Gabe about that."

"When would I start?"

"The minute you say yes. Dr. Green is already on board—you'll get full internship credit, graduate on time. Believe me, you'll learn a *lot* doing this job." Ruby smirked again. "I know I have. Had to transfer everything to the University of Paris, and I'll graduate this fall. If I can get the paperwork done in time. That's one area where you can help."

"How can I refuse such a great offer? Yes, Ruby, I'll accept the position."

Relief softened Ruby's expression. "I appreciate it, Linda. Thank you." She pulled up more files. "Speaking of paperwork, fill this stuff out. After you sign the last one, you're employed by the Martiniere Group. Salary starts today."

The wine and charcuterie arrived while Linda reviewed and signed documents. Ruby poured three glasses of wine, and sipped on hers.

At last, Linda signed the final document and set the stylus down. She picked up her wine glass and eyed Ruby. "All right, it's done. So just how super-secret *is* this position?"

Ruby laughed. "Oh, you can tell people you're my executive assistant. Just not the specifics of what you're working on." Her face tightened. "You will be assigned a security detail from now on—in fact, they'll take you home. Probably should call your parents as soon as possible and talk to them about the potential need for increased protection, because of your work."

"They have their own security, but I'll talk to Dad." Linda took a big sip off of her wine. "How quickly should I pack up?"

"Personal items and things you don't want others handling— this weekend. Movers will handle the rest on Monday. Gabe and I are staying at Mist Knoll with Justine and Donald. We'll pick you up on Monday, go to LA for a week, and you can start learning those labs. Then Paris."

"Hit the ground running, hmm?" Linda picked up a slab of faux pepperoni and wrapped it around an olive.

"Best way to learn this whole twisted setup, because otherwise it's just overwhelming." Ruby raised her glass. "To a productive and hopefully better future. Welcome to the Martiniere Group."

Linda arched a brow at that comment, but raised her own glass. "I hope this doesn't turn out to be a mistake. Some of those side comments you make worry me."

Ruby sighed. "I'm sorry, Linda. I'm hurting, tired, and today has been difficult until now. A firehose of information that is more than I can manage. One reason why I need an executive assistant. Someone I can trust who is capable of tracking details." She picked up her phone and frowned. "Gabe's running late. I hope everything's all right. That he just got sucked into discussing a good potential project with one of his finalist candidates. He hasn't triggered security alerts—yet." A tiny smile twitched her lips. "That's how we got together. Mutual research obsessions."

"How are your grandparents?"

"Doing well enough. Gabe's parents live on the ranch with Gramps and Granma now. The four of them are constantly scheming about convincing us to have kids." Ruby's lips tightened. "Gabe and I decided, no kids, when we got married, and we're still in that frame of mind." She shook her head. "Just too much to do. What about your family?"

"Oh, my sister is making up for both of us on the kid front. She's up to four now." Now it was Linda's turn to tighten her lips. "Her husband's gotten pretty high up in the Real Truthers."

"So it's a damn good thing you're getting out of the country, perhaps?" Ruby raised a brow.

Linda snorted. "Not quite that drastic. Yet. But yes, Clyde has his eye on higher office. Which means he feels free to stick his nose into my business at all times, so that I don't embarrass him."

"Lovely, just lovely." A chime sounded. Ruby looked at her phone and her face softened. "Gabe's on his way. Good."

"You keep track of each other's movements when you're not together?" Something she needed to know as Ruby's executive assistant.

"Yes. In detail, with fast-key alert systems. Just in case one or the other of us has to ride to the other's rescue." Ruby set the phone down with another sigh, that long stare coming into her eyes again. "Now that you're on board, I can tell you more. Gabe and I keep a low profile in the US for legal reasons. Part of that corporate war piece. Gabe ordered assassinations on people who were trying to kill us. I put my name on that decision as well. Then—I killed Philip Martiniere and Vera Braun when they attacked us in August. I was cleared from those acts in December. But the assassination orders? Still working through *those* legalities. If we were poor, we'd be in prison by now. One reason why we're based in France at the moment. The Martiniere claim to royalty is over four centuries extinct, but the Family holds some weight in certain circles there, especially given positive public opinion about Gabe. Philip Martiniere was not well-regarded."

"What, you're having to deal with legalities over assassination orders while those who were trying to kill you aren't?"

Doesn't money—especially the Martiniere billions—make a difference?

A weary smile from Ruby. "The people who tried to assassinate us are dead, Linda. That was Walter Braun, Frank Braun, Philip Martiniere and Vera Braun. Our assassins got Walter and Frank—but the Braun assassins killed several of our people in the process. Nearly blew up me, Gabe, and his parents at one point—literally, there was a bomb—thank God for the presence of security." She exhaled. "Which reminds me. You should check with your parents right away and let them know about your new position, ask about their security status. Gabe will want to know this afternoon, so we can get things set up."

"I'll do that."

Ruby pushed herself up, reaching for her cane. "I'm headed to the door to meet Gabe. Give you some privacy to have that talk. Needs to happen just that soon."

"Thanks."

LINDA CALLED HER FATHER AT HIS BANK OFFICE—EARLY ENOUGH that he wouldn't have gone home to enjoy a sunny spring Friday afternoon. "So I have a job now," she announced after they exchanged pleasantries.

"Oh?"

"Remember my friend Ruby Barkley? She just hired me to be her executive assistant."

"She's the one who married Gabriel Martiniere, right?"

"Right."

"But executive assistant—I thought you wanted to work in robotics."

"Ruby is in charge of the Martiniere Group R & D division. I'm going to be dealing with their labs, and will be part of a new project—details are confidential."

Her father whistled. "That's huge. I've been hearing rumors

about the Martiniere Group doing something big. Congratulations. And—well, where will you be working?"

"Paris. France. Europe. Some US work, but mostly Europe, Southwest Asia, and North Africa."

A long exhale. "I hate to see you go so far away, but—all things considered, I'm glad for you."

"It solves one big problem." And for that she was eternally grateful to Ruby. Even if this job turned out to be totally nuts—it got her out of the US and away from Clyde.

And if she didn't like it? Well, six months to a year as Ruby's assistant on *this* project would set her up for something new that wasn't based in the US.

"Does it ever. You're starting after graduation?"

"No. I've already started."

"That's fast. What about graduation?"

"Apparently, the job counts as an internship, and I'll be graduating on time."

Her father laughed. "Well, that's good news. When are you taking off?"

"Monday for certain. A week in Los Angeles, then to Paris. I'll be based there."

"Expensive city. Do you need funding to find housing?"

"Six-figure salary that started today, Dad. Housing allowance. Clothing allowance. Security detail. Which reminds me. Because of the nature of my job, you and Mom need heightened security. There's been—corporate wars going on. Do you need help with personal protection? The Martinieres will provide it."

"What on earth are you doing?"

"Can't tell you. But—" Linda exhaled. "I'm supposed to find out if you need help from the Group. I imagine that the concern is kidnapping, as leverage since I'm so close to Ruby and Gabe."

"You're on a first name basis with the head of the Martiniere Group, already." Her father's voice was a mix of rueful and pleased.

"I assume I am. I haven't talked to him yet. Just Ruby. And since I work for his wife, well…."

"Oh Linda. I had no idea this was even possible. Congratulations. Are you going to call your mother?"

"If I have time—Dad, can you tell her? I have to pack, and there's an event, and—" the door opened and Ruby and Gabe entered, arms around each other. "Security needs?"

"I think we're good. I'll review with my people, and get back to you."

"All right. I have to go." Linda hung up, and took a deep breath.

Now it begins.

CHAPTER 2

THE MARTINIERE HIMSELF
APRIL, 2030

LINDA ROSE. GABRIEL MARTINIERE—*GABE*—DETACHED HIMSELF from Ruby and bowed to her.

She returned it. Oh, he was still as handsome as ever, with the same roguish good looks that had put Linda off her stride during her Martiniere Grant finalist interview. However, this close, in brighter light, he looked much older than he had the year before. Lines scored his face. Sallow skin clung tightly over his cheekbones. A trace of sweat glimmered on his forehead.

Nearly died, did die once on the way to the hospital. Ruby's words came back to Linda.

August. Eight months ago.

Well, Gabe definitely looked as if he had gone through a harrowing experience. But was there something else wrong with him? Shouldn't he be better by now? Did Ruby need her for more than just being an executive assistant? Ruby and Gabe were living in exile—did she also need a friend close by?

If that's the case—then I'm definitely glad I took the job.

Ruby guided Gabe to a chair and pulled another one over. He tried to raise his right leg to put it on the chair. It quivered before he could lift it high enough, and he dropped it back to the floor with a painful hiss. Ruby clucked, then tugged at his pant leg. Gabe tried again, his face tight and paling. This time, Ruby picked up his leg and eased it on the chair, then straightened up, breathing hard.

I thought Ruby looked in rough shape, but damn. Gabe does not look good.

He pulled Ruby close and they rested their foreheads against each other, like they had in the hallway. Linda glanced away, once again feeling like an intruder. Then the *thonk* of Ruby resting her leg on the extra chair as she sat down reassured Linda that it was safe to look.

Gabe met her gaze steadily. "Ruby says you've accepted the position. I'm glad. I hoped *you* would take it."

"It's—one of those dream offers. I couldn't turn it down."

He exhaled. "I am *very* glad you're part of the team. Welcome aboard. Now. Before we get too relaxed. Does your family need security?"

"My parents are covered, and my sister's husband—" Linda hesitated.

"Clyde Newsome. I'm not worried about protecting *him*." A brief, contemptuous smirk tightened Gabe's lips, then faded. "Yes, you've been vetted in advance. Normal for the Group. You were easy because we just had to update from last year's checks for the Martiniere Grant."

"I passed, even in spite of Clyde?"

"I know about Newsome and his ambitions. You sure your sister's safe with the man? And that your parents aren't in danger?"

Linda spread her hands. "Sara made the choice to marry Clyde. They have four kids. He appears to be treating her right. And my parents—well, my father knows how to negotiate his way through difficult situations. He will let me know if they need more support."

Ruby and Gabe exchanged a glance that seemed to wordlessly convey information.

"I'll ask my sister Justine and her husband Donald to keep an eye on them, just in case," Gabe said. "If you hear of any problems, let me know, please—Donald and Justine have their ways of helping women in trouble, especially women with kids who are tied to powerful men." His mouth twisted again. "Foolish for Tine and Don to be activists like that here in the US, with Tine so close to having their baby. I wish she'd have it in France."

"Gabe, you can't always be the protective big brother," Ruby murmured. "Justine and Donald are adults. They can make their own choices. Donald also has access to Knowles and Atwood resources."

Gabe ran a hand through his hair. "I know. I worry. Things are getting too weird politically, even with Philip dead. I just—" he shrugged. "I'm concerned. I don't like seeing my close family exposed to potential problems."

"They have Donald's mother Barbie watching out for them, too."

"You're right. Barbie Atwood isn't anyone to trifle with. All the same, I'm going to worry, all right, Rubes?" His voice sharpened and Ruby frowned at him. He sighed. "Sorry. I'm just so damn frustrated. Last year was so excellent for Grant recruitment, between finding Jeff Swait in Arkansas, then having the four of you to choose between here. But this year? Nothing. I didn't pick any of the candidates. I called my sisters, canceled out of dinner. Sorry, Linda, but I'm exhausted. We can hang out here for a while, but dinner—"

"I'm sure that Justine doesn't mind," Ruby said.

"Neither does Louisa." Gabe pinched the bridge of his nose.

"Does not finding a candidate happen often?" Linda asked. No qualified candidates from Oregon State to be one of the Martiniere Grant finalists this year? That had to be unusual.

Well, she *had* overheard Dr. Green complaining, behind a slightly ajar door, about the quality of the junior class students, the ones who would normally be considered for the Martiniere Grant to fund their senior year projects. Had noticed it in the questions and comments asked in even the higher division classes.

Ruby wasn't the only ag robotics student who hadn't come back this year.

"It's not the usual situation." Gabe rubbed his face.

"Enrollment is down," Ruby said. "What do you think, Linda? You're good at extrapolating observations from data."

Linda pursed her lips, suddenly very aware of Gabe's focus on her. A test? "I would say that about a quarter of last year's juniors and sophomores didn't come back this fall, and while there have been students transferring in, there aren't as many as those who didn't come back. Numbers have been down in classes—the college needed to drop some sections of freshman and sophomore sequences. But I wouldn't know about numbers at that level. Just the juniors and seniors. Seminars are smaller. It's been good, on the one hand, for getting more direct experience. On the other—classes have been canceled."

"Any idea why?" Gabe leaned forward slightly.

"I wish I knew. I suspect finances to be one factor. Tuition jumped up again this year." Linda tapped her fingers on the chair arm. "But that doesn't explain everything. There's been a lot of downright stupid questions in upper-division classes from those transfer students. Some don't know their first-year basics. Huge holes in knowledge. The brightest students are among those who didn't return—and some of those are people with money."

"It matches what Justine and Louisa have been saying about students in their classes as well." Ruby chewed her lower lip. Once again, she and Gabe exchanged a glance that appeared to contain an entire conversation.

"Political unrest?" Gabe's voice went softer.

Ruby reached for a piece of faux pepperoni. "How many students got burned out in last summer's fires? Biggest conflagrations in five years. Last fall's bread riots. Growing homeless enclaves. The Feds tightening down on dissent. How many ended up in jail?"

"That last part is a big chunk of what's happening, Ruby."

Linda found herself lowering her voice even more. "Remember Ollie and Perry? Not in classes this year."

The two men had been the other Oregon State 2029 Martiniere Grant candidates.

Ruby nodded. "They didn't come back? Well, I could see Perry getting into political trouble—but Ollie? He's all about being part of the system."

"They both transferred to Canadian schools—at least that's what I heard."

Ruby's brows shot up. "*Both* of them?"

"Clyde said something about Ollie's family being unacceptable Real Truther Party members. And Perry's fiancée was detained for reproductive rights advocacy."

Gabe nodded. "I heard about Perrin's girlfriend Sally through Justine and Donald. They managed to get her to Canada —sounds like he followed her." He shook his head. "Canada's not going to be far enough away when things finally blow up." He furrowed his brows. "My executive assistant Armand Martiniere—your counterpart, now, Linda—is working on relocation for our most vulnerable researchers. I hope it won't disturb your packing if he drops in to talk to you tomorrow. He'll have your visa paperwork."

"Not at all." With the compensation she was getting? Availability was part of the job. And getting that visa paperwork correct was crucial, at least to prevent Clyde from pulling some sort of scheme to keep her in the US.

"At some point the relocation may need to include my sister Louisa and her companion Remy Trask." Gabe frowned. "They want to get married, and same-sex marriage will make them a target."

"Thunder County is a safer location for them as a couple, at least for now," Ruby said. "Remy is from an old County family. Combined with your parents' presence at the Double R, and Remy's role as our personal attorney, that means that no one currently in power in the County is going to mess with them."

"For now, anyway. Until the goons in power turn their attention to places like Thunder County—and don't kid yourself, the Martiniere presence there means it will get their attention, sooner rather than later. Even now, if Louisa and Remy are together outside of the County, then their relationship becomes problematic." Gabe ran a hand through his hair. "And since Louisa needs to be doing our promotional work—"

"It will work out, Gabe. Louisa and Remy aren't stupid, and if Remy sees trouble coming, she knows who to call for help."

"True," Gabe sighed. "I just worry."

All right. Linda was getting a sense of one dynamic shaping her job. Once someone came within Gabriel Martiniere's sphere of influence, he started worrying about their safety—which meant Ruby needed to worry, too. Did that extend to people outside of his immediate contact list?

Well, she would know more once she talked to Armand—Martiniere, so obviously a family member.

"Of course, you worry, Gabe." Ruby patted his arm. "You wouldn't be who you are if you didn't."

"Part of being the Martiniere."

"Absolutely. Change of subject. Linda, Armand will also help coordinate your shipping as well as your visa paperwork," Ruby said. "Part of your training is learning those routines so you can help Armand. Gabe and I are still moving our things to France. I didn't have the time needed to make it happen sooner rather than later. Part of what we're doing at the Double R on Sunday is packing up what's left there." She pushed herself up. "I'll be back. Gabe, did you want to eat anything more besides this platter?"

"I'm good with it, maybe another, smaller one. Tine and Donald are planning to feed all of us tonight. That includes you, if you'd like, Linda."

"I don't want to intrude on family," Linda said as Ruby left.

Gabe shrugged. "Given the position you're holding with

Ruby, you're going to be close enough to us to be Family anyway. Keep that in mind."

"It seems that the definition of *Family* is very loose." Oh, she heard that capital F in *Family* all right. Ruby had remarked on that emphasis during her early involvement with Gabe.

That brought a wide, genuine smile from him. "Oh yes. I suppose it's my version of hearkening back to our royal ancestors, unlike my biofather's approach, which was all about trying to turn himself into—oh God, I don't know what Philip wanted to be. Not what I am." The smile faded. "Seriously, Linda. As Ruby's executive assistant, you've probably started to figure out that this isn't exactly the typical position."

"I have."

"Good. Not surprising, given your background." He impatiently pushed back a lock of curly black hair that had fallen into his eyes. "Ruby's been resisting the necessity of getting an assistant, and she really needs one. I'm worried about her workload and health."

"*Both* of you look pretty skinny, compared to a year ago."

They worried about each other's health. That must be nice, to have someone who wasn't a parent who cared about them.

"Side effect of everything we've gone through during the past few months." Gabe rolled his eyes. "Ruby beats me around the head and shoulders when I start running myself into the ground, but she won't listen when I express the same concerns about her. I have a history of overwork and collapse. She—has gotten worse about it in the past few months. Even if I bring up her family history, with that cousin who died from working himself to death, she won't listen. She's getting frantic about the Group grain crop projections."

"I know. She showed them to me."

"*I* think they're skewed toward the dire side. But I have more experience with the Group and the data they produce than Ruby. Which is neither here nor there when it comes to her analysis, because she may be right after all."

"Ruby was pretty good in classroom and lab sims."

"Exactly. Which is why I'm being careful about reining her in. I may be too close to the Group to get the same conclusions from the data that she is. All the same—I will appreciate anything you can do to help her take it easy. *Anything.* Don't work yourself to death but please—take what burden you can reasonably assume from her. Even the little things." He pinched the bridge of his nose. "I know that worry about me drives her, as well as the stats she sees. I just—if she goes down, I go with her. Ruby is my heart and soul. And I wish she would think more about herself."

"I will do my best."

Again with that big, warm smile. "I appreciate it, Linda."

Ruby returned. "I know this puts some pressure on you, Linda, but do you think you could come to the Double R with us on Sunday, then to Los Angeles? That would allow you and Armand to work together on what needs to be shipped from the ranch. Justine and Louisa have offered to come over and help you pack tomorrow, if you'd like. I can be there too. Gives you a chance to interact with Gabe's sisters in a less formal setting."

"It will also get us back to Paris more quickly," Gabe added. "We can all catch our breath and take a few days *off* while Linda settles in." He glowered at Ruby. She turned her head away from his gaze, focusing on Linda.

"I'll take any help you can provide," Linda said. "Not that I have a lot of things anymore. The last year has been—edifying. I've been paring back on possessions."

Just in case I had to emulate Ollie and Perry in making a run for Canada.

But France would be even better.

"It's been that bad." Ruby's lips tightened.

"Yes."

"Then it's a damn good thing I could help you. Otherwise, we'd both be in the same situation. If it hadn't been for Gabe—"

"Let's not go there," Gabe interrupted. "Rubes. Really. This is supposed to be a celebration of Linda joining the Group. Let's focus on that, all right? We'll have lots of time to talk about the other stuff." He pinched the bridge of his nose again.

Ruby exhaled. "You're right." She raised her wineglass. "Welcome aboard, Linda. I am thrilled that you're working with us. And it sounds like it's a good thing for you as well."

"Oh, it is. And I'm looking forward to tomorrow."

"We'll bring wine and have Justine ration it out so we don't get *too* plastered *too* soon." Ruby grinned. "Since she can't drink right now, she's perfect for that job. She'll bring *good* coffee, too."

"Sounds like a good time." Linda nibbled on a slice of fake cheeze.

Oh, this was *so* going to be an interesting job.

And—even better—no matter how much power Clyde Newsome was able to accumulate with his ties to the Real Truther Party, there was no way on earth that he could touch her. Not as long as she worked for the Martinieres.

CHAPTER 3

A MEETING OF COUNTERPARTS

IT WAS A *VERY* GOOD THING THAT LINDA WAS USUALLY UP BY SIX, NO matter how noisy her apartment complex was the night before. One of the drawbacks of living in a complex catering to well-off students—if she had her preference, Linda would have chosen a residence where the other students were focused on working and studying. Not the bastion of the privileged.

But her father was worried about safety and security. He insisted on paying for what he thought was the safer place for her to live.

If only he knew.

Just one of the many things she couldn't quite explain to her parents about student life. Linda had *enjoyed* sending her notice to the otherwise non-responsive complex manager last night, along with payment for the rest of her lease—*just go ahead and pay them off and don't worry about it,* Gabe had said yesterday afternoon. *Don't get sucked into arguing deposit details. If the place is as bad as Ruby says, then while I hate giving them money, once they get a whiff that you're Martiniere-connected, they'll want to argue and drag it out in hopes of getting more out of us.*

So she had done just that. Everything was settled, and she had also sent compensation to her father to cover the deposits she probably wouldn't be getting back. No matter how clean she left the place.

Linda dressed, then checked email while gulping faux coffee and chewing on a stale muffin. Just in case she already was getting notices from her new work.

She was.

Greetings, Ms. Coates.

When we meet to process your visa paperwork and coordinate the shipping of your belongings, would it be an imposition to go through Group orientation tasks as well? I understand that Ruby, Justine, and Louisa will be present at your apartment to help you pack. There are some orientation tasks we need to perform where their presence would be helpful.

Regards,
Armand Martiniere

Not surprising, since Ruby and Gabe had already mentioned this possibility.

Dear Mr. Martiniere,
  No difficulties at all. I will be prepared.

Regards,
Linda Coates

Then Linda went to her bedroom to finish packing. Her door-comm buzzed. Linda checked the time. Eight. The Martinieres must be early birds as well.

At least she *hoped* this was Ruby, Justine, and Louisa, and not Clyde trying to talk her into doing some bizarre religious Saturday thing with Sara.

Laughter came from the speaker when she switched it on, multiple women's voices, none of them Sara—who wouldn't be laughing, anyway. Not when she was doing something with Clyde. It had been far too long since Clyde allowed Sara to be alone with Linda.

Linda relaxed. *Good.*

"So who's here?"

"Me," Ruby said. "And Justine, and Louisa, plus our security staff. Do you need packing materials? Boxes?"

Linda looked around the cramped living room. While she had saved some packing boxes, there wasn't space in the tiny one-bedroom apartment to store more than a few broken-down boxes. And tape plus packing material? None. She had already decided that one of today's tasks would have to be an expedition to get those items.

She sighed. "Heavens yes, Ruby. I hadn't started accumulating boxes for the post-graduation move yet, and I don't have anything else on hand."

"Then it's a good thing that Justine collected a batch of packing materials left over from her move to Mist Knoll. We'll bring them up. Should we have an escort who isn't carrying things?"

Ruby remembers the old days.

More than once, Ruby had arrived fuming for a study session with Linda because one of the other building residents had tried to get handsy with her in either elevator or stairwell. Not a good idea with a woman used to handling pushy horses, who regularly wore cowboy boots with pointy toes. Linda had overheard mutters about bruised shins from some of *those* jerks after a Ruby visit.

"Mmm, better have an escort up." Even though this *was* one of the nicer secured buildings near campus, some of the other residents were—well, it *was* Saturday morning and allegedly safe. All the same, Linda didn't trust that it would be all clear. Even on Saturday morning. Some of the men might be staggering home from Friday night parties.

No need to start off my tenure with the Martinieres by getting one of them accosted by a drunk!

"All right."

Linda buzzed them in. She thought about making coffee, then didn't. After all, Ruby *had* said that Justine was bringing good coffee, hadn't she?

More laughter at the door before Ruby's firm, decisive knock —*that* hadn't changed. Linda opened the door and the three women swarmed through, giggling, followed by three security staff carrying packing supplies.

Lance Helgessen saluted Linda. "Should we remain outside the door? After some of Ruby's stories, I'm concerned."

"Everyone's safe once they're in the apartment," Linda said. "I've just had incidents in the hallways."

Helgessen nodded sharply. "Understood. We'll be outside. Call us when someone needs to leave."

"We will." Ruby made a face, as if she had smelled something bad. "This place hasn't changed any in the past year," she added after Helgessen left. Today, she was dressed like Linda was accustomed to see Ruby wearing—long red hair in a braid, jeans with knee brace on top, and a snap-button Western shirt, this one a green and blue paisley print. And her pointy-toed boots. "Except that security scared the jerks off or something. Was hoping for one last chance at edifying the fools."

"I'm very glad this is my last weekend here. I think they're still drunk and in bed." Linda had stayed up late sorting her clothing, because her headphones weren't powerful enough to block out the cacophony of a springtime party night. Last night had been one of the wilder occasions.

"I bet."

Justine Martiniere-Atwood, huge in late-stage pregnancy,

carrying a brightly printed cloth bag, waddled toward the kitchen. "I brought an extra French press because I *have* to drink decaf, but I can make *real* coffee for the rest of you."

"Thank you." Linda followed Justine and pulled her *good* coffeemaker out of its storage cubicle. "I didn't think you would want to drink my faux instant coffee."

"Oh God, no. Not even faux decaf." Justine scowled. "The hardest thing about pregnancy has been giving up wine and coffee. So I want *good* decaf. Hopefully I'll be able to drink coffee again when nursing." She rubbed her belly. "Little girl, what your mama has given up for you needs to count for something. Keep the teen angst down to a dull roar, all right? I promise not to emulate your maternal grandfather." Then she started grinding coffee beans.

Linda joined Ruby and Louisa in the living room. They were assembling boxes.

"Welcome to the madhouse." Louisa grinned at Linda. "Call me Weeza if you'd like, in informal settings—that's my Family nickname. Once you get settled in Paris, we'll talk about Ruby's PR platform—you'll be working with me on that. Maybe the two of us working together can actually get the woman to do more than the bare minimum to promote her programs."

Ruby rolled her eyes. "Publicity is one of those obnoxious necessities."

"And you're pretty darn good at it, when you make up your mind to cooperate." Louisa turned to study the piles Linda had organized in the living room space. "So how much of this goes? If I were you, I wouldn't worry about the furniture."

"Disposing of furniture on short notice is a challenge," Linda said. "Especially some of this old stuff. I just hate to have someone haul it off to the dump. Some is useable, some was left behind when I moved in."

"The Group can handle donation and disposal." Ruby started assembling a box, reaching for tape to secure its bottom. "Same for food items. Import regulations. Whether you end up at The

Residence or the Hôtel Martiniere, there's a full kitchen on site. Smaller kitchens in the suites. Easy enough to get food delivery set up, both cooked meals and groceries."

"I have some preferred utensils and dishes."

"Bring them with us. Armand will know more about the shipping schedules, but anything you want to have on hand right away should come with you. There's room on the plane."

"Nice pans," Louisa said, studying Linda's collection of cooking utensils that were stacked, ready for packing, on the table.

Ruby eyed the collection of items that Linda had assembled. "You *have* been cutting back, or did you start packing last night? I remember you had some really pretty porcelains."

"*Had* is the operative word." Linda sighed and picked up a sheet of newsprint to start wrapping her dishes. "Tony broke some of those in November, while I was kicking him out of my life. I sent the rest to Sara."

By then, Linda had started to realize that she might need to be able to leave things behind on short notice. Since her pretty things were family heirlooms, it made sense to pass most of them to Sara. And, hopefully, it was unlikely that Clyde would forbid her sister to have them on display, using the excuse of vanity. Sara deserved *something* pretty in her life. Something not controlled by Clyde.

"Aw, shit. I always liked them." Ruby perked up. "The chateau comes with some very nice decorative items—paintings, knick-knacks, et cetera—that have been packed away. Feel free to browse through them for your suite."

"I'm not sure—"

"Eh, if it were me, I'd move into the Residence with Ruby and Gabe," Louisa said. "Right by the Bois de Boulogne in Passy, quiet, private—yeah, the Hôtel Martiniere is private, and in the city, but you'd just be there with Uncle Gerry and his family. And it's a lot bigger than the chateau. The Hôtel is a spooky place when it's not filled with the Family at Christmas." She shivered. "Sometimes I think the old pile is haunted. Several centuries worth of ghosts."

Ruby snorted. "Gabe's mom Angelica says the same thing, but I think it's PTSD after all those years dealing with that ass Philip, pestering her and Saul at Christmas."

"Um, I'm not sure," Linda said. *Did* she want to live in the same house as her boss? Always easily on call?

On the other hand—the commute would be nonexistent. And she could always change her mind once she was more familiar with Paris.

Justine entered the living room and eased herself down carefully in the rocking chair that had belonged to Linda's grandmother. "I also suggest you live in the Residence. The rooms are bigger and you won't have to deal with the entire Family descending on the place during Christmas—just us." Justine pulled out her phone. "Here's some pictures—not of Ruby and Gabe's quarters, but one of the other suites. The chateau's security, electronics, and HVAC are also more up-to-date than the Hôtel Martiniere."

Hmm. Now that was useful information—and a point in favor of staying in the Residence.

Linda took the phone and scrolled through the pictures.

The suite pictured *was* lovely, with high ceilings, a modern kitchen, and plenty of space. And the interior design—oh, Linda could see herself living in that pastel-toned, airy, elegant suite with graceful, curving lines, wood accents, and floral motifs. Great-grandma Coates's rocking chair would not be out of place. And oh, that gorgeous bedroom. She could stand to wake up there—and feel like an old-timey movie star.

"Art Nouveau?" she asked.

"Gabe prefers that to heavy, dark, gloomy surroundings," Ruby said. "As do I. The whole interior of the Residence is decorated in that style. Apparently it was the preference of a previous Martiniere in the late nineteenth century. They redid the interiors in Art Nouveau."

"The Hôtel Martiniere is Empire-themed," Justine said.

"Well, *that's* enough to convince me to at least *try* living in the chateau."

"Another Art Nouveau fan." Louisa smirked. "I knew it."

"Linda has excellent taste." Ruby got up. "And I'm getting coffee, because it must be ready and I need it this morning." She hobbled into the kitchen, followed by Linda and Louisa. "Cups in the same place, Linda? Or are they all in the living room with your other dishes?"

"Same place as always. I left four mugs in the kitchen for today."

Ruby pulled them out of the cabinet.

Louisa took one look at the illustrations on each mug and laughed. "Let's see. Cowboy chuckwagon barista. Cow in tropical print swim trunks. Two Thelwell bucking ponies. I detect a theme—and it's just like the collection that Ruby has!"

Ruby and Linda grinned at each other.

"Well, might be because funny mugs were the best gift I could afford to give Linda. And then it became a thing."

"Did it ever." Fond memories of Christmas spent in the apartment with her friend. Ruby stayed in Corvallis during the holidays because the trip home to the Double R was risky in winter, and she needed to work. Linda remained because—well—after Sara married Clyde, Christmas with her family was fraught.

The land mines at the Coates home in Roseburg might be figurative rather than literal, but they were definitely present. If not Sara and Clyde, then her parents' drinking—all and all, nearly as risky as Ruby driving I-84 by herself during the height of winter raider season, especially given the intensity of recent winter storms.

Besides, Linda was not about to let her best friend go through Christmas alone—or expect Ruby to put up with her family's weirdness. Especially since for Ruby *going somewhere* meant taking time away from her job working at the stable, which also provided her with a tiny studio apartment.

Ruby reached for one of the Thelwell mugs. "I'm gonna take this one and the French press out to Justine so she can at least have her decaf. Don't drink up all the regular coffee before I get back!"

She started to hobble off, wincing.

Linda suddenly remembered Gabe's words.

I will appreciate anything you can do to help her take it easy.

"Ruby. Let me do that for you."

Louisa groaned.

"Oh good God," Ruby grumbled, and turned to face Linda, her face set hard. "I'm sure Gabe has already had a talk with you about *me* overdoing. Listen. I have to move around. I'm foregoing formal physical therapy today, *because* I am getting my steps in by helping you pack, and I'll do my exercises later. So can we *please* not worry about it?"

"Sure." Linda flinched. That edge in Ruby's voice was new.

Ruby sighed. "Sorry if that sounds sharp. I just—I want to have a little bit of regular life once in a while. Tomorrow at the ranch is going to be tiring, long, and a bit of a challenge. Let's laugh, drink coffee, and then have some wine once we get your things straightened out, all right?" A pleading note came into her voice. "Have some fun?"

"Of course," Linda said softly.

Ruby's expression softened. "Thanks."

"Whew." Louisa exhaled once Ruby left. "That's mild, for Ruby," she whispered. "I thought Gabie was a bad patient, but Ruby?" She rolled her eyes. "The time to watch out for health problems is when Ruby lets you help her with physical things, and doesn't grouch about it. She has those days—you'll know them when you see them."

"Understood." Linda poured coffee into all three mugs. Louisa took the other Thelwell cup and drank half of it, reaching for the pot again.

Perfect excuse to take Ruby's cup to her.

Linda grabbed the cow mug as well as the cowboy barista one. She met Ruby in the doorway and handed her the cowboy barista.

"If I remember correctly, this mug was one of your favorites," she said. "Thought I'd better pour you a cup just in case Lou—*Weeza*—decided she needed to finish the pot."

"You'd better make more coffee, Weeza!" Ruby called.

"What do you think I'm doing? I know better, and after last night, I need plenty myself. You *would* drag me out of bed at this ungodly hour."

"Ungodly hour," Justine muttered. "As if. That's what you get for staying up all night videoing with your girlfriend, Weeza!"

Louisa joined them. "Like you or Ruby don't do the same when you're apart from Don or Gabie?"

"True," Justine conceded. She took a big gulp of her decaf before leaning forward. "All right. How much of this stuff is getting shipped and how much do you want to take with you, Linda? Why don't you stack fragile things that you want to have at your place right away by me? I'll wrap and pack them. At least I can do *something* useful."

LINDA LEARNED THE DETAILS ABOUT THE CONVOLUTED FAMILY relationships as they worked—while Louisa and Justine were Gabe's half-sisters, they were cousins to each other. Louisa and Gabe shared a mother—Angelica, married to Saul. Justine and Gabe shared a father—Philip.

Which led to a detailed discussion of their fathers, the twins Saul and Philip Martiniere.

Ruby rolled her eyes. "I will never, ever understand why on earth Saul and Angelica agreed to the IVF that led to Gabe. Not that I'm complaining—the man I love is incredible. But that choice, and then them letting Philip take Gabe for two years, right after Gabe was told at sixteen that Philip was his father? Everything that happened to Gabe in Philip's house? I can never, ever forget those atrocities after hearing about them. I just— *can't.*" She sighed. "It didn't end up solving the situation within the Family. Philip damn near killed Saul, and he would have done the same to me and Gabe if I hadn't beat him to it."

"But it did give us Gabie," Justine said. "Not having Gabie would have been a loss." She scowled. "My brother Joey, on the other hand—even though I shouldn't speak ill of the dead—"

"True," Ruby conceded.

The doorcomm buzzed. Linda hurried to answer it.

"Armand Martiniere here." The man's voice was slightly accented.

A second voice chimed in—Helgessen. "ID checked and cleared, Linda."

"Thanks." Linda buzzed him in.

"Who's here?" Louisa stuck her head out of the bedroom.

"Armand Martiniere."

"Cousin Armand!" Louisa beamed. "I'm so glad he's working with Gabie. He's an excellent organizer—good at keeping Gabie on track."

"Cousin?" Linda almost felt like she needed a genealogical chart after spending the morning talking about the assorted Martiniere relatives. Especially confusing since many of the male names were repeated in different branches of the Family.

Except for Gabriel. He appeared to be the only one, at least in several generations.

Louisa nodded. "Armand's father Yves is—let's see, gotta think about it for a minute—not the son of Donna and Louis, our grandparents—Justine, you know more about the Family genealogy than I do. Was Yves Louis's brother, or Charles's?"

"Great-uncle Bertrand is the connection!" Justine yelled from the bedroom. "Yves is the son of Grandfather Louis's brother Bertrand, so Yves is the brother of *that* family's Charles. Don't ask me what degree of cousin that makes him. First cousin once removed? Second cousin? After a while, it's easier to just call them all *cousin* and not worry about degrees of connection. After all, it's not like we're reinstating the monarchy or anything like that."

After Justine's statement, when Linda opened the door, she expected another brown-to-black-haired Martiniere, like Gabe, Louisa or Justine. But Armand Martiniere—with that piercing-gaze Martiniere aspect about him—had ash blond, almost light brown hair. Long, lean face; tanned, athletic appearance—*do all the Martinieres look like they should be on a sports team?*—and a wide smile matched with gray-blue eyes.

While he wore the same uniform of crew-neck shirt and chinos along with boat shoes that most of the male residents of the apartment complex sported, it looked natural on him, not an affectation that didn't fit quite right over burly, beer-bloated bellies. He carried a sleek aluminum attaché briefcase, a second bag slung over his shoulder.

"Linda Coates?" He bowed to her; his words faintly accented.

"Yes. And you must be Armand Martiniere." She bowed back, then gestured for him to enter.

"Cousin Armand!" Louisa rushed out of the bedroom. They embraced.

"You are looking lovely, Cousin Weeza," Armand said. "Your new love is working out?"

"Mmm, well, she's not so new anymore. We've been a couple almost as long as Don and Tine have been married."

"Eight months is still a new relationship," Armand pronounced, but a grin softened the ponderous tone of his voice.

Ruby and Justine joined them.

Armand bowed to Ruby. "A pleasure, as always, Ruby."

She laughed. "As if we hadn't already seen each other at breakfast, Armand!"

"But it is a new circumstance. And even though I also saw Justine at breakfast—" he broke off to hug her. "One never knows when the little one might decide to make an appearance."

"She still needs to be in there for another six weeks," Justine said. "Don't be giving her ideas, Armand!"

"She is your daughter so she will be gorgeous, and will do as she decides, no matter what any of us tell her, just like her mother." Armand checked the rows of boxes in the living room as Justine chuckled. "Good. Everything is labeled and sorted."

"We'll have the bedroom and bathroom finished shortly," Ruby said. "So if you want to go through orientation and visa requirements with Linda without the distraction of our presence —" she waved to the bedroom. "Weeza, Tine, let's go back to work."

Armand's expression went neutral as the three women filed back into the bedroom. "Thank you for accepting Ruby's offer, Linda. Gabe asked me to go through the company orientation with you. We do not need to do it all today, since I understand you are traveling with us, starting tomorrow?"

"Yes."

He looked around. "Mm—is there someplace where we can sit?"

"Let me clear off the table." Linda moved the detritus of leftover paper wrap, rolls of packing tape, and laundry markers to the side, then pulled up two chairs.

"First." Armand sat down, pulling out a tablet from his bag. He tapped on it and swung it over to her. "Your visa paperwork. Go ahead and fill it out."

When she was finished, she carefully pushed the tablet back to him. He scanned it quickly, then nodded, pushing *send*. Then he set the briefcase upright on the table.

"That should take care of *that* issue. Now. Let's set you up in our systems."

"Sounds good."

"This is your official traveling office. Access is through both fingerprint and facial recognition." He pointed to the space under the briefcase's handle. "Tap that twice with your right index finger, then follow the instructions."

Linda followed the directions. A faint warmth heated her fingertip. Then a silvery hologram shimmered over the briefcase.

"Look here—" a female voice droned as a pair of red dots appeared. "And say your full name."

Linda focused on the dots and said her name. The hologram faded.

"Very good," Armand said. "Now you may open the brief-case. You will need to go through that sequence each time, but it is keyed to you alone now."

Linda cocked a brow at him. "Am I in a thriller movie or something?"

Armand laughed. "No." His expression became solemn. "But as the executive assistants to the Martiniere and his wife, we are working with proprietary materials. Better secure than regretful."

"Understood." Linda rested the briefcase on its side, popped the latches, and opened it.

Half of the briefcase was padded and held a computer tablet with attached keyboard, plus a phone. Assorted small boxes, a letter-sized tablet with yellow paper, and a clear pouch holding various office supplies including scissors, stapler, staples, a *good* staple remover, file folders, labeler, tape, highlighters, pencils, and pens filled the other side.

She raised her brows. "You weren't kidding about this being a portable office."

"I took the liberty of assembling the supplies myself. All of these items have been useful to me when traveling with Gabe and Ruby."

"Thank you."

Armand picked up the phone. "This is your corporate phone. Highest security, already programmed to link into Martiniere networks. Satellite capacity if you need it, will serve as a hotspot when you are in the field. You can program it to access your personal number as well as your corporate number, without revealing your location."

"Sounds quite useful."

"Especially given your connections to Clyde Newsome. But we can talk about that in a little bit. Let's personalize the phone for you."

Armand walked her through the process.

"So does this mean I don't need to use my personal phone?"

"If you want to keep your own phone, then Serg Vygotsky needs to install appropriate anti-tracking security measures on it. You and I are too close to Ruby and Gabe to allow outside services to track our locations."

"I'm good with just this phone. What should I do with my personal phone?"

"Turn it off, ship it to where you will be staying."

"Then I'll do that, after I make sure I can access my contact list." She ran through the protocols that switched the Martiniere phone to her personal number, and back again. "Done." She sighed, half-smiling. "Next?" She looked up.

Armand eyed her appraisingly. "I see why Ruby speaks so highly of your skills."

Linda blushed.

Armand reached into the briefcase and pulled out the tablet. "Next, this, and then we can discuss shipping as well as your brother-in-law."

Linda made a face.

He laughed. "I understand that Clyde Newsome is not a pleasant subject?"

"Only if you're discussing shipping him off to the Pleistocene. Or some other appropriately prehistoric caveman location."

"I wish!" Armand laughed again, then rested the tablet on the keyboard support. "Same process as with the phone."

"Good." She went through the setup process with a few prompts from Armand. Then she checked the assorted apps—

many were tied to proprietary Martiniere products, including agricultural data tracking programs as well as robotics programs. "Powerful little tablet," she said finally.

"There is a secondary protective hard case exclusively for field work," Armand said. "We do not usually bring it into the US, but we can pick one up once you are in Paris." He exhaled. "This went much more quickly than I expected. Now let's get the other three in here for network link setups. Justine and Donald for financial management, Louisa for publicity and promotion, and Ruby for everything else." He rose. "I will be right back."

Linda poked at the tablet, continuing to explore the links. Louisa joined her first, activating her network links and taking Linda through them for access verification. Then Justine, and finally Ruby.

"All right." Ruby glanced at the clock. "I'd say it's time for a lunch break. We've just about finished packing, Linda. Then it's just routing boxes, and sitting back to chat—"

She scowled as her phone buzzed and pulled it out of a jean pocket. "What? Oh, damn. I suppose we can go in the bedroom if he insists on seeing Linda. But you come up with him, Lance." Ruby tightened her lips. "Linda, Clyde is here and raising a fit because security won't let him buzz you. Do you want to talk to him, or shall they send him away?"

Linda sighed. "I'd better talk to him." Clyde had probably heard about her new job, and wanted to harangue her about joining the Martiniere Group. Best for Sara's sake and for her parents that she indulge him one last time.

"Just a minute." Armand pulled out one of the small boxes. "Linda, we need to put your tracker on, because there is absolutely no way that I will risk you having any exposure to Newsome without this tool being activated." He popped out a gray bracelet that looked like a fitness tracker. "It has chameleon capabilities, so it is not easily noticed. New technology, developed in the last six months."

Linda snapped the bracelet on her wrist, noticing that it

immediately changed color to match her skin tone. "Wear this all the time?"

"Yes." Armand tapped the bracelet's top. "Martiniere Security product. It tracks your location and blocks everything but our trackers. Fingertip here."

She pressed the area he indicated.

"Now, if anyone tries to take it off besides you, it sends out an alarm. And you set the alarm off yourself by pressing *here* and *here*." He pointed to three sites on the side of the bracelet, which illuminated when Linda held her fingertip over it.

"We need to hurry things up," Ruby said. "He's making a big scene. We either have to send him away or let him talk to Linda, because he has reinforcements on the way." She handed the phone to Linda.

"Do not let him up here if we can avoid it," Armand said, voice tense. "Not with Ruby present. He has been agitating to have Ruby and Gabe arrested."

"Got it." Linda took the phone. "It's Linda." Clyde's raised voice chanting some sort of incoherent prayer in the background made it hard for her to hear Helgessen. "Go ahead and put him on," she said.

"Linda? What on earth are you doing with those godless Martinieres?" Clyde growled.

"Working for them, Clyde."

"You can't do that! They'll pervert you."

"On the contrary. They're paying me well, and I'll be doing the sort of work I trained to do."

"Hah! Your best destiny is to give up this college baloney and marry Tony."

Linda rolled her eyes. "Clyde. I am a legal adult. I have no interest in marrying Tony. I *do* have an interest in working for my friend Ruby, designing biobots to counter climate change."

"Unnatural woman!"

"That's me all right," she quipped.

"You belong under your father's headship until you marry.

And if he won't assert his headship, then as your brother-in-law—"

"As my brother-in-law, you have no authority over me. Period. Now. Stop making a scene and *leave*. Dad already knows that I've taken this job, and he approves."

Voices. Sounds of a scuffle.

"Hey! Hey!" Clyde yelled. "I'm still talking to her! Don't take the phone—"

Helgessen's voice responded. "Do we need to continue this further, Linda?"

"No. That's quite enough," Linda said. "Go ahead and escort him off the premises." She sighed. "I suppose he'll try again once you leave."

"He's not good enough to get past security," Helgessen said. "If you want your security stationed outside your door, rather than on the perimeter, we can do that."

"I think it's the best idea."

"Then I will implement that procedure." Helgessen hung up.

Linda exhaled. "I'm sorry," she said to everyone.

Ruby shrugged as Linda handed the phone back to her. "No better than some of my Barkley relatives. He's more powerful, however, and that can be problematic. Rumor has it that Philip's constituents in the Real Truthers have now become Clyde's adherents."

"That's not a rumor," Linda said. "Clyde was bragging about it at Christmas."

Armand raised his brows at her. "Can you tell me more?"

"Clyde is the Real Truther state party chair, and he's running for Governor. No primary opposition, so he's focused on the general election. The national party is cultivating him as a potential vice-presidential candidate. His brags include showing off comms from high-level Truther organizers whenever he can. It's legitimate."

"Are you sure you're safe staying here tonight?" Justine asked. "Another hour or so, and we can have everything ready to go. Might want to have the movers start work this afternoon, and you spend the night with us at Mist Knoll. Might be safer."

Linda considered the prospect of no longer needing to worry about Saturday nights. "You know, that sounds like a good idea. And since everything is settled with the manager—"

"Then I will make it happen," Armand said.

Linda heaved a relieved sigh. If she knew Armand better, she'd be willing to hug him in relief.

CHAPTER 4
DISCLOSURES AT THE DOUBLE R
APRIL, 2030

GABE'S FACE WAS TENSE AND TIGHT WHEN HE AND DONALD MET Linda, Ruby, Justine, and Armand in the foyer of the main house at Mist Knoll that afternoon, once Linda's apartment had been cleared of everything by the Group's movers. His expression softened after he took Ruby in his arms, kissed her, and nuzzled her neck briefly.

Justine and Donald awkwardly embraced. Justine leaned against Donald's side and rubbed her belly as he held her close.

"Why the glower, Gabie?" she asked.

"I am *very* glad that Linda's staying with us tonight," Gabe said. "Both from what Lance reported and from the ruckus that Newsome's been raising ever since then."

"How bad is it?" Linda steeled herself. She wouldn't feel safe until they were on the plane to Paris, at this rate.

Gabe rolled his eyes. "Nothing major that we can't deal with. Alleging undue influence on Linda by us, trying to tie it *somehow* to the assassination orders I issued last summer. Corporate Legal is dealing with the bureaucrats, but—we'll be staying Sunday night at the Double R, day trip to LA, leaving for Paris on Monday evening. Very brief business session in LA on Monday, introducing you to the lab principals, Linda. Just to be safe, in case Newsome gets some bright ideas about arresting all of us."

"I'm sorry."

"Don't be." He fixed her with a stern gaze.

"Gabie, don't scare her with that glare of yours," Justine said. "It's not Linda's fault."

"Not intending to." Gabe rubbed his face. "Just—learning new things every day. Newsome will grab at any means to harass me and Ruby right now due to our role in Philip's death. Linda, were you aware that your brother-in-law was the chair of Philip's presidential campaign's exploratory committee? I certainly wasn't, until today." His scowl deepened. "Too much about that damn Real Truther party is kept hidden. A lot of that internal structure doesn't come popping up in even the most detailed searches, because they aren't complying with disclosure regulations. If there's one thing the Truthers seem to be good at, it's maintaining a conspiracy in fact, rather than just being hype."

"I didn't know that Clyde was that deeply involved in Philip Martiniere's campaign," Linda said slowly. "I'm not certain my father knows, either. It's surprising. Normally, Clyde would be bragging all over the place about his role."

"Apparently the hush-hush part is tied to that religious cult they're part of," Gabe sighed. "Philip and Clyde were anointed by the elders—church leadership, I guess—as part of Philip's campaign organizing. Philip as primary, Clyde as secondary. I just learned that today. It was super-secret."

Linda and Armand exchanged glances. "*That's* why Clyde's making such a fuss," she said. "I get it now. Anointing by the elders is a *huge* thing in their church. I know that much. And leadership authority anointing is even more secretive. That would give him more power within church structures as well as any secular structures associated with the church."

Armand scowled. "Gabe, there are significant aspects of Philip's political organization that we are overlooking. Inner cadre information about the Electric Born religious cult tied into the Real Truthers political organization is one piece that we do not understand. It could end up causing us more than a few problems." He eyed Linda. "I would be interested in whatever you can remember of what Clyde has said, Linda. Even the tiniest piece of information can help. You may know more than you think."

"I'll try. Maybe I'll call my dad and see how things are going. I don't know how much he'll tell me, but it's worth the effort."

"First," Justine pronounced, "you need to get settled in. Come on, I'll show you around, Linda. Dinner is at eight."

"Sure." Linda reached for the handle of the roller bag she had brought inside—everything else that was traveling with her was in security's hands.

Armand took hold of the handle. "Go ahead." He gestured to Justine. "I know which suite is yours and can drop it off on the way to mine."

"A suite? I rate a *suite*?"

Ruby chuckled as Gabe swung her away, heading toward one of the hallways branching off of the foyer. "Not the biggest one, but yes. Welcome to the Martiniere life, Linda. Gabe and I believe that our support staff should be comfortable as well as decently paid. It's not entirely all bonbons and decadence, but— hard work has its rewards."

"I guess so," Linda murmured, as she turned to follow Justine down that same hallway.

***

Hard work has its rewards, indeed.

Linda flopped on the loveseat in her suite after a tour of Mist Knoll, taking it all in. Understated luxury, but luxury nonetheless.

A low wall separated the queen-sized bed from a large living space that contained a big screen, the comfortable loveseat she stretched out on, plus a desk and worktable. The bathroom held a large soaking tub as well as a standalone shower.

It *was* similar in some respects to the residential suites that she and Sara had stayed in when their father brought them along for work trips during their teen years.

But the decorative details—ah, that was the difference. A colorful mural representing the Mist Knoll vineyard, with Mt. Jefferson in the background, covered one wall. Instead of generic hotel pressboard furniture in neutral colors, the wooden furniture was solid wood with light veneers, fabrics in lavender and green.

Armand was in the neighboring suite, and Ruby and Gabe stayed in the largest one at the end of this wing. Mist Knoll's central area contained the kitchen, dining room, and great room. A swimming pool, workout room, library, and offices for Justine and Donald made up the basement. And while security screens shaded the windows of her suite, Linda could still look out at the vineyards and the Cascades to the east.

Overall, pleasant.

But enjoying her surroundings wasn't getting this call made. Much as she wanted to check out the swimming pool, she *had* promised to contact her father.

Linda checked the time. Six in the evening on a late April Saturday meant that her dad had finished his rounds of the golf course and was settling into his library at home. Her mother was cocooning in her room with the appropriate spring cocktail while streaming whatever series she was following at the moment. Clyde and Sara would be nowhere near the house, since Saturday evenings involved pre-church Bible studies.

A good time to talk to her dad.

She pressed his call link.

"Hey, darling." No slurring in her father's voice, so this hadn't been a heavy drinking day on the course. "How's the new job going?"

"Just fine, for what little I've done so far. Which has mostly been visa paperwork, orientation, and packing up my apartment, with Ruby's help."

"You didn't need to pay me back for the deposits."

"Eh, I wanted to. Getting onto my own feet and all that." Linda hesitated. "There is an issue. Clyde raised a fuss while we were packing today. Security wouldn't let him in the building. I hope he hasn't been bothering you and Mom."

Her father sighed. "He called me full of all sorts of fury because you're working for the Martinieres."

"What is his problem?" She hesitated. "By the way, this is a secure phone, at least on my end."

"Not so secure for me. Clyde's been in here recently." Another sigh. "You know about the assassination contracts put out on Frank and Walter Braun by Gabriel Martiniere?"

"Yes, Ruby told me about them. And that she had signed off as well."

"Clyde is concerned that your working for the Martinieres will negatively impact his political career because of those contracts." A third sigh. "Don't let his rhetoric stop you. Yes, he's trying to control you like he does Sara. I told him that where you worked was not his business, and that he should leave you alone."

"I just don't get why he thinks my working for Ruby will impact his politics. Neither Ruby nor Gabe are planning to run for office, and they're working through the legalities around those contracts."

"It's how that Electric Born cult he's part of works. They're focused on men being in power. Plus, the Martinieres are politically Catholic. Maybe not so much in the practice of their faith, but Gabriel Martiniere has been meeting with Church leadership in the past two months. Political connections."

Hmm. That should be interesting. Ruby wasn't practicing any faith when I knew her.

"I don't see how that would be an issue," she said, keeping her voice low. "I haven't seen any evidence of any sort of Church involvement around the Martinieres so far. No talk of going to services—Mass, I guess. No one's wearing crosses or talking religious like Clyde and Sara do all the time."

"Honey, Catholic and Jewish political conspiracy theories are something that Clyde and the Electric Born hook into hard." Yet another sigh from her father. "It's an old trope that goes back for years in American political history. There are reasons why we've only had two Catholic and no Jewish Presidents." A pause. "You understand? Remember our trips with your grandmother?"

"Got it, Dad."

He didn't respond, but remained silent.

He didn't *have* to say anything.

Her father had been proud of Grandma Jenni's political achievements. Grandma Jenni took Linda to her office in the State Legislature while Sara and their mother went to church camp with Grandmother Norma. Jenni Coates had been outspoken in her advocacy for equal rights and voting access.

But Grandma Jenni had died under mysterious and violent circumstances. Linda's skin crawled at the memory.

The calls to the house before Grandma Jenni's death, promising increasingly explicit details about how they would kill her. Emails. Texts. Increased security presence, including on-site patrols for the first time. How her father had turned secretive, and her mother suddenly started drinking more.

The, out of the blue, right after Grandma Jenni's death, Sara married Clyde, when they hadn't dated *at all*. If anything, Sara complained about Clyde before their engagement. When she slipped out of church camp to gossip with Linda some nights—Grandma Jenni's old place was next to the camp—she had grumbled about Clyde Newsome's overbearing attention to her.

He's a creep had been her most frequent objection.

And yet—Sara had married Clyde, right after Grandma Jenni's death.

That drama had ruptured Linda's family. For her father to refer to *trips with your grandmother* in connection with Presidential religious affiliations—oh, she was being warned that this was a dangerous Electric Born religious issue, *big time*. A previously arranged code.

"I understand, Dad," she repeated, after the silence between them grew too long to bear. "I'll call you when I'm settled in Paris."

"That sounds good." The relief in his voice was obvious.

They chatted further, before Linda hung up. She stared out the window, fretting.

But what could she do, besides stay safe?

Linda shook her head. She needed to do something after talking to her father.

Did she have enough time to swim before dinner? It was late, scheduled for eight. Justine *had* said informal dress code.

Yes. Enough time for a good swim and a soak in the hot tub after. Linda gathered up her swim gear and a change of clothing, then headed for the pool. She changed in one of the rooms provided next to the pool, lathering her hair with cheap conditioner and sliding a silicone cap over it—one swim team trick to keeping her hair nice while lap swimming.

As she went out to the pool, she spotted another swimmer, male, in goggles and swim cap as well as training suit, working through laps—possibly Armand, maybe Donald. Both men were fairer-skinned than Gabe.

Linda slipped into the pool, waiting until the other swimmer reached the wall before pushing off, so he was aware of her presence. Even with lane lines, she always wanted to check in with other swimmers when using a smaller pool like this.

Armand clung to the wall and pushed his goggles up on his swim cap as she ducked her goggles in the water before putting them on, to reduce fogging.

"Getting some swim time in?"

"I try to swim at least a mile several times a week."

He nodded. "Another reason to choose the Residence over the big house. While the big house—the Hôtel Martiniere—has a very nice workout room, it does not have a pool. Gabe and Ruby had a pool put in at the chateau—part of their ongoing physical therapy after Philip damn near killed them."

"That's good." A therapy pool. Probably warmer than most, possibly smaller, probably slow water, but— "Hot tub there as well?"

At least she would be able to keep up with her workouts and blow off some steam. Swimming had always been Linda's exercise of choice. The pool at her former apartment wasn't that good, and the other residents harassed her for being serious about swimming and not partying, so she had gone to the university pool complex for her workouts. But that wasn't always enough, and, if she needed a late-night swim, leaving the apartment complex was downright unsafe.

Having a *good* pool on the premises was a perk. And if there was a hot tub—even better.

"Sauna and hot tub." He grinned. "Might as well go for the full decadence, right? Though they have their therapeutic uses, which was why they got installed in the first place." He pulled his goggles back down. "Need to get more laps in."

Linda adjusted her goggles, then pushed off, swimming in an adjacent lane. Soon enough she was into the rhythm of swimming laps; first freestyle, then breast stroke, butterfly, and finally back stroke. The Mist Knoll pool was "fast water," or at least what her high school swim team used to call "fast water"— water that was the right depth and temperature to swim quickly, coupled with a pool-level perimeter overflow gutter that reduced wave action.

This pool was designed for serious swimmers, even down to the design of the lane lines. Not long enough to be a competition pool, but for its size—very nice for lap swimming.

Armand finished before Linda and sat on the side of the pool, waiting as she finished.

"You are a good swimmer," he said as she pushed up her goggles.

"High school swim team. Not good enough for college or Olympic competition, but—I still like it."

He shrugged. "You are very efficient. And fast."

She pulled herself out and sat on the wall. "I needed to blow off some steam, and this is good fast water."

"Surprised you had that much energy after all the packing."

"Oh, having plenty of help made it easy." Linda paused. "I called Dad. He—pretty much warned me off talking about Clyde with him. Electric Born issues. Any time he refers to my grandmother Jenni, in the context he did—it's enough to tell me that things are serious and that he won't talk."

Armand's mouth tightened. "I am sorry."

She sighed again. "I did learn a little bit that you can pass on to Gabe. Part of Clyde's issues have to do Gabe's contacts with Catholic political leadership, as well as the legal problems around the assassination contracts. And then Dad referenced my Grandma Jenni—which means he won't say anything more. Prearranged code."

"Oh? I know Jenni Coates died under suspicious circumstances."

"We don't know for certain, but rumors suggest that Grandma Jenni's death was orchestrated by a religious terrorist group. Never been proven."

"Tied to the Electric Born? Rumors suggest they have performed political assassinations."

Linda nodded, staring down at the pool water and not at Armand, almost wanting to dive back in and swim another intense set of laps. But that would be a mistake, tired as she now felt.

"Dad referenced visits to Grandma Jenni, and the fact that there have been only two Catholic presidents, and no Jewish ones. Grandma Jenni was investigating the Electric Born's potential involvement in political intimidation incidents during the 2024 election before her—death. The presidential references explicitly mean the Electric Born in the codes Dad devised after what happened to Grandma Jenni."

"I am sorry," Armand repeated.

"My sister married Clyde right after Grandma Jenni's death. Things went to shit in my family. At least I had robotics competitions and swim team."

"It is a better outlet than most. I swam competitively before college, too. Not fast enough for higher-level competition. But on a rough day, swimming helps work out a lot of the tensions."

The slap-slap of flip-flop sandals alerted them to the arrival of more people.

"I see we're not the only ones thinking about a dip before dinner," Ruby said dryly.

"Eh, we have just finished," Armand said. "Pool is all yours."

"Actually, after physical therapy, all I want is the hot tub," Gabe said. "Come join us."

They followed Ruby and Gabe to the spacious hot tub. Neither Gabe's baggy swim trunks nor Ruby's one-piece racerback suit hid the still-red gunshot and surgery scars on their bodies. The knobby bumps on their abdomens testified to healed broken ribs.

Damn. That they're functioning and sane—apparently—says one hell of a lot.

Unlike Armand and Linda, neither Ruby nor Gabe wore a swim cap or carried goggles. They steadied each other as they entered the hot tub, Armand and Linda hanging back until Ruby and Gabe were settled and snuggling close together.

"Ah," Gabe sighed, leaning his head back. "Here tonight. The Double R tomorrow. Los Angeles, then a long flight, and back home. I never thought I'd consider France to be *home*. But after everything—"

"You know, maybe we should talk about something else," Ruby said quietly. "We've been discussing politics all day, and it's time to take a break. What do you think of this pool, Linda?"

"It's very nice. A good fast pool."

"Donald and Justine spend a lot of time around it during working hours. Work for a while, jump in the pool and swim a few laps, then back to work. Justine's slowed down now that she's pregnant, but she still swims," Ruby said. "It'll be interesting to see how she handles their pool life with a child."

"Oh, they'll start teaching their daughter how to swim soon enough." Gabe chuckled. "I wouldn't be surprised if Justine has already planned a water birth. It certainly fits how she and Don operate."

Linda slid down lower in the water, rotating her shoulders. Swimming hadn't completely eliminated the tension in her upper back. There was a nice powerful jet nearby that would just about work to loosen it up—but it was awfully near Armand, closer than she wanted to be. All the same, the warm water was helping ease the tensions from that last discussion. And he wouldn't get handsy if that was his inclination, not with Gabe and Ruby right there.

Armand moved aside. "A good shoulder jet right here. Looks like you need it."

"Thank you." Linda heaved a relieved sigh and eased into the spot.

She was still closer to Armand than she had been. But he was scrupulously polite, keeping hands and feet to himself.

Such a relief. Linda closed her eyes and let herself completely relax.

Two more days. Then she would definitely be out of Clyde's reach. Hopefully things would be easier for her parents after that. Clyde's behavior made her suspect that he had plans to marry her off to some Electric Born functionary.

Tony? Possibly.

It was just about the only reason she could imagine for Clyde to be so concerned about her future.

Unless—

No. She was most explicitly *not* going to consider that possibility. Besides, Clyde was devoted to Sara. And the Electric Born weren't into polygamy.

Were they?

———

DESPITE THE LATE DINNER, THEY LEFT MIST KNOLL AND CORVALLIS early in the morning. Linda thought she knew what to expect at the ranch—she had visited Ruby several times during the summers. But the short flight and the landing at the ranch revealed a lot of changes.

An airstrip, for one. Previous trips had involved a drive that took most of the day. The flight from Corvallis to Lakeside—the Double R itself, as it turned out—was less than an hour.

Several hangars lined the east side of the landing strip. As Linda left the plane, blinking in the bright Eastern Oregon sun, she realized there were more ranch buildings than there had been when she last visited it. A *lot* more. Modular structures lined up behind the hangars.

The airstrip was a short distance from the ranch house. The buildings Linda recognized—the main house, three stories high, the horse barn with attached arena, the run-down ranch manager's house and the bunkhouse—were freshly painted and in good repair.

Well, that made sense. Ruby, Gabe and his sisters had taken refuge on the ranch for several months after Philip Martiniere attacked his brother Saul, the man Gabe acknowledged as father instead of his biofather Philip. And Ruby *had* said her in-laws now lived at the ranch, along with her grandparents.

An older couple who weren't Ruby's grandparents waited by one of the hangars. A man in a wheelchair, the woman standing tall and elegant behind it.

That must be Saul and Angelica Martiniere.

"Mama. Papa." Gabe confirmed Linda's assumption as he hobbled over to them, kissing his mother's cheeks, then bending to hug his father. Ruby followed his lead. Then Gabe turned, gesturing to Linda and Armand. "Linda, my parents, Saul and Angelica Martiniere. Mama, Papa, this is Ruby's new executive assistant, Linda Coates."

Linda bowed to them. Saul nodded and Angelica bowed.

"Pleased to meet you," Angelica said.

"Welcome to the Martiniere Group," Saul said. "You said you were spending the night, Gabie?"

"Some difficulties with politicians," Gabe said smoothly. "It's best that Ruby and I get out of the country fairly soon. We'll introduce Linda to the LA lab heads before we go."

Saul sighed. "I saw your report to the Board, son. Sooner or later, we'll get it all straightened out."

Angelica raised her brows at Ruby. The two women stepped aside, and Linda followed, figuring that she should probably keep track of something that involved Ruby unless otherwise informed.

"Your grandmother isn't doing well," Angelica said softly to Ruby. She glanced at Linda. "You know what's going on, Linda?"

She nodded. "I've visited the ranch before."

"Linda is an old college friend. She knows that Granma has end-stage cancer." Ruby frowned. "How bad is it, Angelica?"

"Let's just say that it's a good thing you and Gabie are spending the night."

Ruby closed her eyes tightly, and shuddered. "How long do you think she has?"

"Weeks, at best. Ruth has been looking forward to this visit."

Ruby blinked again, then shook her head. "I wish—" she sighed. "Well. Fuck. This can't be changed. And Gramps?"

"Saul and I are taking turns sitting with your grandmother so that he gets some rest. We're here for him."

Another tight squeeze of Ruby's eyelids. Then a hard swallow. "I am so fucking glad that you and Saul are here to help, Angelica. Thank you."

Angelica laid a hand on Ruby's arm. "It's what family does for each other, Ruby. Especially within the Family."

"I guess I'd better get up there, then. They'll have heard the plane coming in." Ruby and Angelica headed toward the house, Linda following behind them.

As they passed Gabe, Saul, and Armand, Linda overheard Saul. "Gabriel. We are safe here, at least for now."

"I don't trust the Truthers," Gabe said. "I devoutly wish that once Ruby's grandmother passes, you two and her grandfather join us in France."

"I didn't run from your biofather when he was alive, Gabriel. I refuse to let his surviving lackeys drive me from the United States, before I am ready to leave."

"You're permanently in a wheelchair as a result," Gabe sighed. "And I'm not in much better shape."

Then she was past the men and couldn't hear anything more.

Ruby slowed as they climbed the slight rise from the airstrip to the main house. "Damn this knee," she grumbled, leaning hard on her cane.

"The surgery didn't work?" Angelica asked.

"I need a second replacement. This time we're doing it in France, not Los Angeles. Though Gabe is talking to someone in Germany who he thinks might be a better surgeon."

"Have you scheduled it yet?"

"Can't. Spring planting, and both Gabe and I are heavily involved in new product releases. Probably this summer."

"But you have Linda's assistance now."

"It will take all of us to get the new bots launched and shipped on time. Which is another reason to get back to France rather than linger in Los Angeles. This last cold snap has slowed farmers, especially in Ukraine, but right now it's a situation where we need to be on board and ready to roll."

"It was much easier for us when Saul was the Martiniere," Angelica said. "Neither of us were as involved in research and launch of new products as you and Gabie are."

"And the climate situation wasn't as dire then as it is now." Ruby stopped at the steps leading to the back door.

"Should we go around to the front and use the ramp?" Angelica asked.

Ruby shook her head. She inhaled deeply, then exhaled. "All right. I can do this." She climbed the stairs, grasping the railing tightly and using it to pull herself along, pausing at each step.

Angelica fell back, walking with Linda.

Ruby's grandfather, Ron Ryder, waited inside the kitchen. *This* room was much as Linda remembered it being, just with the addition of a fresh coat of pale yellow paint and light-green trim. New white vinyl sheet tile replaced the old stained floor covering. But otherwise, it was much the same, with the old green Formica and chrome kitchen table underneath one window.

Ron hugged Ruby. "I'm glad you made it."

She straightened up. "I am too, Gramps."

"She's very frail. I think she's been holding on so she can see you one last time."

"That bad."

Ron nodded. He rested one hand on Ruby's shoulder as she buried her head in one hand and sniffled. Then she raised her head, dashing away the tears running down her cheeks, gulping for several breaths. She hobbled over to the sink and splashed water on her face. After wiping it dry, she clenched her cane harder.

"All right. I'm ready."

"Do you want me to stay here?" Linda asked.

Ruby's lips tightened. "No. Please come with me. Granma will want to say hello, too, Linda. And I—I—" she choked. "Angelica. Both of you. Please." She raised her chin high, and slowly, carefully, hobbled to the swinging door that separated the kitchen from the hallway that led to the first-floor bedroom, offices, and living room.

Ruth Ryder lay in a queen-sized hospital bed, gazing out the window. Her face was blank, expressionless. A pale blue turban covered her head, matching her nightgown. She turned clouded blue eyes toward them, and a joyful smile transformed her entire face, bringing life into it.

Linda bit her lip at how pale and fragile Ruth appeared, a contrast from the still active although thin woman she had first known. Then, Ruth's skin had been still tanned, still firm. Now it was lined and soft, pale with age spots, skin sagging as a testimony to the amount of weight she had lost.

"Ruby. I'm so happy to see you," Ruth rasped. She reached up to stroke Ruby's cheek with claw-like fingers as Ruby bent over to kiss Ruth's forehead.

"I'm happy to see you too, Granma," Ruby said. "Do you remember my friend Linda Coates? She's my new executive assistant."

"Absolutely." Ruth extended her trembling hand and Linda squeezed it gently before easing it back down. "I'm very happy to see that you're working with Ruby."

"I'm glad to be doing it," Linda said awkwardly.

Ruby gently stroked her grandmother's cheek. "Granma. I'm afraid we just have today and tonight. Gabe and I have to leave the country again."

"So Angelica tells me." Ruth looked beyond them, smiling at Angelica. "I'm just glad to see you once again. But you're still so skinny." Her voice sharpened. "Hasn't that husband of yours been feeding you? You're almost too thin to have babies."

"Oh Granma." Ruby shook her head, but a rueful smile twitched her lips. "We're still going through physical therapy. I need another knee surgery. And no babies are in the works, I'm sorry to say."

"Well, sit down and tell me what you've been doing."

Angelica retrieved a chair and slid it over to Ruby. Then she gently took Linda's arm. "Ruby, do you need to supervise what packing needs to be done, or can Gabriel do it?"

Ruby looked away from Ruth. "No. That—should be fine.

Linda, Armand has the packing list. You'll—know what to do. Please send Gabe in when he gets to the house."

"We will." Angelica guided Linda out. She exhaled heavily once she closed the door behind them. "Just so you know," she said softly as they walked down the hallway. "I don't expect Ruth to live for another week. I—was at my mother's deathbed. I know this scenario. I think Ruth has been hanging on so she can see Ruby one last time. You—and Gabriel—are going to be the ones with her when it happens, and since you're one of her friends—"

"Thanks." Linda swallowed hard. "I'll be there for her.

More and more she was beginning to understand just why Ruby had wanted to hire *her*, rather than someone else.

Ruby needed a friend who was close to her, as much as she did an assistant who knew their way around ag robotics.

RUBY AND GABE SPENT MOST OF THE DAY CLOSETED WITH RUTH AND Ron. Linda and Armand worked on the third floor, which had apparently been Ruby and Gabe's combined bedroom and office area. Most of what they sorted through were memorabilia from Ruby's rodeo days, and a few paper records from the short period they had spent at the ranch before Philip's attack.

Ruby came upstairs after lunch. Linda and Armand were sorting through storage in the attic space connected to the second bedroom, which had been Ruby and Gabe's office. At this point they were into Ryder family records and collectables, including photo albums.

"How much of your personal family stuff do you want shipped?" Linda asked.

"All of it." Ruby's voice was flat. "Old family heirlooms. Everything of that sort. Once—eventually Angelica and Saul will move into this house, and it'll be a research center, with housing for interns. I don't know how soon I'll be back, if ever, once

Gramps is gone. I have Justine working on shipping Gabe's Midnight horse and my Sunshine to France. She'll handle that, she has the connections. At least they'll be safe. Oh God, Linda. I wish Gramps would commit to coming to France for his last years—" She choked.

Linda hugged Ruby. She leaned her head on Linda's chest and cried, while Linda murmured soothing words. Armand slipped out of the room.

"Oh fuck. Fuck," Ruby finally groaned. "She's going to die soon. I know it. I won't be here—can't be, it's not safe. She said she was proud of me. That I was soaring higher than she had ever expected from me, but that I needed to leave and not look behind." Ruby dashed tears away with the back of her hand.

"Things will get better. Eventually."

"She wants us to have kids. But Gabe and I decided in January that it wouldn't happen. He's had a vasectomy. Me a tubal ligation. We aren't going to leave hostages to fate—Justine and Donald's kids can step up to leadership. Maybe even their daughter. Though Gabe's worried because of whatever toxic legacy he and Justine may have inherited from Philip." Ruby sniffled. "But *God*, Linda. I can't tell Granma—or Gramps—that. Going to be hard enough to tell Saul and Angelica. Neither one of us—not with Philip's psychopathy, not with my father's insanity—want to take that risk with a child. Doubly risky. At least Donald's family is reasonably sane. Justine and Don's children have a chance."

Linda's heart ached for her friend. Oh, she understood the reasons for making that choice not to have children. Especially these days.

Ruby's braver than I am.

Not that she had that sterilization option open to her as a single woman, at least here in the US.

"Worse yet, I don't know if I can return to the ranch anymore," Ruby whispered. "I just remember what it was like— after—" More gulping, more tears. "I had a panic attack when

Gabe and I tried to look at Homestead field in November, before the snow. It hit right where Philip Martiniere and Vera Braun jumped us. I just kept seeing Gabe all bloody, dying, and Philip aiming a rifle at me while I rode him down. Gabe—it doesn't seem to bother him, but being here just brings the horror back to me."

"I'm sorry."

"I loved this place. I never thought I would leave it. But seeing the man I love almost dying here, on one of my favorite stretches to ride horses—aw *fuck*, Linda. That's ruined now. And France isn't home yet. I don't *have* a home. The Residence is lovely, but it's not mine. It's Gabe's. It's beautiful, but it's not home. That fucker Philip Martiniere took my childhood home from me, just as much as if he bankrupted Gramps and kicked me off the place."

"I know how you feel," Linda murmured. "Clyde Newsome's done that to me. Oh, Mom and Dad still live in the house, but going there? The place is bugged. Dad's security does weekly sweeps, but they always find new listening devices. I'm followed around Roseburg, and it's the dangerous ones that are doing it, the militia guys affiliated with the churches. I'm sure Clyde had people watching and listening at my apartment."

Ruby straightened up, brushing tears away, face tightening. "Linda, that fucker wants *you*. Has to be the case."

"But why? He has Sara. I think he loves her, and he sure seems to be committed to that damn Electric Born theology. They *can't* screw around."

"Like hell." Ruby laughed bitterly. "Their sainted Philip Martiniere? He was screwing Vera Braun. And she was just one of many lovers he had. What he did to Gabe—" she choked. "It's all a fucking lie, Linda. I wish I had known that you were in Clyde Newsome's sights earlier. I'd have gotten you out as soon as I realized what a sham the Electric Born are."

"Oh God. Sara—" *Should* she warn her sister?

"They brainwash their wives to accept their infidelity, even to the point of taking second and third wives. What Gabe's told me about Philip's wife Renate and how Philip manipulated her would make your hair stand on end." Ruby shook her head, and shuddered.

"How on earth do they get away with it?"

"Lies. Lots and lots of lies. God. I just—oh, I don't want to think about this anymore. I spend too much time thinking about it already." Ruby exhaled, looking around. "You and Armand have made a lot of progress. That's good. Thank you." Another exhale. "I have to get back to Granma. Just needed to take a break."

"I'm here, whenever you need to talk."

"Thank you. And thank you for taking the job. I hope you can stand our drama."

"Well, you now have a damn good idea of the drama I'm living with."

Ruby smiled weakly. "Damn, woman, I've missed having you around. At least now we can help each other." She looked around again, and sighed. Then she straightened her shoulders and left.

Linda waited a few minutes, then decided to go downstairs and get some water, almost running into Armand as she entered the office area.

"Sorry—" She rocked back and lost her balance.

"Sorry—" He steadied Linda, dropping his hands quickly once she was upright. "Is Ruby all right—at least as much as she can be, given the circumstances?"

"She's aware her grandmother will most likely die soon." Linda shook her head. "She doesn't think of the ranch as her home anymore. Armand, she *loved* the Double R. She always talked about coming back once she had made a name for herself."

"She and Gabriel have gone through a lot and this is where the worst of it happened. Trauma is—" Armand fumbled for words. "Neither of them are over it. Not really. And both Gabe and Ruby drive themselves so hard."

Linda bit her lip and nodded. "It's up to us to slow them down. Keep them from flaming out far too early."

Now it was his turn to tighten his lips and nod. "I am glad you see this as well."

"She and I were best friends. I can't miss the changes in her." Linda swallowed hard. Time to change the subject, ask the question now nagging at her. "You're the expert on the Electric Born, right?"

He nodded again.

"Ruby thinks that Clyde wants me. That the Electric Born men take more than one wife. Is she right?"

"It is not legal, yet—but yes."

"*God.*" Linda wrapped her arms around herself to stifle yet another shudder. "That explains too damn much."

"And that is why you are under the highest security protection until we are clear of this damned country," Armand said. The vehemence in his voice startled Linda. "Women like you, Linda Coates, should be prized and cherished—not just for your intellect and courage, but for who you are. Not relegated to the status of a secondary wife or concubine. Not paraded around as status symbols. Those Electric Born *couchons*, those *connards*, those small-dicked, tiny-brained abominations terrified because they can't match the integrity of the everyday woman on the street—" He scowled, his glower reminiscent of Gabe's. "I apologize."

"Don't," she said. "And thank you."

"Armand?" Gabe called from downstairs. "Need you to check on something."

"On my way." He smiled faintly at Linda. "As you can tell, I have very strong feelings about men like your brother-in-law."

"I'm glad you do."

"I would not be doing this job for Gabriel otherwise." He bowed formally to her, then turned and left.

Linda raised her brows.

Yes, this position with the Martinieres was going to be very interesting, indeed.

And she definitely had a lot to think about, after everything she had just learned.

CHAPTER 5
A COMFORTABLE EXILE
APRIL, 2030

THE RESIDENCE.

Pictures didn't do justice to the reality of living in an Art Nouveau palace in France. Jet-lagged as she was, her new surroundings didn't make much of an impression on Linda until she woke up in her suite the first morning in France. She looked around and blinked, momentarily taken aback.

Gorgeous. Like something out of a movie. Green and gold-shaded drapes. Light blue walls. The bedroom alone felt as big as her entire one-bedroom apartment in Corvallis, and it held not just a big dresser and armoire, both in a light-shaded wood Linda couldn't identify, but also a matching vanity with a wood-framed round mirror.

All soothing. All elegant.

Boxes to be unpacked all around her, *true*, but she was *here*. Working for Ruby. In this gorgeous setting.

I need fancier nightgowns and robes. Something slinky, that fits the setting.

Why not treat herself?

Linda slipped out of bed and went into her suite's full kitchen to make coffee. *Real* coffee, not faux. The kitchen appliances were small and modern, but the cabinets and moldings were, if not the original, excellent replications. The kitchen opened into a small living area, and past that were double doors that shut off the office from the living room.

Once Linda had made coffee and filled one of her Thelwell mugs, she went into her office.

Airy. Light. Another set of glass doors led to outside, blinds enclosed within the glass that were controlled by sliders—actually, the entire room was surrounded by windows with blinds set in them.

Wouldn't that be a security problem? Linda looked closer. The glass shimmered. She had to squint to see the faint sparkle of security nanosensors in the sunlight. Not so bright that they would interfere with looking outside, but strong enough to raise protective screens and block audio and visual surveillance. And those blinds—Linda tentatively moved one of the two sliders.

"Outside left door disarmed," an electronic voice droned.

Ah. Security shutters. Something she had read about but not seen before. That slider raised the blinds. Linda lowered it.

"Armed."

Linda repeated the process with the smaller slider. The voice reacted in the same manner. This slider opened the blinds. By checking the edges, Linda spotted how they fit together. Nanolocking mechanisms. Top-of-the-line security—then again, what would she expect to find in the house of someone like Gabriel Martiniere?

All right, then. A secure office. With as much natural light as she might want. Now she needed to figure out all of the controls —first of all, determine if she would need to deal with that annoying automated voice every time she fiddled with a blind.

Instructions were somewhere around here. Probably part of that further orientation Armand had referenced on the flight to Paris.

Linda eyed the desk—a sit-stand L-shaped desk with a projection disc instead of screens. Tablet rest. Horizontal two-drawer filing cabinet under the desktop. Wooden bookshelf next to it that held supplies and binders, but had space for more books.

Printers, both regular and small 3-D.

Her favorite office chair. A small glass-topped round table with two chairs that could be working space, or a place for tea with one other person. Armchair in one corner. Space for plants, if she wanted to have some (and was here often enough to take care of them). One of the many regrets she had about her Corvallis apartment was that it didn't have enough light to grow houseplants.

Yes. Put out some of the ornaments she had kept, her pictures on the walls—there was even a whiteboard on the wall next to the desk. An easel with smartpaper and smartboard leaned against the wall underneath the whiteboard, secured with big hooks.

Definitely looked like a comfortable working space.

She just had to unpack the boxes that had accumulated in here as well.

Boxes!

Just dealing with boxes would take up a good chunk of today. To Linda's surprise, *all* her stuff was here, even the items she had shipped.

Must be an in-house Martiniere shipper.

And it didn't hurt that her things shipped with the bosses'.

Part of the things to do after they arrived yesterday afternoon had included cross-checking the shipping manifests. Linda had a bleary image of Ruby and Gabe's much larger wing, which included big offices for both of them, as well as a small lab setup where Ruby could print and trial her bot designs.

Once they were done checking the shipping manifests, it was all Linda could do to change into her ratty Oregon State sweats and fall into bed.

At least she didn't need to worry about feeding herself this morning. Ruby and Gabe had scheduled a formal business breakfast, to introduce Linda to the Group leaders in Paris.

Business casual, both Ruby and Armand advised.

Linda could manage that without worry. After another cup of coffee and a shower, she paired a peach-shaded sleeveless tunic with tan slacks, and tan flats. Light makeup. Grandmother's pearl earrings. Her hair—well, Ruby or someone would be able to set her up with a stylist for an easy-to-care cut that would be current and appropriate. For now, Linda put it up in a twist and secured it with hair sticks.

She collected phone and tablet, then hesitated. Should she bring them? After a moment's consideration, she texted Armand.

He responded quickly.

—Whichever you prefer for quick notes. The most that will happen at these breakfasts is a request to perform some action, usually confirmed via email afterward. No deep examinations. Gabe will clearly specify if it's to be a working breakfast where you'll need the wider range of the tablet. Ruby doesn't allow that to happen very often.

—Thanks, she sent back. Phone, then.

She slipped the phone into her pocket and went out the door.

Armand stepped out of the suite across the hallway. "Perfect timing." He smiled.

"I guess so." She had been too tired to pay attention about who went where when they arrived yesterday. "And honestly— yes. I'm not sure I know where to go, exactly."

"Eh, it is not difficult, once you learn your way around." They walked down the hallway. "But after the whirlwind trip we've had, I confess to being a bit disoriented as well."

They reached the grand foyer. A clatter of dishes and chorus of voices came from their right, just as an elegant, older man who strongly resembled Gabe entered the foyer from their left.

"Allo, Armand," the man said.

"Bonjour, Gerard," Armand said. He gestured to Linda, continuing in English. "Gerard, may I introduce you to Linda Coates, Ruby's new executive assistant? Linda, this is Gerard Martiniere, head of the Martiniere Group operations in France."

Linda bowed. "Pleased to meet you, Mr. Martiniere."

"Ah, call me Gerry," Gerard said. "And the honor is mine as well." He bowed back. "So you were one of last year's Martiniere Grant candidates. Tell me about your project."

"It's not as elaborate as Ruby's bot," Linda said diffidently, before launching into a description of her soil quality and contamination tester. Armand led as she and Gerard spoke.

"Gerry, you beat me to Ruby's assistant!" another older man called in English as they entered the large, glassed-in solarium where breakfast was being served. His laugh belied any upset, however.

"Only because once you get your claws in her, Artie, I will not be able to get a word in edgewise," Gerard retorted, the same laughing tone in his voice. He continued around the long table to sit next to Artie.

Artie must be Arthur Martiniere.

Gabe and Ruby sat at the head of the wide oak table covered with a lace cloth, empty chairs around the corners next to them. Linda surveyed the other attendees—clearly she, Armand, and Gerard were the last to arrive. Fourteen people in all, counting herself. A young couple sat next to Arthur, an older woman beside them. She chatted energetically in French with another older woman on the other side of the table, hands waving to emphasize her point. Another young couple, then two men, the younger next to the empty seat by Ruby.

"Go ahead and sit next to Ruby," Armand said when she hesitated. "I am usually in the empty seat between Gabe and Gerard." He smiled. "Seating doesn't change that much at these functions."

"Thanks."

Another smile and nod before he continued to his seat.

"Good morning." Ruby picked up a carafe as Linda sat down. "Coffee?"

"Have you ever known me to turn down coffee?"

Ruby laughed, and poured. "Never. So did you get some rest?"

"I did. And the suite is—amazing. I feel like I need to upgrade my sleepwear to do the place justice."

"Oh, I had the same reaction my first morning in the Residence. I'm glad it's not just me." Ruby lowered her voice. "It was a good thing I had that time living in Los Angeles before coming here because—wow. The LA house is beautiful, especially when it's not shuttered down for security purposes—which unfortunately wasn't the case when Gabe and I were there. But it was still a culture shock coming here. I—kinda wondered if it was just because I came from the ranch."

"No." Although her parents' house was nothing like this, or possibly even like the LA house. They lived in a two-story daylight basement design from the 1980s, in a development with a homeowner's association. Classic small-town suburbia. "You and Gabe have a house in Los Angeles, too?"

Well, they were billionaires, after all.

"Technically, it's Saul and Angelica's." Ruby sipped her coffee. "But I don't think they're planning to leave the ranch anytime soon." She shuddered. "I don't intend to live in LA. Memories."

Gabe cleared his throat, then tapped his water glass. "Now that our last attendees have arrived, it's time for introductions." He nodded to Ruby.

Ruby fumbled for her cane—her leg had been hurting a lot by the time they were done checking the shipping manifests yesterday—and stood, leaning hard on it. Apparently, the night's rest hadn't helped ease her pain.

"I would like to introduce my executive assistant, Linda Coates. We were in the ag robotics program together at Oregon State, and Linda was one of my competitors for the Martiniere Grant last year." That wicked half-smile of Ruby's appeared. "So who better to hire to help me with monitoring research and development? Linda knows my prototype RubyBot very well, since she had input into the design. Plus she has some interesting field data collection bot ideas."

Applause and calls of greeting came from the others.

"Linda's damn good at programming and organizing," Ruby continued. "And with her help, I'm hoping that we can get that microdrone biobot complex up and running within a few weeks. *After* she gets a couple of days to settle in." She eyed the others before sitting down.

"Family introductions, now," Gabe said, also sitting.

Linda made mental notes with each introduction. The "Artie" next to Gerard was, indeed, Arthur Martiniere, director of the Martiniere labs in France. Arthur's son Charles, second in command of the French labs, and his wife Solange sat next to Arthur. The two older women at the end of the table were Madeline and Jeannette Martiniere, Gabe's aunts. Then Gerard's son David, with his wife Therese, and last of all, the two next to Linda, Piotr and Serg Vygotsky—of Vygotsky Security, the commercial side of Martiniere security.

Though, from what Linda had already discerned through observation and conversations, Vygotsky Security handled security arrangements for the high-level Martiniere heirs. Not in-house Martiniere security. Lance Helgessen was Vygotsky-connected, not Martiniere.

Interesting.

Once introductions were done, food was served. Linda was still jet-lagged enough that keeping track of the platters of food being passed around took up much of her attention, rather than the conversations that swirled around her in English and French. The crepes were oh-so-tempting, and she took three—only one chocolate, but the fruit enticed her as well.

"What does your schedule look like?" Serg Vygotsky asked after she had taken a few bites. "I need to walk you through the details of your security systems."

Linda set down her fork. "I saw the security shutters and the nanosensors. I didn't realize the technology was that far along."

"Not available to the general public, yet," Serg said. "I noticed you experimented a little bit this morning. When I'm on site, I get all the notifications. Someone will always be monitoring, usually Lance Helgessen if I'm not here and Gabe is at the Residence. My suite is next to yours, in case you have any problems."

"Oh. All right. Is there some means of dealing with that damned automated voice, or is it a necessary part of the system?" Linda picked up her fork and took another bite of the cherry-filled crepe.

Serg chuckled. "I'll show you the keypad sequences, if you'd prefer to use those."

"I really would. I'm used to them. And because of—circumstances, I'm accustomed to security system routines."

"Good. So, a time?"

Linda shrugged. "I'm unpacking and getting settled in, so any time today will work."

"Perhaps after we're done here?"

"Sure."

"Do you carry a weapon or other protective devices?" Serg sipped from his water glass.

"I haven't carried anything stronger than protective spray. I know how to use a handgun, but haven't shot much."

Serg nodded. "Then I want to do a security and safety assessment. Doesn't need to be today, but within the week, before you leave the Residence grounds. Even with security around you, it's best that you have some sort of personal protection."

"Serg, Linda has pretty good instincts," Ruby said.

"She needs more than protective spray." Serg frowned.

"I need training, I know that," Linda said. "But my father discouraged me carrying anything more. I suppose it's because my grandmother carried, and it didn't save her."

"We'll do our best to ensure you aren't put into that position. But if you are—" A real smile spread across Serg's face. "You'll have the finest tools that Vygotsky Security has to offer."

Linda went from her security system briefing directly to her security and safety assessment, starting in her apartment. Since Serg was firm about her going through it before she left the Residence—well, she had never taken well to being confined.

"Don't change," Serg said when she picked up her sweats. "I want to assess your performance in working attire—" He feinted and grabbed her arm to twist it behind her back.

What the—?

Linda responded like she would to one of the grabber attacks in her old apartment complex. Quick stomp of the heel on his instep, shove *into* him, and—

Serg let go and backed off, raising his hands. "Good. Good. You've had some training and you don't hold back. Better yet, you have good reflexes. Fast, and we can drill them to be faster."

"I've had practice. Grabby men in my apartment complex." She shivered. "Ruby used to kick them in the shins with her pointy-toe cowboy boots, that she wore specially for dealing with the assholes."

Serg chuckled. "I can just see Ruby doing that—*have* seen her do it, in training, even with her knee the way it is. Too bad you don't have sharp edges on the heels and toes of your shoes. That's a good move for you."

"I'd like to have that option."

"That can be arranged. Custom but stylish shoes, like Justine and Ruby have." Serg bowed and swept his hand toward the door. "Let me show you the training space. We'll do the *rest* of your assessment there."

Linda bent over and brushed a smear off the toe of her right flat. "Still in work clothing?"

"For this initial assessment, yes. I want to see what you can do now. Then we'll go about setting you up with weapons. Things that work with your style and preference. Once we do that, you're cleared to leave the premises. With security support, of course."

Ooookay.

A level of security that she would expect in the US.

"Are things that bad here?"

Serg paused as they reached the grand foyer. He waved his wrist in front of a square in the wall. A faint shimmer, and an automatic door opened, revealing a well-lit staircase descending into the basement. He gestured to Linda to go through.

"You need to wave your security bracelet there—" he pointed to another square after the door closed, illuminated in red.

It faded when Linda complied.

"Always make sure that the concealing field is activated after you go through the door, when coming to the training and physical therapy spaces," Serg continued. "In worse cases, this area can serve as a safe room or bunker. This entrance also conceals an evacuation route."

"How will I know where to go?"

"Illumination keyed to your phone and bracelet."

"I feel like I'm in a spy movie."

Serg laughed. "Just wait until I've issued your weapons."

But he hadn't answered her question about how safe the Residence was.

Linda returned to her suite with three security kits that included pistols, Tasers, and smaller, more directed versions of her protective spray. Antidotes for common knockout and sedative gases. One set to go in the safe by her bed, activated by her touch. Another in her office—the same. And a third to go with her whenever she left the Residence—*and I'd advise you to carry one weapon on you at all times, even here,* Serg had added.

A Hermès bag like Ruby's, in Linda's preferred peach shade, finished the collection. The bag hid a protective travel case for her tablet, and first aid supplies, plus slots for Taser, pistol, sprays, and antidotes.

Plus Serg had her scheduled for daily weapons practice.

He still hadn't answered her question about how bad things were. Linda sighed and looked around the living area.

Well, there has to be a downside to this dream job. On the other hand, now I can defend myself if I need to.

That was a significant improvement over her situation just a few days ago.

At least she knew more about her new home and worksite. The swimming pool was by the workout and training rooms, so she could swim before her evening meal, change and shower downstairs.

Meals. Most of the time she was on her own, unless Ruby and Gabe sponsored a meal. Not a problem—Linda preferred that arrangement. Her cupboards and refrigerator had been stocked with fresh items, based on a list she had given Armand when they were in Los Angeles. Serg had gone through the process of secure order and delivery systems after her assessment—Linda could go to shops as long as she took security staff with her, or send an order to security and have it delivered.

Might as well save the time. Order, and have it delivered.

Clothing. She had an appointment with Ruby's tailor for tomorrow afternoon—to have clothing fitted that would be both stylish and secure. Hair stylist just before that.

Sara—before Clyde in her life—would have been jealous. Now she just wore the lumpy brown sack dresses favored by the Electric Born women.

Linda shook her head to dismiss thoughts of her sister. She had too much to do. But a wistful longing for *what might have been* still went through her.

Grandma Jenni would have been proud of me.

Though she could just imagine Grandmother Norma spluttering to Mother and Sara about how awful it was that Linda was off in France, working for *a Catholic.* A Martiniere, no less.

Enough!

She had far too much to do to brood about things she couldn't change. Ruby wanted to meet around five, so Linda needed to get her office organized. Tomorrow would be a regular working day.

Linda secured the office and bedroom security kits. The Hermès bag went on the kitchen counter, so she could grab it quickly on her way out the door. Then she went to her office. The rest of her things could wait, but the sooner she got her office in order, the better.

After adjusting her security settings to her preferred combination of voice and fingerprint authorizations, Linda set about unpacking. Electronics. The few paper books she held onto, for various reasons—Grandma Jenni's memoir, photography art books about the Cascades and Crater Lake, the memoir of a woman homesteader on the Rogue River—went on the bookshelf, along with Grandma Jenni's last official portrait. She had just started unpacking small ornaments when her door chimed.

"Armand Martiniere."

"Open," Linda directed.

"Linda?"

"Back here." She continued to unwrap the first ornament, a Duncan and Miller clear glass bride's basket that had belonged to Great-grandmother Eloise, Grandma Jenni's mother. Rare, but only slightly valuable, worth more as a family trinket than anything collectable. Sometimes Linda used it for flowers, but more often of late it had held paper clips, a couple of pens, her tablet pen, and other odds and ends on her desk.

Linda put it on the bookcase. Maybe she would use it for flowers *here*. Apparently ordering flowers through the food security service was not only normal but expected. She would need to think about what she wanted to get.

Armand raised his brows as he entered her office. "You have been very busy."

"I work better when my office is in order, and it sounds like tomorrow is going to be off and running when it comes to work."

A half-smile. "I like an orderly office as well. Serg told me you had been approved to go off-site. Since it is approaching one, I wondered if you would like to join me for a late lunch, along with with our subordinates who work in the Residence's offices?"

"I would love to do that, Armand." Plus it got her away from *boxes* for a while. "See where they work, as well. Are they in Ruby and Gabe's wing? I saw those offices yesterday, along with Ruby's lab."

"No, the offices in Ruby and Gabe's wing are just personal setups, like ours. The main labs and Residence offices are in a separate building." He grinned. "Orientation in the offices after lunch?"

"Sure." Linda hesitated before she continued. Would he take this personally? *Probably not. He seems to like structure as much as I do.* "I'm surprised at how informal this orientation is."

Armand nodded. "There is a lot to cover for your position. Residence orientation. Residence offices orientation. Labs. We have formal training sessions for lower-level workers, but you and I have so many responsibilities that we will be getting you oriented over the next couple of weeks. I had to create my own orientation because of the sheer volume of things I needed to know and connections I needed to make, so I am trying to apply what I learned and did not learn during that process to make it easier for you."

"That makes sense. I appreciate the thoughtfulness, Armand."

A bigger smile. "Thank you." His smile took on an impish slant. "Are you planning to swim today?"

"I meet with Ruby at five, so after that."

"Well then, perhaps we should move on to the next stage of your orientation so that you will have time to finish getting your office organized before then." Armand's eyes twinkled. "I swim around six-is. That's usually a quiet time in the pool."

"Well, then, let's get going." Linda glanced around her office.

Maybe she would get this part of her life in order today.

SURPRISINGLY, EVEN WITH TAKING THE TIME FOR LUNCH, LINDA finished setting up her office and got around to organizing the kitchen and living room before it was time to meet with Ruby. That allowed her time to think about the lunch with the office subordinates.

Not all the workers went out to lunch with them—there were lab workers, and others who needed to remain on site. Security workers. Comm workers. Information technology. And more.

Linda took the time to focus on each person as she was introduced to them. There were quite a few low-level Martiniere relatives, many, like her, refugees from the United States. Distant cousins. The Martiniere Group strove to provide for its own, and as long as one was a competent worker, just about anyone with a connection to the Martinieres could find a job—somewhere in the organization. Even if it was only something like janitorial work.

Part of the Group's origins in a Family Association after the Revolution, Armand explained afterward. *The American and British branches went out of their way to help French relatives fleeing the guillotine. Now—well, we are returning the favor, at least for the Americans.*

Noblesse oblige? That seemed to be a recurring theme with the Martinieres.

"Ruby Barkley Martiniere," her comm chimed. Linda jumped, and checked the time. Four-fifty. So she wasn't running late.

"Hi, Ruby."

"Hey." Ruby sounded harassed. "Mind if I come to your place for our meeting? I need to get out of these quarters."

Thank God I mucked out the office first!

"Come right on over. My office is set up."

Ruby laughed. "Thought that would be the case." Her voice was lighter. "I'll be right there."

"Herbal tea? Or something stronger? I plan to go swimming

after so I won't join you, but *someone* put a nice bottle of bourbon in my liquor cabinet."

"Oh no, the usual tea will be just fine. I—probably shouldn't have anything right now, either. On my way."

All right, then.

Ruby shared Linda's preference for spearmint tea over peppermint. Linda dug out her tea set and teas—another thing to be grateful for, packing assistance that paid attention to the need to *properly* label boxes—and brewed tea. By the time Ruby arrived, it was steeping nicely. Linda had the little glass table set with her tea service, the blinds opened far enough to admit light but not glare from the afternoon sun.

Ruby was on crutches when Linda opened the door. "Twisted my knee the wrong way in PT," she grumbled as she limped in. "Slacked for too many days in a row."

"I'm sorry."

"Oh, I'm running on painkillers. Will be tomorrow as well." Ruby hobbled to Linda's office. She straightened up, looking around, and exhaled, rolling her shoulders, muscles relaxing, before she continued to one of the chairs around the table and sank into it, putting her crutches next to the chair. "This is nice. All you really need now are plants."

"I have plans to get some. I've missed having plants around."

"Yeah, that dark apartment of yours was about like my barn cave was. I have a few starts I can share."

"Thanks." Linda dragged the other chair around so that Ruby could prop up her leg, then set her tablet on the table, before bringing her office chair over.

Ruby leaned her head against the back of her chair as Linda poured the tea. Her hand trembled as she picked up her cup. Ruby set it back down in the saucer, flexed her fingers, exhaled heavily yet again, then picked up the cup, this time her hand steady.

"There are *days*," she said finally. "Between jet lag, screwing up my knee *again*, a setback with the RubyBot, and—" she closed her eyes tight. "Gramps called half an hour ago. Granma's gone into a coma, and her doctor doesn't think she'll make it another twelve hours."

"I'm sorry." Linda rested her hand on Ruby's.

Ruby wrapped both of her hands around Linda's. "I—" she opened her eyes and shook her head. "Gabe's having a rough day as well. Pain, but they can't locate the source. I wish to fuck those damn doctors would find out what's causing it. He finally took enough muscle relaxant to knock him out for the night, so I couldn't share this with him. Not when he's getting some sleep."

Linda put her other hand on Ruby's. They sat in silence for a few minutes, Ruby blinking hard as silent tears trickled down her cheeks. At last, Ruby heaved the heaviest sigh of all.

"I am one hell of a lucky woman," she said softly. "But don't kid yourself. I've paid a price—still am paying—for this good fortune. If there's one thing I've learned by becoming a Martiniere, it's that good fortune also requires a willingness to pay the price." Another shake of her head. "I knew that Granma wasn't going to last the week. That Sunday was our last time. And it's probably best that I'm not there. That I remember her being happy to see me, and her joy that I managed to escape Thunder County. But *oh God*, Linda—"

"Do you need to take more days off? I can arrange your schedule so that you aren't loaded with so many meetings tomorrow."

Linda had been *appalled* by Ruby's schedule when she finally got access to it. No downtime, things scheduled back-to-back— one thing her dad had pounded into Linda when she worked as his receptionist and scheduler was the need for processing time between meetings. And so many of them were people who didn't need to see Ruby in person, but could accomplish more by meeting with lower-level associates.

"Fewer meetings would be good. I can't afford to duck every-thing, especially if Gabe is down tomorrow—which seems likely."

"So let's look at priorities. I don't know enough yet to defi-nitely decide what can be relayed to others, but I have some ideas. I did lunch with the main office and met people there."

"Good." Ruby released Linda's hand and pulled her tablet out of her handbag. Linda keyed hers up.

It took them half an hour to allocate meetings and therapy schedules appropriately.

Ruby was much more relaxed when they finished. "It really helps to have someone else's perspective. I was panicking at the thought of—just—overload. You sure you want to take on that coding review? There's a lot to it."

"And just which one of us got through those faster in class?"

Ruby snorted. "Of course. You spot the programming errors quicker than I do." She looked around the office again. "Would it be too much of an imposition if we made this a regular meeting site? Me come here, rather than you to me?"

Linda shrugged. "It's my office. Not an issue."

"We'll still end up doing the next-day-planning in my office sometimes. No way around it. But I need to get out."

"*Angelica Ramirez Martiniere.*" Ruby's phone.

Ruby flinched, closing her eyes tight. "Oh God. This is it." She exhaled before answering. "Yes, Angelica?" A pause. "All right. How is Gramps doing?" She tapped her fingers on the tabletop. "Oh. I see. Gabe's asleep. He's had a bad day between jet lag and pain. Finally got him to take his meds. We'll—thank you for handling everything, Angelica. Thank you so much. When Gramps wakes up, tell him I will call. And—thank you for being there, when I couldn't."

Ruby set her phone carefully on the table, hand quivering. She leaned her head against the back of her chair again, then rubbed her eyes.

"Your grandmother?"

Ruby nodded. "Gramps was up with her all night before she passed away. He's worn out. Angelica and Saul are staying in the main house with him right now. There'll be a small service, nothing big."

"We can arrange something here, if you'd like."

"Let me think about what I want to do." Ruby sighed. "I'm glad we opened up my schedule. I'm not going to be good for much tomorrow. I can give myself that, at least." She fumbled for her crutches.

Linda helped Ruby get situated on the crutches and walked with her friend to the door. She hugged Ruby.

"Are you going to be all right?"

Ruby nodded. "I only took half my painkiller before coming over here. I'll take the rest, and crash with Gabe. Oh God, Linda —thank you. Thank you for taking the job. Thank you for doing what is above and beyond what is normally expected for a job like this—" She broke off. "I'll be available for meetings tomorrow afternoon. If you could move the bank meeting to the afternoon?"

"I will," Linda promised.

Her heart ached for her friend as Ruby hobbled away. Linda watched until Ruby had gone into the grand foyer, on her way back to the wing she shared with Gabe. Then she crossed the hallway and knocked on Armand's door. He was wearing sweats and looked strained and tired, phone in one hand.

Not surprising, if Gabe has had a bad day. Wonder how many appointments Armand has had to move?

"Linda! What a surprise."

"I thought I'd better let you know. Ruby just got the call from her mother-in-law, while we were meeting. Her grandmother's died."

"Oh damn. All right."

"I had already cleared most of her schedule for tomorrow morning."

"Then I will do the same for Gabe. I was in the process of adjusting his schedule for tomorrow, but this means I need to do more." Armand rubbed his forehead. "Thank you for letting me know, Linda." He sighed, and closed the door.

Linda returned to her suite.

This was a comfortable exile, all right.

But exile had a price.

What happens when it's Dad? Mom? Sara?

She didn't give two hoots about Grandmother Norma but the rest of her family—

Will I ever be able to go home again?

CHAPTER 6

LIVING THE NEW LIFE

FOR THE FIRST TIME *EVER*, LINDA WAS GRATEFUL FOR A PIECE OF advice that Clyde had given her. It might be the *only* time his advice had value, but it was definitely of use now.

Get experience in practical media technology, he had said. *Not just content but production.*

While she didn't want to think about exactly *why* Clyde had given her that advice, Linda's experience as a media production volunteer for assorted radio and video broadcasts in both high school and college helped with handling the chaos following Ruth Ryder's death. Neither Justine nor Ruby were able to be present at Ruth's funeral, but both wanted to watch and speak. Plus, the ending would conclude with a recorded announcement to be sent out for public consumption.

Ruby and Justine already had technology built into auditoriums that allowed high-speed, high-quality multiple shared input/output projection screens to work. That wasn't the problem. Getting something set up at the Double R Ranch—especially since they needed big portable interactive projection capacity because the ceremony would be outdoors—now *that* made things interesting. Add in the time difference, and recent upgrades to the ranch's connectivity that still might not be enough bandwidth for *two* big screen projections with good resolution, and....

"This is tech we always talked about putting in at the ranch, while we were stuck there during the battle with Philip," Louisa said in a meeting with Linda and Armand the evening after Ruth's death, running her fingers through her hair as she scowled at something to the side of the projection. "But then Gabie nearly died, Ruby was hurt so bad, and we were free to leave the ranch, so it didn't happen. We don't have the time now to do more than cobble up a makeshift."

"Send me the specs and I'll get a permanent setup started." Upgrades at the Double R were Ruby's domain, so part of Linda's duties. "Needs to happen in the long term."

"Sending now."

Linda pulled up a screen, inputting tech requirements to sort through the list of Martiniere-approved vendors that were closest to Northeastern Oregon. Then it was her turn to scowl at the results. Tech from *Seattle?* Not even *Portland?*

"I'm surprised that Saul and Angelica haven't requested this tech before now."

Louisa sighed. "Mama and Papa are still pretty shut down when it comes to connecting outside of their close circle. While Gabie and Ruby *had* to be in the world because of Gabie's responsibilities, that's not the case for our parents. Mama took over monitoring Ruth and Ron, with Papa's help, and that's kept their focus on the ranch."

"Makes sense." Linda paused. Should she say more?

"I worry about Gabie and Ruby. They're functional, but—" Louisa sighed.

"I know what you mean." She didn't have to say more as Armand nodded in agreement.

Then the conversation veered to more tech requirements.

ARMAND HANDLED THE ORGANIZATIONAL DETAILS ON THEIR END OF the event.

"Am I ever glad that you are on board and handling the tech," he said the second night after Ruth's death. They had finished their swim workouts and were sitting in the hot tub. "Comm tech is not my strength."

"You're better at event coordination than I am." Yesterday evening, Linda had located the *perfect* shoulder and neck jet that pummeled her muscles into relaxing so she could have a pleasant if early bedtime. So where was it now?

"Complementary strengths. That is good." Armand leaned his head back, closing his eyes. "Oh. The jet closest to the one you are looking for is over there." He gestured to one closer to him. "I have the best jet and right now I am going to be selfish. Give me a few more minutes and we can switch."

"Oh, you—!" Linda splashed him.

Armand laughed, opening his eyes, and flicked water back at her. Then he settled into the jet again. "I did not realize that Ruby's grandmother had made so many connections within the Family."

"Saul and Angelica live on the ranch. Gabe and Ruby, Justine and Donald, and Louisa spent last summer there. That means a lot of secondary Martiniere connections."

"And if there is one thing the Family does well, it is spawning a horde of secondary connections." Armand straightened up. "Swap jets?"

"You bet." Oh, she could just *anticipate* the pounding of that good jet.

One ankle-level jet unexpectedly increased in intensity as Linda stood to change positions. The sudden push against her leg made her wobble. Armand caught her by the shoulders. The contact sent tingles throughout her.

He inhaled sharply, cheeks faintly pink. Or was that just from the hot tub?

"You all right?"

She nodded. "Thanks."

They settled back at their respective jets. Linda closed her eyes, savoring the pummeling of the water.

Focusing on finding *just the right space* for her muscles to get worked over was an excellent distraction from what had just happened.

THE NEXT DAY WAS THE FUNERAL DAY—OR NIGHT, AS THE TIMING OF the service worked out between Paris and Oregon. Linda spent the day tweaking tech with Louisa at the Double R and Donald at Mist Knoll—early morning for them, afternoon for her. She slipped out early for her swim, but no hot tub—best to carry the energy into the event rather than relax. Armand was already grinding through his laps when she reached the pool, along with a couple other staff members also trying to grab some exercise before the funeral.

Business casual dress for the event, since both she and Armand would be syncing and running tech in the control booth.

This *had* to come off just right for her friend.

Soon enough, they were settled in the booth, waiting for the feeds to start.

"Let's start with the Residence," Louisa said.

Linda brought up the screens and camera for the Residence. Gabe and Ruby sat front and center in the small auditorium in the Residence offices. Gerard, David, and several other Parisian Family members were with them.

"Justine and Donald."

Justine and Donald's projection shimmered on half the front screen in the Residence's auditorium.

"Interactive available?" Donald asked.

"Available," Linda confirmed.

"And now—going live at the Double R," Louisa said.

The screen came up from the cemetery next to the ranch's backyard. Linda held her breath as it fuzzed, then sharpened. Whew. She roughly estimated that about thirty people were present for the graveside service—restricted list, due to Angelica and Saul's presence, and mostly Ruth Ryder's friends and local relatives.

The system checks worked. Transmission and reception good from all three locations.

The service began. It was generic Protestant, with the preacher from Lakeside Community Church officiating. Ron Ryder sat between Angelica and Saul, holding their hands, as the preacher briefly spoke about Ruth's contributions to the community.

Then it was time for others. Several of Ruth's friends talked about her involvement with local women's service organizations. Another about her family.

Angelica rose. She patted Ron's hand, then proceeded to the podium.

"We didn't know Ruth Ryder as well as those of you who knew her for a lifetime. But the Martiniere Family owes Ruth— and her husband Ron—a very great debt." She gulped. "Thanks to Ruth and Ron, I have a marvelous daughter-in-law. Ruth went out of her way to be hospitable to her granddaughter's in-laws. When we were in danger, when we needed a refuge, Ruth and Ron offered their home. Ruth ensured we were comfortable, safe, and welcome. And she provided a wonderful example to Saul of how to handle limited mobility with grace, courage, and skill." Another hard swallow. "Our lives—and the world—are much diminished by her loss."

Ruby shivered and sniffled. Gabe wrapped his arm around her shoulders, brushing his lips against her temple, holding her tight as Justine spoke after Angelica.

And then it was their turn.

The big one.

As staff swiftly set up a podium, Ruby rose slowly, carefully, and walked onto the stage, not using her cane or crutches. Linda held her breath.

Would it work? Would Ruby make it to the podium without falling? She had barely made it that far yesterday, in physical therapy. One reason why staff lingered after the podium was set up and connected—nearby support, should Ruby need it.

She didn't.

Linda exhaled, and checked the switches. Everything was running just fine.

"Thank you." Ruby's voice quavered as she grasped the podium. "Thank you, everyone. Gramps, I wish I was there to hug you and hold your hand—Angelica and Saul, thank you for being with my grandparents when I couldn't." She drew a deep breath. "I've not just lost a grandmother. I've lost someone who has stood in the place of my mother for my entire life. But Granma was more than that. She was my greatest advocate. She encouraged me to reach high. Not just for rodeo titles but for a life beyond Thunder County. She—" Ruby gulped and buried her head in her hands, leaning on the podium.

Gabe rose. He hobbled to Ruby, rested his cane against the podium, and took her in his arms. Ruby laid her head on his chest for a moment, then raised it. Gabe smiled, brushing the tears from her eyes, then kissed her, keeping his arm around her as he faced the podium, clutching it with his free hand.

"I'll pick it up from there." He signaled to Armand and Linda.

Linda flipped the recording switches, holding her breath. They worked.

Good.

Gabe cleared his throat before speaking. "Ruth Ryder shaped the woman of my heart. On our first meeting, Ruth asked me to help Ruby soar. To move beyond the ranch and Thunder County. I'd like to believe that I've done my best to see that happen." He exhaled. "Ruth's contributions go beyond Ruby. She was a generous and giving soul and—well, one thing that she and I discussed in private, the last time I saw her, was a means for helping young women soar and achieve. I haven't been able to progress as quickly as I would like, but I want to announce that the Martiniere Foundation will be setting up the Ruth Ryder Fellowship Fund, with the intent of helping young American women in rural areas achieve their educational and career goals. Interested women should contact the Foundation via email, at RuthRyderFund at Martiniere Foundation dot com, for more information. We will begin issuing funds as soon as possible."

Armand brought up the screen with the email address, bright red lettering on a blue background.

And there it is. The big announcement.

Gabe signaled again. Linda switched off the recording. After the ceremony was done, she would check it, then send the recording out not just to the general Martiniere Group streaming feed but to media.

"Ehh. Here we go." Armand slumped back in his chair, rubbing his forehead. "Another means to annoy and irritate the Real Truthers. Necessary but dangerous. I worry about Gabe's safety. It is like he is *daring* them to attack him."

"*Both* of them are like that, not just Gabe."

Armand gestured toward the stage. "I support this fund. I support everything they want to do. But Gabe wants to fix it all at once—climate change, political oppression—and I worry that it is too much."

"It's like a runaway horse."

"Like yesterday's meeting."

Linda sighed. At yesterday's Martiniere Group Board meeting, Gabe proclaimed that he and Ruby wanted to announce the Ruth Ryder fund at Ruth's funeral.

Start working on the specs for the fund, Ruby had directed. *I can't focus on it right now, but please get the process started. Include Louisa, Justine, and Barbie Atwood.*

Two hours later, the fund organizing committee met. Linda

added Armand to the meeting, at his request, so he could monitor for Gabe and give input on Gabe's behalf.

I don't think we're going to have the political turnaround Gabriel anticipates that quickly, Barbie Atwood had pronounced as they discussed the issues while defining criteria. *This may become primarily a fund to finance women fleeing the United States to seek asylum. That need has the potential to overwhelm many others.*

If anyone would know about the political possibilities in what existed of the US political system, it would be Barbie Atwood, with her involvement with the women's rights group Real Lives for Women.

Justine had bit her lip but hadn't argued with Barbie. The meeting had ended with some rough guidelines and—wrestling with the definition of "young women," "educational and career goals," and "rural areas".

If I end up funding mass exoduses from the US for women of all ages in Ruth Ryder's name, so be it, had been Gabe's tight-lipped pronouncement when Linda and Armand reported the results of that meeting to him. *I will do what it takes to help.*

So here they were. The Fund was announced.

Ruby and Gabe returned to their seats. The preacher approached the podium for a final prayer.

"There are ways to work around the Truthers and stay in the community that can be rewarded," Linda said. "Non-political activities that nonetheless help improve women's survival in a repressive society. Ruby found a means, even before Gabe came into her life. So did I. It's difficult, but not exactly *The Handmaid's Tale.*"

Yet.

Armand raised an eyebrow. "How so?"

"Involvement in community service organizations that aren't church-related, like Ruth was. Athletes, like I was. For Ruby, rodeo queening. The women who will be going for an award like this will know what to say to dispel suspicions of anyone like Clyde, because they've grown up under this baloney."

"Those are the ones who stay. What about those who want to leave? I think Barbie Atwood is right. We will get swamped by young women who want out of the United States."

"Nothing wrong with that. Honestly, if I could find a means to finance a *get out of here now* asylum fund in the name of my grandmother Jessi, I would. I just wouldn't want to make it as prominent as Gabe and Ruby will end up making this one."

"We will see how things go."

The last hymn ended. Linda and Armand went through the signoffs as the Residence attendees filed out of the auditorium. Linda slumped back in her seat once everything was finished.

"What a day."

"Agreed." Armand stretched. "I do not usually do this, but I plan to take a flask down to the hot tub, along with a big jug of water. Not a major drinking spree, just enough to unwind a little bit. A couple of swallows."

Linda considered. Was this an invitation, or not, and should she accept it?

"I happen to have a flask as well."

"Well, perhaps your flask—and water—should join my flask and water around the hot tub. Unwind. We might be the only ones down there—or not. Whichever is the case, you are welcome to join me."

"Then I will. After I get this recording vetted and sent out."

He grinned.

<hr>

LINDA CONTEMPLATED HER SWIMSUITS. THREE OF THEM WERE ONE-piece training suits, newer versions of the ones she had worn on swim team. But there was a fourth—a tankini, barely worn, for special occasions when she was around the pool for reasons other than exercising. Dark blue with a lighter-shaded floral design on the top, boyshort bottom, and a matching coverup.

Might this be an occasion to wear something that wasn't her usual training suit?

Why not?

No need for goggles, or swim cap if she wasn't swimming. The stylist recommended by Gabe's Aunt Jeannette had cut Linda's hair into a short blunt style, easy to wash and maintain —her longer hair would have required a cap even for soaking.

Linda filled her small flask with good whisky, grabbed her water jug and other things she needed, then headed for the pool.

Armand was already in the hot tub. He had pulled two lounge chairs close, dropping his towel, flask, and water on one. Linda put her things on the other and slipped in.

"No one else around?"

Armand shrugged. "The others left before you got here—just Yvette and Henri. Long day, so many people just wanted to go home. No blame to them for that choice, and it leaves this space open for those of us who live here."

"I'm just getting used to the notion that the Residence isn't a very fancy hotel."

Armand laughed. "Honestly? I think that is nearly everyone's reaction. Well, perhaps not Gabe and Serg, but the rest of us? It takes a while to get used to living and working here."

"You, me, and Ruby, then."

"Pretty much. Louisa and Justine have their own suites in Gabe and Ruby's wing, and Piotr Vygotsky—Serg's father—has a suite next to mine."

"I'd have thought you would be accustomed to all this." Linda waved a hand.

Armand was silent for a few minutes, before he sighed. "The life of high-level Martinieres is different from the rest of us. After all, by US standards, your family is fairly well-off. And yet *all this*, as you put it, is more than you are used to. That's the situation I am in, as well."

"How so? If I'm not being too snoopy."

"Eh, I know more about you than you probably do me, so it

is only fair that you ask. I am from the Canadian Martinieres. My grandfather Bertrand was born in Paris, but moved to Quebec. Louis—Gabe's grandfather, Grandfather Bertrand's brother—sent Bertrand to Canada to manage the family financial interests of Louis's wife Donna—Gabe's grandmother, commonly called Donna-gran by the family. She had various inheritances from her family, and needed an in-country financial manager during Louis's tenure as the Martiniere. My father was raised in Quebec City, and my mother is from there. I grew up on Donna's estate."

He's Canadian, not French. All right, that explains why he speaks formally for the most part, as if English isn't his first language. Even if it is—

"What does that make you? A high-level heir or a lower-level heir?"

"Lower-level—well, somewhat in between. High-level heirs are the Martiniere's close family. Justine and Louisa are the highest-level heirs, because they are Gabe's sisters. After them are Gerard, Peter, Madeline, Melusine, and Jeannette—Gabe's uncles and aunts. Their children are lower-level heirs, like the rest of us, unless we are the children of the local Head of Family."

"Sounds kind of complicated to track."

"It is all about inheritance and who is eligible to become the Martiniere-in-waiting and then the Martiniere. In an emergency, I can draw a small stipend out of the Martiniere Family Trust, but otherwise? The name buys me a slot somewhere in the business as long as I am competent. Inheritance is primarily through my direct family connections, and their shares in the Trust."

"So the Group leadership is hereditary."

"Sort of." The hot tub shut off and Armand sighed again. "Much as I'd like another round of soaking—I probably shouldn't. Unless you want to soak longer?"

"Eh, I hear a flask calling my name." She could drag out the hot tub time, but a drink sounded better.

"Mine as well."

They climbed out of the hot tub. After rinsing off in the poolside shower and drying, Linda slipped into her coverup—fleece, to keep her warm. She noticed that Armand, too, had worn something other than a training suit—in this case, long, baggy swim trunks.

He toasted her with his flask. "To a successful event."

"I'll drink to that." After taking a swallow, she followed it with several big gulps of water. "The recording looked good, and I was able to send it out without any problems."

"Good. To continue," Armand said, putting his water down. "If Gabe wanted, he could move the title of Martiniere-in-waiting—essentially, his potential successor and current second-in-command—to another Family branch. He has somewhat done that now, by appointing Gerard's son David to be the Martiniere-in-waiting."

"Is the Martiniere always a man? I would have thought Justine or Louisa would be next in line."

"Yes. Salic Law tradition." Armand rolled his eyes. "Gabe wants to change that, but Gabe wants to change a lot of things. He has to be mindful of the battles he chooses, and Justine suggested that now was not the time." He took another swallow from his flask. "And so much for *that* lecture. That is the drawback of living on site. Always talking shop."

"Can't beat the commute, however."

"Agreed."

A companionable silence fell between them.

"So," Armand said finally. "I have learned a lot about Linda the colleague. What do you do for fun?"

Linda laughed. "You know, I've almost forgotten about fun because I was so focused on doing well in college. I used to paint a little bit. Nothing fancy, mostly watercolors. Then I started playing around with fabric art, translating my sketches into wall hangings and things like that. Another of those good ways to hide out from people like Clyde. They'll think *oh, she isn't danger-ous, she does that artsy quilting stuff. Maybe I'll buy a piece to give to the wife.*"

"An artist, hmm? I have dabbled with sketching. When I first came to Paris, I would go into the city and draw. Or the museums."

"The museum staff don't mind?"

"Lots of people do it." Armand shifted to his side. "It is a time-honored practice."

"I would like to start going to museums," Linda said wistfully. "I need to figure out how to get into the city. Call security for a car and escort?"

"Pretty much. Which one would you want to see first?"

"I imagine the Louvre is pretty crowded most of the time."

"Oh, there are ways to find times when it is not that busy, and there are other lovely museums as well." Armand arched a brow. "I was planning to visit the Musée Marmottan Monet on Saturday. It is close, not really going into the central city. Would you care to join me?"

"I love Monet's work. Certainly!"

"Then, perhaps, some sketching along the Seine afterward? It is a novelty to find someone else who likes to sketch that I do not have to put through a security vetting. I am curious about how you would translate a sketch into fabric art or wall hangings."

"I could walk you through my process. If you're interested."

"Yes." He stretched. "Two o'clock on Saturday. Museum and sketching."

"Sounds good."

"And with that, I think I've unwound sufficiently. Good night, Linda."

"Good night, Armand."

Linda chewed her lip thoughtfully.

An artist, hmm?

And that mention of *security vetting*. She hadn't considered that aspect of socializing outside of the Group.

Not that she had much time to look around, whether she was looking for friends or—more.

On the other hand, after the blowup with Tony, she wasn't in any hurry to replace him.

But Armand liked art. That *was* interesting.

SATURDAY WENT WELL. THEY ENDED UP SKETCHING A SECTION OF the park's forest. Armand teased Linda about the shape of the trees she sketched.

"I don't need a detailed outline for something I'm translating over to fabric," she said. "Abstract representations work well for my style."

He grinned, and showed her his version. "I am hopeless with landscapes. Architecture, and some faces come out better. But I keep trying." He quickly flipped past one sketch that looked like a face.

"What's that? You sketch people as well?"

"People I know. But this one—well, the proportions are all wrong. It embarrasses me. You will laugh." He closed his sketchbook firmly.

"You should see how badly I botch *my* people sketches."

Armand hesitated. Then he opened his sketchbook and flipped back to that face. "Please do not be—oh, I don't know. Insulted? Embarrassed?"

Linda studied the sketch. Clearly her, concentrating on her own work. Despite Armand's disclaimers, she liked it.

"I'm flattered. You make me look better than I am."

"That is what you think." Armand closed the sketchbook. "It is not right. I need to think about it. I hope you do not mind that I sketched you, but the light was just right on your face." He sighed. "I do not always get the proportions correct. It feels dead to me. I was not able to catch that expression, the life in your face, your smile, the way I wanted to do."

"You're better at portraits than I am, especially as quickly as you sketched me."

He ducked his head, flushing slightly. "Thank you. You flatter me."

"I'd like to see a final version someday."

"When I think that I have finally gotten your expression correct, then yes—I will share it with you."

And that was it for sharing sketches that day. But they set up another sketching date for Saturday, this time venturing into the city to the Musée d'Orsay.

Linda hoped she might get to see a further version of Armand's sketch of her then.

THE NEXT WEEK WAS FULL OF RUBYBOT CODING WORK. RUBY plunged hard into coding, trying to bury her emotions from her grandmother's funeral. She and Linda worked late into the evenings, tweaking programming and testing their code.

They moved from Ruby's private lab to the Residence labs midday on Tuesday, after their sims continued to work.

Time to make nanobiobot prototypes and see if the sims were correct. Trial-and-error 3D printing took up the rest of the day and into Wednesday.

Gabe and Cousin Arthur stopped by during the late afternoons to check on their progress.

"When Artie says we're ready for limited field-test distribution, that will pretty much be it for development," Ruby said during lunch on Thursday, ordered in from the Group's favorite bistro. "Minor tweaking only after that."

"If we ever get there," Linda grumbled.

"Oh, we will. We're closer than you think." Ruby grinned.

That sounded promising. Ruby was usually accurate about estimating progress. Linda returned to work with renewed enthusiasm.

RUBY'S CONFIDENCE WAS JUSTIFIED ON FRIDAY AFTERNOON WHEN Arthur pronounced the RubyBot ready for limited field-test distribution.

Field work.

Excitement pulsed through Linda as she scheduled the first field test for Monday morning. It wasn't going to be anything big—just a day trip to one of the Martiniere contract fields near Paris to release these early versions. The RubyBot alone was undergoing the field test, not the portable growbox setup that they eventually hoped to cultivate the RubyBots in. The grow-boxes were proving to be more complex to standardize for non-technical use than the RubyBot alone.

All the same, it was a baby step toward what they hoped the RubyBot would become. Linda spent Friday afternoon in the Residence labs programming dronecams, both for release moni-toring and publicity shots.

Someone knocked on the open lab door. Linda looked up as Armand entered.

"Congratulations. You and Ruby have been busy this week."

Linda had been swimming later than Armand the past few days, as she and Ruby bashed through the programming, so she hadn't seen him other than quick glimpses. Otherwise, she had been in the lab with Ruby.

"Thanks." Linda put down the drone she was working on. "Ruby and I have been notorious for going on programming tears, back when we were in college. Tying up a lab for hours on end—it's nice not needing to wrestle with others for access. And knowing I could leave my work secured without having to pack it up and lug it off after each session. That makes a big difference in time spent working, if I don't have to do setup and takedown."

"Oh, I imagine it is a huge difference. Not a lab person myself, but I can certainly understand being able to leave work secured. So. I was wondering if you would like to change our museum and sketching plans for tomorrow? Go out for dinner and something afterward instead, to celebrate? Gabe was planning something special for Ruby, and I realized that you should also have that opportunity. After all, you have been working just as hard."

Linda pursed her lips thoughtfully. "What kind of dinner, and how big an event?"

"We could stay local, or we could go all the way into the city. Even clubbing, if you would like."

"I'm not a big fan of clubbing. But perhaps a nice restaurant —I'll let you pick it since you know more about what's available than I do. Are there any gallery openings near a restaurant, or galleries we can visit?"

Armand raised his brows. "This *is* Paris, my dear."

"Then dinner and a gallery. I don't know that I want to start buying art for my walls yet, but it doesn't hurt to be shopping."

"Early dinner or later?"

"Early. Perhaps six-ish?"

"Sounds good. Any cuisine preferences?"

Linda smiled at him before picking up the drone again. "Surprise me."

"I will."

Was this or wasn't this a date? Linda went back and forth about it the next day.

Dinner and a gallery. It *sounded* like a date, more than the informality of going to a museum and sketching afterward.

And yet—Armand had referred to Gabe and Ruby doing something special. Was this dinner on the company account or what? Had it been Armand's idea, or Gabe's? Maybe even Ruby's suggestion?

Linda, it doesn't matter. You're having a nice dinner with a colleague to celebrate a major work accomplishment. In Paris. Just settle down and enjoy it. No obligations. Even if he is attractive, and nice, and....

She pulled herself up sharp. Of course, she liked Armand. He was organized, efficient, and pleasant to work with. Someone who liked to swim and sketch, just like she did.

That was all this was.

Friendship. Not a date.

CHAPTER 7

QUESTIONS UPON QUESTIONS
MAY, 2030

SATURDAY WAS WARM ENOUGH THAT LINDA SETTLED ON AN ELEGANT but comfortable cotton retro dress for dinner with Armand, one of her new outfits. Sleeveless with a fitted bodice large enough that she could add in a sleek, form-fitting bulletproof vest underneath if needed, full knee-length skirt, white background with a lush magenta-toned floral pattern. Along with the dress, she wore her new white flats—the special ones with sharp-edged heels and toes.

And, of course, the Hermès bag.

She tossed a lacy shawl over her shoulders when Armand knocked on the door.

"Very nice." He grinned.

"I can say the same for you."

Armand wore a light tan double-breasted suit with light blue pocket square and matching tie. "We are going to a local Italian restaurant, with a lovely view of the Seine and the city. Michelin-rated."

"Italian?" She raised her brows. "Not French?"

"Very *nice* Italian. Multiple good cuisines here." He lowered his voice as they approached the door. "You are armed—besides your bag, right?"

"Yes." She didn't feel like giving him the details about the pistol in a thigh holster, or the Taser in another. The full skirts that were currently in style hid a *lot*, as Grandma Jenni had taught her. "And I have the permits for them."

"Good."

Security stood by a waiting SUV. Armand helped her inside, then joined her.

"Excited for Monday?"

"Oh yes." Linda looked away from the window. Between moving in, Ruth's funeral, and then this week pounding away at the RubyBot, she hadn't been able to leave the Residence for more than a couple of excursions to the closest bistro. She was more than ready to get out, do a little sightseeing.

And now, with the golden glow of early evening spilling over the city, the realization was finally starting to hit her.

I live here now. Paris. France.

Would she ever get tired of the lights of the Eiffel Tower?

They arrived and Armand helped her out of the SUV. Once inside the restaurant, they were escorted to a table overlooking the river. A bottle of champagne, already in an ice bucket, waited for them.

"I took the liberty of ordering a libation ahead of time when I made the reservation," Armand said. "After all, this is a celebration."

"Thank you."

While she *should* be blasé and unconcerned, Linda couldn't keep from grinning big as their server uncorked the champagne, then poured.

This.

This was the sort of thing she had been working toward. A life of her own. She hadn't envisioned working in Europe, much less Paris, but—*if only Grandma Jenni could see me now.*

"You look happy," Armand said after they placed their orders.

"I still have to pinch myself to make sure I'm not dreaming. This position allows me to do everything I went to school for. That I'm based in Paris is sheer gravy."

Armand raised his champagne glass. "If your past week's work with Ruby is any example, the Group will easily benefit from what you two come up with. I am envious."

"How so?"

He shrugged. "I can't create devices like you and Ruby can. Or Gabe, though he doesn't spend much time doing it these days —too busy administering the Group."

"Your knowledge of administration is just as important." She raised her glass. "We are a team. Ruby and Gabe; you and me. The four of us contribute to the advancement of the Group, them as leaders, us as their support. We *have* to be productive."

"Ah, but we should drink to you first. To Linda, who together with Ruby is helping the Group launch into a new era."

Linda sipped her champagne, then raised her glass again. "Another toast. To Armand, who sees the patterns of organization and makes them work. Ruby and I couldn't have accomplished this much in this short a time without you and Gabe coordinating the supplies and support we needed."

He smiled at that, his cheeks flushing. But he sipped his champagne without argument.

"I'll be right back." Linda eyed her bag. Did she really need to take it with her to the restroom? "Can you watch my bag?"

"I will guard it," Armand said. "Especially since security will follow you to the restroom. Not that you should need any support from them here."

She nodded. As Linda stood, two men wearing Martiniere security outfits—house security, not Vygotsky—rose from the back of the room to follow her. Different from the security in the SUV. She wondered about that. Were those men standing watch outside?

For a moment, she almost turned back to get her bag.

No. I have the tracking bracelet, the Taser and a pistol. If that's not enough—

Linda looked around until she spotted the restroom sign—down a hallway that was darker than she liked. "Please don't crowd me," she said as one of the men moved closer when she entered the hallway, almost stepping on her heels.

Something's not right—

He grabbed her shoulders as the other man tried to put something across her face. Linda hit the emergency buttons on her security bracelet. Then she screamed and kicked back. A stinging sensation burned sharply in one arm; the world turned wobbly around her. Her muscles didn't want to cooperate, much less let her grab either her pistol or the Taser. Linda fought as best she could, flailing with feet and hands even as numbness flowed through her and she sagged into darkness....

Linda woke to the sharp burn of another shot. She lay on the bare vinyl floor, Armand bending over her, injector pen in hand, his expression concerned. Security—not the men who had jumped her, but not the men who had accompanied them in the SUV either—stood behind Armand. Lance Helgessen's voice issued orders in French, but she couldn't quite understand him. Her brain felt full of fuzz and refused to translate his words. Helgessen snapped something in her direction and she stared at him.

"Do you understand what *I* am saying?" Armand frowned at her.

Linda coughed. "Yes." Why was her throat so sore?

"*Good.* She is all right, Lance."

"Not processing French right now," she croaked. "Couldn't understand what Lance said."

Helgessen frowned, then squatted next to Armand. "Look at my finger." He held an index finger up. "Don't turn your head, follow with your eyes." His lips tightened as he moved his finger around. He pulled a medical scanner pen out, pricked her finger with it to extract a drop of blood, and scowled at the readout projected over the medpen. "She needs more antidote."

"She is already maxed out."

"It can go higher."

"Lance—"

"I'll take the responsibility. I have more experience with these knockout drugs." Helgessen took the injector from Armand, tapping up the dose before giving Linda a second shot. "Injections work differently from inhaled agents. Linda, do you remember getting an injection during the attack?"

She frowned, trying to remember as Helgessen held his finger up again for her eyes to follow. He grunted with satisfaction this time.

"I'm not sure," she said finally. "There was something on a cloth the one man put over my nose, but then everything started going numb and dark."

"Medpen data suggests there was an injection as well as an inhaled knockout agent," Helgessen said. "Perhaps even with a short-term memory impact."

"It happened so fast."

"That's another confirmation of an injected agent." Helgessen checked Linda's pulse, then pricked her finger again, nodding at the readout, his features relaxing. "Better. But we should arrange for someone to keep an eye on you tonight, Linda. You're gonna be wobbly for a while. Normal. A delayed reaction may be possible. Remote, no indicators from the medpen that it's likely, but better to be safe than sorry."

"I can watch her," Armand said. "My couch folds down into a bed, and I can sleep in my recliner. Linda, I am so sorry about this."

"As am I." Helgessen's scowl returned. "Vygotsky Security *only* for you from now on, Linda. The same for you, Armand. No general Martiniere security. The two of you are too close to Gabe and Ruby to take chances, and this incident confirms my assertion that regular Group security is *not* reliable for high-level heirs and their support staff. I've already issued the change orders in Piotr's name. He's on his way back from Canada, and is he *ever* pissed about this."

"How did it happen?" Linda tried to stand, but staggered.

"Here." Armand wrapped his arm around her waist. Helgessen did the same on her other side. The world reeled around her and she clutched at them.

Why wouldn't they answer her question?

"Will it bother you to be blindfolded?" Helgessen asked. "Vertigo is a nasty side effect of both the knockout drug and the antidote."

"I am here with you," Armand said. "I will stay with you the whole time."

"Better than getting dizzy and puking—not that I have anything but champagne to throw up right now. Damn it. I was looking forward to this nice dinner."

"It is boxed up, and in the vehicle," Armand said. "No more champagne for you tonight, I am afraid, but the rest of the meal is ready for you."

"After a couple of hours. No food right away." Helgessen fitted a cloth around Linda's head. "How does that feel? Too tight? Too loose?"

"It feels all right."

She leaned more against Armand than Helgessen as they walked to the SUV. In return, Armand tightened his grip on her.

As they helped Linda into the vehicle and the blindfold briefly slipped, she glimpsed a smear of blood on the toe of her left shoe.

Good.

So at least one of her kicks had landed.

Mɪᴛᴢɪ, ᴏɴᴇ ᴏꜰ Hᴇʟɢᴇssᴇɴ's sᴇᴄᴜʀɪᴛʏ ᴛᴇᴀᴍ, ʜᴇʟᴘᴇᴅ Lɪɴᴅᴀ ᴄʜᴀɴɢᴇ out of her dress and into sweats once they returned to the Residence. She guided Linda back to Armand's suite. Then Armand, Mitzi, and Helgessen fussed over Linda and got her settled in Armand's recliner.

"Easier than trying to prop her up on your couch, Armand," Helgessen said. "Linda, you all right with sleeping in the recliner? An upright position is better for the dose you got, both from the drug and the antidote."

"Should I see a doctor?"

"Only if you start having breathing problems in the next few hours." Helgessen squatted by the recliner, looking up into her face. "The combination of alcohol with no food means that the drugs they used hit you harder than usual."

"What happened?" Helgessen hadn't answered her question earlier—would he now?

"Your attackers took out our inside team," Helgessen said curtly. "No idea where the regulars went—they've disappeared. Didn't want to say anything in public."

"The attackers weren't anyone I had seen in security before."

Helgessen nodded. "Confirmed from the restaurant's security videos. No one we've ever employed. Waiting for identity confirmation. We don't know what happened to the two they replaced—that took place out of sight of cams, which is another worry." He paused. "Even more concerning, the drugs they used on you indicate a link with the Electric Born—a product of Electric Born-affiliated labs, created in collaboration with Philip Martiniere."

"I didn't think the Electric Born were active outside of the US." Was this the answer to the question about *how bad are things here* that Serg had evaded during her security evaluation?

"They haven't been, in the past. We're still—" Helgessen's words were cut off by a knock on the door, followed by Ruby limping into the living room.

"Is she all right—oh good, Linda, you're sitting up and oriented. What the hell happened, Lance?"

"Infiltration of the general Martiniere security services," Helgessen said. "Like I've been concerned about, but haven't been able to prove until now."

"Who's responsible?" Ruby's lips tightened. "Is this an attempt to sabotage our Monday release?"

"Possibly. However, there's a suggestion of Electric Born involvement, which implies a political motive, not corporate competition. The drugs used on Linda are some they developed with Philip's help."

"*That* motherfucker just won't let go of us, even though he's dead." Ruby's fists clenched. "Damn it."

Linda focused on Ruby—nicely dressed, like she had also been having a nice dinner. "I'm sorry if I wrecked your dinner, Ruby."

"It would be a lot more wrecked if something happened to you." Gabe hobbled into the living room. "Piotr tells me you suspect Electric Born involvement, Lance."

"Absolutely." Helgessen raised one hand as his comm chimed. He turned away, flicking up a security screen that blurred his voice.

"You two all right?" Gabe put his arm around Ruby's waist, peering at Linda with a worried expression.

"*I'm* fine," Armand said. "They jumped Linda on her way to the restroom. I heard her yell, then her security bracelet alarm went off. I grabbed her bag, ran to the restroom with restaurant staff on my heels, just as the attackers were trying to drag Linda down the hallway and out the emergency exit. They dropped her and ran when I pulled my Taser."

"Should not have happened," Ruby snapped. "God damn it. Who the hell is our leak in security? This keeps happening. Repeatedly. How did Philip and that Vera get onto the Double R? Or the other incidents we've had?"

"It's someone who is either allied with the Electric Born, was a follower of Philip, or was tied to Vera's family," Gabe said. "Don't forget her mafiya connections."

"Or not," Helgessen said, returning to them. "Authorities have apprehended the attackers. Lucky that both Armand and the restaurant staff got a good look at them and gave good descriptions, as well as a couple of clear views on security cams. The attackers were masquerading as servers first, supposedly substitutes sent by a temp service."

"So?" Gabe straightened up and crossed his arms. "Who are they connected to?"

"The US Embassy," Helgessen growled. "Like the last set that bothered us."

"Zimmerman again?" Gabe glowered at Helgessen, suddenly seeming bigger and more menacing.

"No, Zimmerman's gone. McNeil this time. They're part of her security contingent. Contract employees, not regular."

McNeil. Female. That name stirred a memory.

"Are you talking about Harriet McNeil?" Linda asked.

"What do you know about her?" Gabe turned his glare on Linda.

That penetrating gaze—

She didn't flinch away from Gabe's scrutiny. "Clyde has mentioned her a few times. Isn't she the Real Truther party chair?"

"She's currently the Ambassador's press secretary. Have we heard anything about her role in the Real Truthers?" Gabe turned to Armand.

"She flounced from the Party in quite a dramatic manner five months ago," Armand said. "No *obvious* connections since then. The Ambassador's a Classic Democrat. No known political ties there."

"I'll have a chat with the Ambassador about her choice of employees," Gabe growled.

"No," Ruby said. "I'll deal with it, *Gabriel.* No need for the

Martiniere to get involved, especially since it was *my* employee and friend who was affected."

They glared at each other.

Then Gabe sighed. "You're right, Rubes. But this situation just pisses me off."

"Me as well, but we have to be reasonable as long as we're still US citizens. You may have dual citizenship, but I don't yet."

"As citizens we have rights, even in exile, when dealing with *our* government. But all right. Get this whole mess straightened out."

"I will." Ruby studied Linda and Armand. "How long will Linda be down, Lance? Do we need to reschedule our Monday bot release? Is that one of the gases that could trigger an out-of-sequence menstrual cycle?"

Linda struggled upright. "I will be there, Ruby. Period."

Ruby turned her scowl on Linda. "Not a good idea to be reckless with this stuff, Linda. Lance?"

"As long as she doesn't have a bad reaction later on tonight, and rests tomorrow, she should be good for Monday. We have to get through tonight and see," Helgessen said. "And no, it's not one of *those*, fortunately."

"I *will be there*, Ruby," Linda insisted.

Gabe snickered. "All right. You and Ruby have a *lot* more in common than it appears at first. Stubborn women."

"Ex-swim team," Armand said mildly. "Ex-competitive athlete."

"Well, we know about *those*, don't we?" Gabe winked at Ruby. "Makes sense. Barrel racer, swim racer…both of you are competitive and takes a lot to keep you down. Armand, you're sitting watch on her? Will make sure Linda takes it easy?"

"Yes."

"Then perhaps we should get out of here and let Linda rest, all right, Rubes?"

Ruby frowned at Gabe. He cocked his head to the right and gave her an innocent-not-so-innocent smile. She sighed.

"All right, *Gabriel*." Her glower softened, and though she tried to keep her mouth in a straight, severe line, the corners turned up slightly and a dimple appeared in her left cheek. She turned to Linda. "Rest. I'll check in on you tomorrow. And you." She turned and fixed a stern glare on Armand. "You make sure she's all right, okay?"

"I will do my best to take care of her," Armand promised.

Ruby and Gabe left. Helgessen fussed over a packet that he left with Armand, pulling him aside to talk quietly.

Linda closed her eyes. The room was still steady around her, but she was tired, and felt detached from herself. A side effect of the drugs in her system, probably.

Electric Born. Harriet McNeil.

There was more behind the attack on her than McNeil's connection to the Real Truthers. There was a tie between Clyde and McNeil. Bigger than the Real Truthers. No matter how hard Linda tried, she couldn't quite make the connection, but she knew it existed.

Significant? Not significant? Her head hurt just thinking about it.

Armand returned, moving quietly. "Here is some water. Sealed glass with a straw. You need to hydrate, more than usual. Are you hungry yet? You might want to wait, however."

The thought of food made her queasy. Linda sighed and opened her eyes, reaching for the big glass with a silicone cover and straw. She didn't realize how thirsty she was until the first swallow of water reached her mouth. Oh. That felt so good on her irritated throat.

"Not hungry yet," she croaked.

Linda drank half the glass before returning it to the side table, then turned on her side, tucking into the fleece blanket that Armand had spread over her.

"Probably best you do not eat, so that you are not throwing up. Did you want a pillow?"

Linda peered through bleary eyes at Armand, perching on the couch, a worried expression on his face as he studied her.

"I'm fine, thanks."

"Keep pushing the fluids. Sooner or later, you will feel like you have the biggest hangover in the world. More fluids makes it feel less intense." A quick smile twitched his lips. "I got hit with this stuff once. Inhaled only, not injection and inhalation, like you experienced. I remember what it feels like."

"Seems like we should be drawing hazard pay." She fumbled for the water glass again. Sleepy. So sleepy.

"It is not a listed benefit, but—yes. You will see a bonus in your next check, tagged *extraordinary services compensation.*"

"Was joking." She drained the glass.

Armand picked it up. "I wasn't."

"Huh." She was too tired to comment.

LINDA WOKE WITH A GASPING START, SITTING UP IN THE RECLINER, gulping for breath.

" Are you all right?" Armand was right there.

She fumbled for her water. He helped her steady it as she drank. Her breathing stabilized.

"Bad dream," she said finally, slumping against the recliner's back, now becoming aware of the pain in her head. She drank more water before continuing. "About Clyde forcing me to marry him. Sara was my matron of honor, and part of the ceremony as well." She shivered. "Grandma Jenni was there, objecting loudly, until one of Clyde's minions shot her. No one flinched. It didn't even stop the ceremony."

Armand settled on the recliner's arm. "That is a nightmare, all right." He tentatively patted her hand.

"Why would Harriet McNeil want to have me kidnapped? Armand, this whole thing doesn't make sense at all. Something's weird."

He nodded. "I agree. We will see what Ruby's inquiries at the Embassy turn up, if anything, given that it is the weekend. I think the Electric Born and Real Truther connections are key. I have not heard anything from Piotr Vygotsky yet to confirm my suspicions, but my best guess is that your brother-in-law is mixed up in this somehow."

Linda shuddered. "Maybe it's just echoes from that dream, but that's the motive that makes the most sense. Why is Clyde so interested in me, Armand? It can't be so superficial as him wanting to be married to a pair of sisters. Can it?"

"It very well could be. The Electric Born operate like that. Sisters marrying the same man, especially if the women possess particular genetic traits that the man thinks will be useful. Or if one sister only produces daughters. They do not condone IVF or artificial insemination, but there are one hell of a lot of other genetic manipulations that they do support."

Sara's only had girls.

That thought sent chills through Linda. "Then Clyde might be looking at a shared trait between me and Sara, hoping that I'll produce male babies without resorting to IVF if he takes me as a second wife."

"Exactly." Armand met her gaze levelly. "I have not been able to find documentation—yet—that suggests the Electric Born have been charting the genomes of their leadership and their spouses. That has only been a rumor. Justine and Donald are investigating the possibility, since they have more connections with those who would know. But it's entirely possible. Race-based eugenics have been a poorly-hidden but commonly-held notion amongst both the Electric Born and the Real Truthers. White babies sired by the proper fathers. Gabriel's existence is contrary to everything they believe. He is the son of their adored Philip, only Gabe's mother was Hispanic, and he was conceived through IVF. Which is another reason why they hate Gabe, and call him the Great Betrayer. It is not just his role in Philip's death; it's who Gabe is."

"God." Linda buried her head in her hands. "I'm surprised Clyde hasn't tried to snatch me before now."

Armand rested a hand on her back. "He may have been waiting for you to graduate before making his move. He would want you to have a degree. That would also fit a pattern. You landing a job—with the Martinieres, no less—and moving out of his reach might be enough for him to try something like this."

"I hope my family's safe." Her father had been just drunk enough the last two times she had called this week that Linda hadn't wanted to bring up the issue of increased security once more.

Maybe she should have said something to him anyway.

"You have done what you could."

"But was it enough?" Linda sighed and shook her head. Then she raised it. "I wonder if I should call now—what time is it there? My brain doesn't want to make that calculation."

"One in the afternoon there."

She chewed her lip, thinking. "One pm on Saturday afternoon. Dad might be on the golf course. I'll call." Linda started to get up but Armand shook his head.

"I will get your phone. And while you're calling, I will heat up our dinner. I imagine you are hungry by now. I certainly am. I snacked, but that was not enough."

That might explain my headache. But why didn't he eat his dinner? Politeness?

Worry about me?

"Thanks, Armand."

He smiled at Linda as he handed over her bag. Somehow, it was a different smile from before. Softer, more intimate.

Or was she just imagining things?

Linda called her father as Armand went to work in the kitchen. No response. She left a message and slumped back in the chair. Call her mother? No, that needed to be saved for an emergency. No way of telling if this was one of her good days or her bad days, not from this far away. No need to get her worried.

She closed her eyes and the world seemed to sway around her.

Oops. Maybe that's not such a good idea.

Linda opened her eyes. "Armand?"

"Are you all right?" Armand returned. "How is your father?"

"I don't know. He didn't answer. Might be out on the golf course. Left a message. I—when I closed my eyes, it was almost like the spins after drinking too much. Still feel disassociated. Is this—is it a sign of a problem?"

"More likely just a combination of substances plus hunger," Armand said. He took her hand. "This help? Sometimes contact can settle the disorientation."

It was something to focus on. Not perfect, but it helped. "Yes —but things are a bit wobbly." Another need made itself felt. "I —need to use the restroom, too." Mitzi had helped her before everyone left, but now—

"Here." Armand eased her to the edge of the recliner, then helped her up. "Do you want me to come in? Counter should help with support if you do not want me there. I can leave the door open and not look."

"Leave the door open."

She made her way to the toilet, somehow. It seemed to take forever to deal with everything and wash her hands. Armand slipped in and scooped her up once she finished.

"How about we sit on the couch until dinner is finished? You can lean against me while you eat."

"Sure."

Dare she admit how nice it felt to be in his arms once they stopped moving? Armand held Linda in his lap. She curled against him and rested her head on his chest, listening to the soothing steady beat of his heart. Her eyelids drooped and she drowsed, feeling *safe*.

The distant timer chime roused her. Armand eased her off of his lap. Linda flopped onto her side, not wanting to sit up. She dozed off again, waking to the clatter of dishes as Armand set them on the coffee table.

"I am sorry it doesn't have the nice presentation but...." His voice trailed off.

Linda pushed herself up. The scent of food made her stomach rumble loudly. She couldn't stop the laughing that broke free; half-anxious, half-humor at the absurdity of all this.

Armand sat and put his arm around her, the concerned expression returning to his face.

"This—is—just—so bizarre!" she finally managed to choke out.

That brought a smile and then laughter from him. He wrapped his arms around her while they laughed.

Linda drew a deep breath when her hilarity finally ebbed. "Sorry. I think I'm a bit—"

"Intoxicated? Yes." But that faint amused smile was still there. "Sometimes laughter is the only way to cope with the weirdness of the world. Feel better?"

"Yes. Yes. And now I can eat."

***

LINDA CURLED AGAINST THE BACK OF THE COUCH WHILE ARMAND dealt with cleaning up, falling asleep once again.

"Should move you back to the recliner," he murmured as he shook her awake.

"Do I have to? Comfortable here. More comfortable leaning against you. Maybe no nightmares."

"Are you sure?"

"Uh-huh."

"Let me set things up so that we can rest, then."

"All right." She closed her eyes as he moved cushions around.

Soon enough, he eased her legs onto the couch and settled

her in the corner, then slid in next to her. Linda exhaled and rested her head on Armand's chest as he took her into his arms.

Once again, the steady beat of his heart lulled her into sleep.

This time, she didn't have dreams, or if she did, they were unmemorable.

She *did* think that at one point Armand's lips gently brushed the top of her head.

But it was probably just her imagination.

CHAPTER 8

NEGOTIATING A RELATIONSHIP

MAY, 2030

LINDA WOKE TO THE SCENT OF COOKING POTATOES, BACON, AND freshly-brewed coffee. She pushed herself upright, pleased to discover that she wasn't wobbly any longer. After a restroom stop, she wandered into the kitchen. Armand's suite was set up slightly different from hers, without the garden view, and his kitchen was separate from the living room. His furniture wasn't all Art Nouveau, either—for example, the couch they had shared last night. Comfortable, big, and definitely *not* Nouveau.

He grinned at her. "Coffee's there—" he pointed to the coffeepot. "And I thought you might appreciate an American breakfast. No eggs, but I can at least provide bacon and potatoes."

"That works." She fixed her coffee and leaned against the counter, cupping her mug in her hands. "Thank you for taking care of me last night."

His face went solemn. "I thought you might prefer to have someone familiar around to watch you, rather than security. You still need to take it easy, especially with the release tomorrow." Now he made a mock-angry face and shook the spatula at her. "You are not escaping my clutches today!"

Linda chuckled. "I'm—not feeling that ambitious, to be honest."

"A good day to settle in and watch videos. There is a storm blowing in, so it is not that nice out."

"Only if you watch the videos with me."

He laughed. "It is Sunday. I usually try to take this day off, even if I work part of the day on Saturdays. So what is your desire? I am a bit short on fluffy downloads, but we could stream something. Or we could play a video game or two, if you are interested."

"Oh, I don't know. I don't feel up to gaming, and I'd like to watch something without a lot of angst. We have enough of that in real life right now."

"I can definitely agree with that." He stirred the potatoes. "Go ahead and sit at the table. Do not push yourself to do more. I speak from experience. My one time dealing with knockout gas was—not pretty, shall we say?"

"All right, all right." Linda eyed the table. A plain yellow tablecloth, two place settings. Two glasses of tomato juice—how would Armand know her preference for tomato juice over orange juice?—wait, he had handled her initial grocery order for the Residence. That would have revealed a lot about her preferences.

Linda sat and watched Armand cook, because he grumbled every time she tried to offer help.

"One concession to bachelor boy life," he said, bringing the pan of potatoes over to the table and setting it on a pad. "Fewer dishes."

Linda laughed. "Not just for bachelor boys. I do it too. So did Ruby."

It was *easy* to laugh around Armand. And that little smile of his when she laughed—

"It is efficient." Armand doled out the bacon, then topped off her coffee. "I *knew* you wouldn't mind. All about the efficiency."

She toasted him with her tomato juice. "What can I say, to the man who held me most of the night because I was disoriented? Thank you, Armand."

"Like I said, I have been in your position. Only with no one familiar around—or at least as familiar as we are after—what has it been? Two weeks? Something like that?"

"Something," she agreed. "It really helped. Head on your chest, listening to your heartbeat, kept me centered."

"I am glad." He looked down at his plate.

An awkward silence fell between them. Linda focused on her food, unsure what to say next.

They were colleagues. Equals. No actual power imbalance, and yet—

Is this really a good idea?

ARMAND'S DOWNLOAD TASTES RAN MORE TO ART-HOUSE FILMS AND obscure cinematography, with a heavy dose of older black and white films. They settled on one of the Marx Brothers movies— she wasn't sure which one—for the first thing they watched, sitting next to each other on the couch, a careful hands-width of space between them.

Until Linda started getting drowsy. She leaned away from Armand—too far away from the couch arm to rest her head on it, but before she teetered too far over, Armand reached over and pulled her into him.

"Okay with this? Has to be more comfortable than lying flat on your side."

"If you are."

"Would not do it if I were uncomfortable. Contact is probably still a good thing. Helps with any long-term after effects."

"Probably," she agreed. She nestled into his side. It *was* more comfortable to lean against Armand. And that faint vanilla scent of his—but that closeness led to an inner argument.

What the hell *are you thinking, Linda Elizabeth Coates? He's a co-worker. A colleague,* her cautious, don't-make-waves side said.

This isn't the standard situation. We're living in the same building, the risk-taking part of her responded. *Family all over the place. The Group already engages in a lot of nepotism, and Gabe married Ruby after she became a Martiniere Grant finalist—don't tell me that wasn't an issue!*

You're not Ruby, and Armand isn't as high up in the Family hierarchy as Gabe. There's still a potentially problematic employment issue.

How? We are equivalent in power. Plus. He cooks. He's a nice man.

But if he knew everything about your family—

He already does. He participated in vetting you before Ruby made the job offer, right?

Linda sighed. Arguing with herself about this wasn't productive or restful.

Armand stroked her forehead with a forefinger. "Everything all right?"

"This is comfortable. Maybe—I don't know," she sighed again.

"Do you want to move to the recliner?"

"No. No. It's just—"

"It is intimate." His voice was quiet. "We work closely together. If you are having the same thoughts I am—"

"I think we are. I'm surprised that the Group's HR department hasn't made a video about work relationships, and issued policies about them. Or have they, and I just haven't encountered them in my orientation yet?"

"Policies exist. But at our level in the organization, with Family involved—it is not a situation that goes to HR." Armand sighed. "If we become serious, then there is a questionnaire I have to take that addresses my intent. Gabe administers it, as the Martiniere. Saul was strict about Family members taking advantage of non-Family employees, and Gabe has continued that policy. I am close enough to being a high-level heir that I fall under the requirement to go through that process if I get involved with a non-Family Martiniere Group worker."

"Oh. Just what does the questionnaire cover?"

"It addresses issues of inheritance, intent, marriage, and

requires swearing an oath not to penalize the other person at work should the relationship fail."

"Just an oath?"

"The Family takes oath-swearing very seriously. Breaking one's word—especially when swearing to the Martiniere himself—is one of the few things that earns immediate banishment from the Group, and possibly disinheritance from the Family."

"Wow."

"It is very old-fashioned, but it works."

She didn't know what to say after that. Armand kept stroking her forehead. Linda closed her eyes, enjoying his gentle touch. It felt so right.

"There is no need to rush into anything," he said finally. "Is there?"

"No." She shifted her weight against him. "We can get to know each other better. I like being around you away from work."

"I like being around you, too. And your recovery day is probably not the best moment to contemplate these issues. Let's just take it one step at a time."

"I'm good with that—as long as I can snuggle up to you. You're *nice* to cuddle with."

Armand laughed. "That might be just the aftereffects of the drugs still working out of your system."

"I don't think so. You're a nice man. You cook. Clearly don't expect someone to wait on you."

"And you are smart. You care about people. You do not think my artistic inclinations are weird."

"How could I, when I have them too?"

"A lot in common." His arm tightened around her. "I regret the reason for—this—today. But I do not regret that it means I have an excuse to do nothing but watch old movies with you, and make sure you get your rest."

"Same here." She yawned. "And I *really* like cuddling with you. You smell good."

Armand laughed. His lips lightly brushed the top of her head—not her imagination this time. She leaned even more into him.

"Sleep, if you need to. I'm here," he murmured.

"Mmmhmm."

Linda's eyelids drooped and she curled into Armand's side, secure.

Safe.

A sensation that had been far too rare over the past seven years.

ONCE LINDA WAS MORE AWAKE, THEY MOVED ON TO OLD CARTOONS —mostly Looney Tunes and Merrie Melodies classics. Gabe, Ruby, and Helgessen slipped in to check on Linda. Ruby and Gabe ended up joining them on the couch to watch cartoons, resting their bad legs on the coffee table. It was a tight fit, but comfortable nonetheless.

At one point, Armand and Gabe got up to make popcorn.

"Getting friendly with Armand, hmm?" Ruby raised one brow while smirking.

Linda shrugged. "We have a lot in common beyond our jobs. Swim team backgrounds. Interest in art. Who knows? We're taking it slow."

Ruby snorted. "*Go slow* may not be as slow as you think it would be with a Martiniere. At least it wasn't for Gabe and me— then again, Armand is not Gabe. Armand strikes me as being less—impulsive? Less driven? More concerned about details in his personal life? Gabe gets sucked into work in a way that I don't think Armand does."

"Armand's a nice man."

"*Nice* is huge. That's what struck me right away about Gabe. But most of the Martiniere men fall into that category—well, with some glaring exceptions. Like Philip. Joseph. Several others who have been kicked out of Family connections for bad behavior."

"The whole Family is nice?"

"So far, that's been true for all but a handful of the Family members I've encountered. Most of them seem to have been raised on a heavy diet of *noblesse oblige*, and they take it seriously. Not just recently, but over several hundred years, enforced by the Family structures and then Family plus the Group. Again, with the blatant exception of Philip and Joseph."

"That's hard to believe."

"There *have* been some stellar bad actors in the Family's past, but they're not as common. Usually one per generation, if that. Mental illness runs in the Family as well—again, Philip as a possible example. Gabe and Justine have been watched very carefully over the years, for fear they might have inherited Philip's psychopathic tendencies." Ruby looked down at her hands, then back up. "Gabe obviously didn't develop those tendencies; neither did Justine. But there are other traits that happen—like Gabe's inclinations toward overwork and depression before he and I got together."

Armand and Gabe returned to the living room with bowls full of popcorn. That ended further discussion about the Family.

But Linda kept mulling over Ruby's statement that *most of them have been raised on a steady diet of noblesse oblige, and they take it seriously.*

It explained a lot about both Gabe and Armand.

<hr>

By evening, Helgessen pronounced Linda as recovered and no longer in need of supervision. Armand insisted on escorting her across the hallway to her suite.

"It has been a nice day, in spite of the circumstances that caused it," he said. "Maybe we should do this again?"

"Safer than going out, apparently."

He laughed. "In some respects, yes." He stroked her temple. "Take care, rest, and I will see you tomorrow."

"Yes."

Their eyes met. His left hand wrapped around hers. She squeezed it.

"Thank you once again for everything, Armand."

"It was a pleasure."

Silence, neither wanting to look away from the other. Linda smiled at Armand, feeling a fluttering deep inside of her as those blue eyes met hers. He raised their twined hands and kissed the back of hers. The touch sent tingles up and down her body.

Oh, I am starting to fall for this man.

Did she really want a relationship of some sort with Armand, something above and beyond work?

He's worth the exploration.

She gently brought their hands to her lips, slipping her hand free just enough so that her kiss landed on his palm. He shivered, his smile widening. Then he eased his hand free of hers, and cupped her cheek. She closed her eyes, leaning into his hand. Oh, the tingles buzzing through her at his touch!

"May I kiss you?" he whispered.

"Yes."

He dropped his hand and leaned in. His lips brushed against hers, careful, precise, their only point of contact. He pulled back.

Her turn now.

Linda kissed him with the same careful restraint. Slow. Delicate. Part of her wanted to grab Armand, drag him to her bed *now.*

But that was how she had started with Tony. No, she wanted more with this man.

Possibly even something lasting.

She could take the time to build a foundation for something long-term.

"Good night," he murmured. "I will see you in the morning. Waiting until you are safely inside."

"In the morning."

She went inside.

Romance had not been on her agenda when she came to Paris.

But now that it appeared to be happening—

THE FIELD TEST TOOK UP MOST OF MONDAY MORNING.

"Be a lot better when we have the mobile growboxes figured out," Ruby muttered as she and Linda monitored the transfer of RubyBots from their growboxes to temperature-controlled trays containing growth medium for transport. "This is awkward as hell."

"Agreed. And requires adequate technology support, as well as the ability to transport these damn trays without spilling."

That had been another part of their work during the past week—figuring out how to transport the biobots from the labs where they had been grown to the field without suffering significant losses. Eventually, the growboxes would deal with that issue, cultivating the biobots and transporting them to the release site.

But for now—the biobots could only survive for a short period without drawing energy from either growth medium or the soil in the fields they had been released in. Growth medium needed to be kept at a certain temperature for optimal use. Soil wasn't an option for the trays, due to the biobot proximity programming that ensured appropriate scattering in the field and was triggered by soil contact.

And they just couldn't dump the biobots into the trays of growth medium for transport. They couldn't be loaded too quickly or too slowly, or allowed to clump up. The transfer from growboxes to growth medium trays required two people, one to monitor the growbox side, the other to observe the tray loading process and ensure the biobots didn't accidentally trigger their proximity programs. Linda and Ruby had figured out over several practices that Ruby was best at the growboxes while Linda was better loading trays.

Once each tray was carefully loaded with biobots, lab staff carried it to a cart, until all five trays for the day's trial were ready. Gabe and Armand arrived as staff loaded the tray cart into a transport van. Ruby and Linda checked the latches holding the trays and cart in place three times.

"Well, I guess that's it," Ruby said. "Off we go."

"Good luck," Gabe said, a wistful expression on his face. "Wish I didn't have so many meetings today. I'd love to see how this release performs."

"We have Armand to take video for you," Ruby said.

"It's not the same as being there."

Gabe and Ruby kissed while Armand and Linda climbed into the van. Because of the bulk of the transport cart and monitoring tech, only one bench seat remained in the van. Linda sat by the window.

"Feeling all right?" Armand took her hand.

She nodded, squeezing his hand. "Just a little nervous. Hoping everything works."

"Same here."

Ruby slid in next to Armand. "Let's do this."

———

LINDA ENDED UP LEANING SLIGHTLY AGAINST ARMAND AS THEY drove from the Residence to the Martiniere testing fields. She didn't feel like talking. Armand held her hand and Ruby focused on her tablet, flipping through something.

"Tired?" he murmured.

"A little."

"I could put my arm around you. Keep you steady."

"You could." She smiled at him. "No objections."

He slipped his arm around her shoulders, and pulled her

close. Linda settled in, trying and failing to focus on the landscape as drowsiness crept over her.

As she had always done on all but the shortest car trips, unless she was driving. The hangover from the weekend didn't help, either.

Ruby had laughed about Linda sleeping in vehicles when they drove further than just around Corvallis. Linda was used to it. Her sleepiness in cars had been a family joke, one that Sara teased Linda about when they were little.

Lin, when are you going to wake up and enjoy the scenery?

I'm trying, Sare, I'm trying.

But Linda never managed to stay awake during a car ride, unless she was driving. Even now that she was an adult.

LINDA STARTLED AWAKE AS THE VAN SLOWED. SHE CHECKED THE time. Only half an hour since they had left the Residence. They turned off on a narrow track along a flat field with a healthy crop of wheat that had grown halfway up to her knees. When they stopped, she straightened up.

As Armand set up the dronecams, Linda and Ruby supervised the staff unloading the cart holding the trays. Then trays were placed along the side of the field at ten-meter intervals, each one with a staff member present to release the bots should the automatic release mechanism fail.

That done, it was time to erect their monitoring equipment.

"Don't know if we have enough bots to cover the entire field if we have any failures," Ruby muttered, tightening her lips.

"We can still track performance in the part of the field that is covered." Linda finished setting up the stand holding her tablet, switching on the monitoring app she had finished tweaking on Saturday.

"It'll have to do." Ruby contemplated her tablet. "Armand, are the drones in place to monitor the release?"

"Just a minute, I have one that is not cooperating. Need to activate a backup." He strode to the van.

"It's always something." Ruby twitched the end of her braid back and forth between the index and middle fingers of her left hand.

"Wouldn't be a field test without a bobble of some sort. Remember what Dr. Green always said."

Ruby chuckled. "Let's hope we don't have anything exploding this time."

"We *are* using a different fuel source." Linda rolled her eyes, remembering *that* field test.

Her bots had blown up like tiny firecrackers in the test field when given the activation signal, on a hot, dry May morning. Linda, Ruby, and the rest of the class had scrambled to put out the tiny spot fires in the field.

Don't want that happening in the height of fire season, had been Dr. Green's mild reproof. *Make sure you have a better fuel source.*

Linda didn't use that fueling mechanism in her designs ever again.

"And it's wetter today than that test field was. Yesterday's rain will be a help."

Armand returned from setting up the replacement dronecam. "All right. We are ready for release."

"Release in three. Two. One." Ruby raised her voice. "Releasing NOW."

Linda focused on her monitors. "Tray #4 is having release issues." She glanced down the row—the assigned staffer knelt next to the tray, fumbling with the manual release. "Ah. There it goes."

She was too far away to see the bots release—a shame, because the ladybug-sized bots were a brilliant bright magenta that looked like a shimmering carpet when they first flooded out of confinement. That color had earned them the name of RubyBot, at Louisa's insistence, for publicity purposes.

Ruby joined Linda. They observed the dispersal of the bots throughout the field on her screen.

"Should be getting more than just location data back from the bots soon." Ruby glanced up, once again playing with the end of her braid.

"There we are. First analysis transmissions."

They studied the results.

"Dispersal works in some form for 85% of the bots—still not getting the entire field, they're not spreading as far apart as they were programmed to do," Ruby said. "That has to be fixed."

"Might be a factor of field conditions." Linda noted *discrepancy between proximity programming and execution* in her separate *Update Notes* app, to be considered for future bot refinements.

"Could be."

"Reports work. Uploading to data center—good!" Linda exhaled. It was one thing to have the bots report to an on-site recorder, but for best tracking, she and Ruby had been striving to program the bots to upload to a satellite. "Aw, dang it, the data doesn't match. Garbled in transmission." She scribbled another note in her *Update* app.

Armand joined them. "Calling dronecams back because the bots have dug into the soil and there is not much to see. Except getting shots of you two at work. So look busy."

"As if we don't always look busy!" Ruby snorted, before grabbing her tablet off of its stand. "Linda, let's see what we can tweak on site. I need to sit."

They ended up sitting in the open back of the van, comparing notes and delving into programming.

SEVERAL HOURS LATER, THEY COULD PRONOUNCE THIS RELEASE AS A limited success. Off-site transmission still needed work, and the bots remained in closer proximity than their programming had been set, which meant that only half of the field was covered.

"If this ends up being a typical proximity issue, that's sure going to affect affordability," Ruby muttered, staring at the field.

"We need to find the site parameters that affect proximity," Linda said. "The data we're getting now might help."

"I hope so."

But the field mapping so far was in great detail. The bots had reported back on conditions and were now introducing microbial dosages intended to reduce soil water loss.

Still at 83% performance. Linda chewed her lip thoughtfully. *Two percent function failure after two hours. We'll see how long they function*—that was the next performance test.

All the same, this was a good beginning.

They piled back into the van as Ruby called Gabe to report.

"Maybe we should have a little celebration tonight?" Armand asked. "Nothing big, drinks and a movie?"

"Sure."

"Your place or mine?"

"It *is* my turn, so my place."

Her phone buzzed. *"Mary Coates."*

What the?

Her mother *never* called. Not by herself. Not from her own phone.

Something's wrong.

"Mom?"

"Linda, have you heard anything from your father?" Her mother's voice was choked, as if she had been crying.

"I—tried to call him on Saturday, and he didn't answer."

Oh God, he hasn't called me back! How could I have forgotten about that?

"Oh God." Her mother gulped. "He hasn't been home since Saturday morning. We didn't have a fight or anything. He just seemed to be his usual self. None of his friends have seen him, either. I—I just thought he was hanging out with Jimmy and Rory. Sometimes their poker games run long, and your dad spends the night with them rather than drive home."

"Did Dad leave a note?"

Armand raised his brows at Linda as Ruby stiffened, turning her attention to Linda as well.

"No. Nothing out of the ordinary. And when I called Rory, he hadn't seen your father since he left work on Friday."

"Just a second, Mom, I'm with people. Ruby, and my counterpart who works for Gabe. May I tell them what's going on?"

"I suppose," her mother sniffled.

"It's my mother. Dad hasn't been home since Saturday morning," she said to Ruby and Armand.

"Is not coming home something he does regularly?" Armand asked.

Linda shook her head. "Not like this. Sometimes his poker games run late, but—Mom talked to his poker buddies. Dad's best friend Rory hasn't seen him since he left work on Friday."

Ruby scowled. "Gabe, I'll call you right back. We have an issue. Security. Linda's father. Tell you when I know more." She hung up and rested her phone on her thigh. "Put her on speaker."

"Mom, I have Ruby and Armand—Gabe's executive assistant —on speaker."

"I don't know that we need to get your work involved." Her mother choked back a sob. "It's just that he never showed up at the golf course. Or the poker game."

Oh, this is getting worse.

"How can I help? Is Clyde doing anything?" Linda tapped her free hand on the seat.

Should I try to go back home? Is this connected to my kidnapping attempt?

"Clyde is—you know Clyde, I don't know if he's taking it seriously or not!" Her mother's voice rose. "He won't let Sara stay with me."

"Should I come—"

"*No.*" Ruby's voice was low and firm. "Mrs. Coates. This is Ruby Barkley Martiniere. My sister-in-law Justine Martiniere-

Atwood is in Corvallis and can help you. I'm texting her now about providing you with a safe, security-cleared companion and a Vygotsky security detail."

"But surely you can spare Linda—"

"Linda is a potential target due to her proximity to me and Gabriel, and the important work we are doing," Ruby said firmly. "As are you and your husband, because you are her parents. Besides, Justine's resources are closer to you than Linda is. You'll have support within a couple of hours. All right?"

"All—all right."

"Mom?"

"Yes." Her mother's voice quavered.

"We'll find him. I promise. You need to stay safe, though, because—"

Armand's hand tightened on her wrist, startling Linda into looking at him. *Do not tell her what happened to you yet*, he mouthed. *No idea if her line is secure.*

"Because I worry." She finished weakly.

"I wish you could be here. I want both you and Sara here." Her mother gulped. "It's scary."

"I've just texted Justine," Ruby broke in. "Advance team is en route to your house, Mrs. Coates. Linda, I've sent IDs to your phone. Will you please forward them to your mother?"

"Yes." Linda quickly pulled them up and sent them to her mother.

Ruby continued. "What about your security, Mrs. Coates? Have they seen your husband since Saturday morning?"

"They—they haven't been here since Friday. At least I haven't seen them. They don't always check in with me, though, even when Thomas is gone."

Shit.

Ruby and Linda frowned at each other. Then Ruby turned back to her phone, fingers flying over it as she texted.

She looked up. "Mrs. Coates, expect the advance team to arrive in half an hour. Let's keep you on the phone until then."

Oh dear God. What are we going to talk about for that long?

Architecture. And interior décor. After that—

Between the three of them, they were able to keep Linda's mother distracted until Justine's security arrived at the Coates house, simultaneous with their own arrival back at the Residence.

Linda said goodbye to her mother and buried her head in her hands. She had been able to banish her worries about what had happened to her father while talking to her mother.

But now—

Armand rubbed her back.

"Take the rest of the day off," Ruby said.

Linda exhaled and sat back up. "No. I need the distraction. Have to work in the main lab anyway, run full-size sims."

"If you're sure—"

"I'm sure." What she really wanted to do was lock herself up alone to scream and wail.

Working for the Martinieres didn't keep Dad safe!

But screaming and wailing wouldn't solve anything.

Working was productive, at least.

CHAPTER 9

FAMILY COMPLICATIONS

CONCENTRATING ON PROGRAMMING SIMS WAS *HARD*, DAMN IT, EVEN in troubleshooting mode. Linda worked in streaks, focusing single-mindedly on the screen and the full-size simulator. Then *something* would snap her attention elsewhere, just long enough to remember *Dad's missing*.

On the other hand, retracing her steps to regain her place after each of those jolts helped her visualize a possible solution to the discrepancies between the proximity programming in simulations and what they had seen in the field that morning. It couldn't be that simple a fix—could it?

"Hey." Gabe's voice startled Linda. He stood in the doorway of her lab space in the main labs—she had left it open. After all, if she wanted to be around people as a distraction from fretting, what purpose did shutting herself off serve?

"Hi." She straightened up. "Come on in."

"Thanks." Gabe closed the door behind him, then hobbled to a chair and dropped into it, lacing his fingers together. "Just updating you on the latest security reports about your family. Ruby's tied up in a lab management meeting, so she asked me to talk to you in her place."

"Dad's been found?" Linda saved her work, fingers trembling.

Please. Please let him be alive.

Gabe's headshake dismissed that possibility. "Unfortunately, no. But your mother is more secure than she was before, with Vygotsky Security replacing your family's previous security. Justine is not happy with what she has seen of their operation."

Linda slumped in her chair. "But no Dad."

"Not yet. The police are useless." Gabe scowled. "I'm also concerned because Newsome has finally allowed your sister to join your mother, after apparently raising a fuss. Then, suddenly —no problem with her showing up at your parents' house, with kids in tow."

"Clyde must have worked out talking points for Sara to use on Mom."

"Very likely. One of them—are you *sure* your father might not have taken off for a weekend? Doesn't have to be with anyone else, not that he's having an affair—just private. Or that he—um —might have—had the intent to harm himself? Those are suggestions being made by both the police and Newsome."

"Short of drinking to the degree that he might get into a wreck, no," Linda said. "But that doesn't fit, either. Dad does his heavy drinking in company, at the poker games. Not alone. And he usually sends a message to Mom when he's staying the night."

Gabe's lips tightened and he nodded. "The problem is that the police think he's off on a solitary bender, based on what they claim his security staff have said. But Vygotsky interviews with your father's friends say otherwise—major discrepancies between them and his security."

"Oh God. This doesn't sound good." Linda buried her head in her hands.

"No. It gets worse." Gabe's voice was flat.

Linda gulped and raised her head. "How much worse?"

"We gained access to a drive-through coffee shop security video that appears to show known Electric Born operatives following your father. And none of his security around him."

Electric Born —oh crud.

"Can you show it to me?"

"Let me pull it up on your tablet."

She handed the tablet over to Gabe. He tapped on it, then pushed it back to her.

Linda watched the video loop several times, her heart sinking as she recognized the men in the car that followed her father's.

"It's elders from the local Electric Born church," she sighed. "Not all of them. They—could have decided to pull an intervention on him. But why? Usually, notice is given to the family, and it's requested—" She stopped as she realized what was happening. "Clyde. Sara. One of them set this up. That's why Clyde allowed Sara and the kids to join Mom. That gets around the family invite and notice provisions the church requires, because Sara's at the house."

"What do you mean by an intervention?" Gabe leaned forward, brows furrowing.

"Religious intervention, usually limited to church members who have gone astray. But Dad's never been a church member."

"You know about it and you're not a church member—are you?" Gabe's frown deepened.

"No, I have more sense than that! I heard enough about interventions from Sara." Linda sank back in her chair. "Damn. This means I should probably go back to Roseburg and get involved. Who knows what the hell they're going to do?"

"Absolutely *not*." Gabe scowled. His brows furrowed and he straightened up in his chair, seeming to loom large. "It's very possible that this is an attempt to lure you back to the US so Clyde can get his hands on you. Kidnapping didn't work. A threat to your family is the next step."

"I can't just let this happen." Linda faced Gabe's glower. "Even if I'm Clyde's target. They're in this mess because of me."

Yeah, Gabe's pissed. Yeah, it's pretty damn intimidating to have the Martiniere himself glaring at me. But we're talking about my family! This affects ME. Not him.

"I'm not saying that *just letting it happen* is what we're going to do." His words came short and sharp, almost snapped. Gabe pulled out his phone. "Armand. What do you know about an Electric Born procedure called an intervention?" A pause. "Linda identified the vehicle behind her father's car at the drive-through as carrying elders of the local church. She thinks an intervention with her father is possible."

Linda clenched her hands, wanting to speak.

Gabe continued. "Get in touch with Justine and Serg with this news, as quickly as possible. Locations? Let me hand you over to Linda." He handed the phone to Linda.

"Linda?" Concern filled Armand's voice.

"Here."

"Are there preferred places where these elders might take your father for an isolated intervention?"

"There's an old church camp somewhere in the Cascades around Diamond Lake—Crescent—maybe Odell Lake. The elders camp—not the one that Grandmother Norma took Mom and Sara to every summer."

"All right. Thank you. Relaying that information now." His voice lowered. "If you do not want to be alone tonight, but do not want me in your space, you are welcome to come to my place."

"I'm not sure I would be in the best of moods to be around others."

"Perfectly understandable. It is all right, no matter what your state of mind is. It won't bother me. I'm just—I am worried about you. Offering a shoulder and the presence of someone else if you need it—or a racing partner in the pool."

"You know, the pool might be just the thing. We'll see after that."

"Usual time?" His voice turned hopeful.

"Unless you hear otherwise."

"Good. Better hand me back over to Gabe."

An odd expression crossed Gabe's face as he took the phone

and resumed talking to Armand. "Justine and Serg know what's happening? Good. Do we need to have that conversation? Not yet—all right. Be careful."

He slipped the phone back into his pocket, that quizzical expression still on his face. Gabe studied Linda, lips tightening, as if he were assessing her value.

"What?" Linda's voice came out sharper than she intended. She didn't *like* that measuring look. It was too much like the fabled *The-Martiniere-Is-Disappointed* expression for her comfort.

Gabe arched a brow at her. "Armand *says* it's not time yet for that intimate relationship questionnaire regarding his intentions toward you. But everything I'm hearing from him—not his words, just his vocal tones and his concern—says that you two are more than just colleagues."

"Nothing reportable has happened. We're taking it slow."

Is this Gabe speaking as the Martiniere concerned about HR issues, or what?

"I thought as much. Armand would have told me otherwise. But." Gabe ran his fingers through his hair, tousling it into greater disarray. "Linda." He paused, grimacing. "Please. Whatever your response to this escalating family issue ends up being, please, *please*, talk to someone before you do anything drastic like returning to the US by yourself. Me. Ruby. Armand. *Someone.* It's not just about your relationship with Ruby." Another pause, before he continued, speaking slowly and thoughtfully. "Armand is one of my favorite cousins. Above and beyond his position as my assistant. I—I don't want to see him hurt, and it's pretty clear to me after this weekend that if something happens to you, it will hurt him."

"I—understand."

So are you warning me off of Armand?

She scowled at Gabe.

I'm not giving him up just because you say so. Even if you are the Martiniere.

"Don't take me wrong." Gabe rumpled his hair again, this

time paradoxically straightening it. "You don't need to frown at me. I approve of your relationship, not that it's my position to express an opinion about it, even as the Martiniere. At least within the Martiniere Group. Now, within the Family—that would be different, but I'm not that kind of person."

"Thank you."

May not be your position but it's clear you have an opinion. So what do you want from me, Gabriel Martiniere? Why bring this up now?

"You two are quite professional in your work behavior from what I've seen so far, and I have no reason to doubt that you will continue to act in that manner. But—I could see Ruby deciding she needs to take action if something like this were happening with her family, and running off to get involved before I knew about it. You're a lot like her. So please. If you decide to do something, get help. Don't do anything alone, and for God's sake, *tell one of us.* Not just for Ruby but for Armand."

"Do you want me to swear an oath or something?"

Another of those quizzical expressions. "You're not a Martiniere, and I wouldn't hold you to that standard. It's just— it's been a short period of time that you have been working for Ruby, but you have many more people here who are concerned about you than you realize. We're trying our best to *do something* about this situation."

"All right," she conceded. "I won't take off and do something stupid without checking in with someone first. I promise."

A flash of a grin, and then Gabe pushed himself up, leaning hard on his cane and wincing. "Thank you." He exhaled, and she noticed a faint sweaty sheen on his forehead. "I will brief you myself about what Vygotsky Security learns. Daily."

"That's not necessary—"

"I *want* to do it." A quick grin. "If it's the Martiniere himself calling so that I can report to you—there *will* be results. More than if it were Armand."

"You don't know Roseburg. Or Douglas County."

"No. But I know a little bit about Thunder County, and Lakeside. A lot more about Los Angeles. Bureaucrats in charge of counties don't like it when a powerful corporate leader *personally* contacts them about something like this. That could reflect poorly on their image. And I can make this an international issue."

"Thank you."

Another quick grin. "You may not be Family—yet—but you're definitely family. Just like Louisa's Remy. *I protect my own.*" He hobbled to the door. "Leave it open, or closed?"

"Open, please."

She stared at the open doorway after Gabe left.

Now what was she going to do?

ARMAND BEAT HER IN SHORT SPRINTS THAT EVENING, AFTER THEY had warmed up. But when they went to longer distances, Linda won their impromptu races. Four laps or more, and she was several strokes ahead of him. They kept racing in each stroke until they got up to eight laps. By then, she was ready to crawl out of the pool, her whirling thoughts finally settling.

"Your turns are better than mine and it shows up at a distance," Armand said as they walked to the hot tub. "They have always been my weakness."

"The few times I won a race, the turns made the difference once we went beyond 100 meters. As long as it was freestyle. Breast stroke, not so good, back stroke, ick, and butterfly—"

"Ugh. Butterfly." He made a face as he held back so that she was first in.

Linda settled at her favorite jet. Armand took the other strong shoulder jet. They sat in silence. His hand delicately brushed against hers. She wrapped her hand around his.

"I would put my arm around you—but do not want to presume," he said. "Especially since this is somewhat public."

"Please," she said. "It's been a rough afternoon. I can use the contact."

Armand slid over and slipped his arm around Linda's waist, pulling her close. She leaned her head against his shoulder.

"You are not worried about being seen?" he asked, as several other staff members entered the pool area.

Linda snorted. "Gabe and I had a conversation. He—and most definitely Ruby—are aware that we're—um—what are we?"

"Colleagues. Friends. Exploring possibilities."

"All of that. Gabe is worried that I'm going to rush back to the US by myself. That came up after I figured out that an intervention might be going on with my parents."

"I would not advise that you consider that possibility at all," Armand said.

"What if it's the only way to ensure that my parents are safe?"

"We will find another option. Somehow." His arm tightened around her.

"Oh God, Armand. Oh God."

Fatigue and emotion finally caught up with Linda, and she sobbed on his chest. Armand wrapped his arms around her, stroking her back. She felt his chest rumble in response to someone asking him something in French, but she still wasn't at the level of fluency where she could understand what was being said without concentrating. Especially as quickly as Armand was speaking.

Another hand on her back. And a second one. Linda raised her head, blinking. Ruby and Gabe stood in the hot tub, on either side of her and Armand. Three other people lingered around the rim, staring down at her and Armand.

Oh God, I've made a scene.

And yet, no one seemed to disapprove or be offended. Concern appeared to be the common expression on everyone's faces, and the other people moved away after Gabe waved them off.

"Are you all right?" Ruby rubbed Linda's upper back soothingly.

"It's just—just—everything." She dropped her head back on Armand's chest, too tired to stay upright.

"Probably shouldn't be alone tonight." Gabe patted Linda's shoulder and sat next to Armand. Ruby remained standing.

"I'm—I'm okay. My family." Linda shook her head. "What a nightmare. You must be thinking—"

Ruby snorted. "You're in good company, Linda. Considering some members of *my* family got co-opted by Philip—your circumstances should turn out better than mine."

"How's that?" Linda turned her head to look at Ruby.

"My Aunt Grace and cousin Jeannie are dead. Jeannie tried to blow us all up, and Grace—well, I don't know what Grace did. But she died, all the same. I don't think your parents or sister are that stupid."

"I hope they aren't—" Linda's voice caught.

"*They aren't.*" Ruby's voice was firm. "Nothing we've seen so far suggests that this is anything more than a straightforward kidnapping, possibly intended to attract you back to the US. Not that any of them—your parents or Sara—are directly involved in bringing harm to you."

"But Clyde—"

"Is not blood kin," Gabe said. "We all have black sheep in our personal connections. Philip. Joseph. You're hardly alone."

Linda shivered, despite the warmth of the water.

"I think it is time we got dressed and had some food." Armand stood and eased her down. "We did a pretty intense workout. Come on. I will fix us some dinner. My place."

"All right," she agreed, too tired to fuss. "But I owe you, big time."

"I'll hold you to that. Just not tonight."

LINDA FELL ASLEEP ON ARMAND'S COUCH AFTER DINNER. SHE didn't particularly notice what she was eating—food was fuel right now, and once she took the first bite of what was definitely delicious, she gobbled it down. And once she was on the couch, snuggled up to Armand, sleep came quickly.

Her phone chime startled her awake in the darkness. *"Justine Martiniere-Atwood."*

Linda shot up, only now aware that Armand was holding her. He grabbed the phone from the coffee table and handed it to her.

"Yes?"

"Sorry to call you in the middle of your night." Justine sounded tired as Linda blinked at the time notification in her screen. 2 AM. That meant 5 PM there.

"That's all right. Is Dad—" Linda turned the speaker on as Armand wrapped his arms around her.

"Found wandering in the woods in the Willamette Pass area. Drunk off his ass, had the crap beat out of him, dehydrated. But alive. And able to move on his own."

"Oh God," she sighed, leaning her head against Armand. "How badly is he hurt?"

"Not too horrible, considering. But between head injuries and intoxication, we may not be able to get the whole story. We think he may have been held at the church camp you told us about." Justine paused. "He may not have been consuming the alcohol willingly. Damn near the edge of alcohol poisoning, and he's been given shots. There's not a lot we know yet—just found him half an hour ago."

Armand inhaled sharply through his teeth. "He resisted intervention."

"Is my mother safe? Does she know about Dad?"

Oh God, if Sara—no, Sara wouldn't. Not to Mom. Would she?

"She's safe, and yes, she knows your dad is all right. There appears to be some complications there as well."

"Oh no."

"Apparently Newsome was not in agreement with your sister going to your parents' house. Either that, or she's resisting his demands that she leave your parents' house. She has requested further security support, and we're providing it."

"Thank you." Linda groaned, rubbing her forehead. "Thank you for telling me right away, even if it is the middle of the night."

"I thought you would want to know as quickly as possible." Justine's voice softened.

"I'd better call. Plan to do something, because if Sara's resisting Clyde—"

"*Don't come back!*" Justine snapped. "Whatever you do. We can handle it without you in the mix, Linda. Still getting things figured out, but whatever happens—Newsome is trying to get you back here. Don't let it happen, not unless you're with Gabriel himself and have a lot of security around you."

"Thank you," Linda repeated.

"You're welcome. Need to go—another call." Justine hung up.

Linda gulped.

Alive.

Armand kissed her temple. "At last. Some good news."

She nodded. "I had better find out what's happening with my mother. But dear God, it's dinner time there. I don't know how drunk she might be." Linda exhaled. "Both my parents are alcoholics, Armand. Functional—until Grandma Jenni's death, at least for my mom. I don't think Dad really started drinking hard until then, either."

"Not surprising. From the accounts I have read, what happened to your grandmother was horrific." Armand snapped on a lamp.

Linda sighed and leaned against him again. "I have to

wonder how much they hid from me. Sara, maybe not much—she was already eighteen, getting ready to go to college, study to be a kindergarten teacher. But the threats—"

Armand patted her shoulder. "Do you want me to leave you alone or do you want me here when you call?"

"Here. And I'm putting it on speaker. Just to make sure I'm not missing a nuance."

He held her as she called.

"Hello?" Sara's voice was guarded.

"Sara! Is Mom—" Linda choked and couldn't say more.

"Vygotsky Security just took her to see Dad. I don't know if he's coming home or staying in the hospital. Mom was in such a hurry that she left her phone at the house. That's why I answered." Sara paused. "She's sober, Lin. And scared stiff."

Chills swept over Linda. Sara hadn't used her nickname for *years*. She had stopped using it after marrying Clyde except when—

"Sare—*are you all right?*"

A sniffle. "I don't know what to do, Lin."

A second use. Not a slip of the tongue.

Nicknames mean danger.

Another quiet code within the Coates family that had been developed after Grandma Jenni's death.

"Oh Sare, what's wrong?"

"I don't know if I want to go home. Things I've heard. Things I've known. Clyde didn't want me to stay with Mom for more than one night, definitely didn't want me to take the kids along, but how could I leave our mother all alone when you're way over there in Europe? One of us has to be here. And I won't leave the girls alone at home. Not with all those politicals drifting through there. I just—" her voice faded into a whimper.

"Oh, Sare," Linda repeated. "Have you talked to Justine?"

Another sniffle. "I don't know if I want to do anything drastic until Dad's safely home. And then there's Mom and Dad. Plus the kids. I mean, Vygotsky's good, but—I don't think *they* will do anything as long as the girls are here." Sara gulped. "Another reason I brought the girls. For my protection as well as theirs."

"*They?*"

"These days I wish I had listened to Grandma Jenni, Lin. Especially when she talked about only two Catholic Presidents and no Jewish ones."

Linda sat up straight, shivering with dread.

Grandma Jenni. Presidential religious affiliations. "Sare."

"Lin. I need to see Dad before I commit to any action." A pause. "I think the girls mean something to Clyde," Sara whispered. "I hope they do."

"If you need a place—"

"I'll know more after I see Dad. And Lin?"

"Yes, Sare?"

"I am so glad that you are still—where you are. Not on a plane here." Sara's voice became firmer. "Not like what was planned."

"You knew." Linda inhaled sharply.

"I overheard Clyde yelling about it. That's—another reason why I came to Mom and Dad's."

"We have to get you out of there."

"*Shhhh! Don't talk like that.*" Sara half-choked, half-sobbed. "Ears. Everywhere."

"Sare."

"Lin." Noises—first a distant buzz, then voices. "Who's there?" Sara's voice quavered.

"Vygotsky," an unfamiliar female voice said. "Bough breaks."

"Oh God, Lin, I have to go, perimeter breach."

"Stay safe, Sare!"

"You too!"

Linda gulped as Sara disconnected.

Before she could say anything, Armand's phone rang. "*Gabriel Martiniere.*"

"Yes, Gabe."

She leaned against Armand's chest, shivering as she listened to him.

"No. Linda knows. Justine called her. She just got off the phone with her sister—there is a perimeter breach at the Coates house."

Silence. Armand stroked Linda's arm.

"Yeah. The situation has become dire. If I understand things correctly, Sara passed on a warning to Linda about the Electric Born—" He raised his brows at her.

Linda nodded.

"Definite. Yes, Linda had her on speaker. And apparently Newsome *was* involved in the attack on Linda. No, neither were explicit. The Coates family apparently has their codes figured out—let's just hope anyone listening is not aware."

A pause. "All right. In the morning. Our morning, not theirs."

He sighed as he put his phone down. "Gabe's calling Justine back to discuss evacuation possibilities for your family, if necessary."

"What a mess." She groaned and buried her head in his chest.

"Worst case, we will try to get them to Canada. Though Gabe does have connections through his mother's family in Mexico as well."

"If they'll even go."

"Why wouldn't they?"

"My mother may not want to leave Grandmother Norma. Sara may have a change of heart about Clyde. And my father—" she took a deep breath. "Dad has always said that he wouldn't leave the United States until he knew for certain who was behind Grandma Jenni's death. Not that he's been doing much to figure it out."

"We will see what the morning brings," Armand said. "Gabe can be pretty damn persuasive if necessary."

She shivered. "But will it be enough?"

"I can't make any promises." He stroked her head. "I wish I could."

Linda groaned. "There's also the discrepancy between what Justine said and what Sara said about her being at Mom and Dad's."

"Not necessarily. It sounds as if Newsome was all right with her spending one night, but after that it became a problem."

"That—and the girls—Armand, what on earth is going on? I thought that while Clyde was hard into his religion and his politics, he wasn't dangerous. But now—he wants *me*. Sara talks like the girls are in danger. And here I am, thousands of miles away, and I can't do anything to help!" Linda sat back up.

"Not by yourself. But you have powerful friends who can help. And that, my dear, is more than you could have done on your own." Armand stroked her cheek.

"I don't know if I'm going to be able to sleep for a while yet. Worrying. Fretting. Fussing." His touch sent fiery tingles through her.

"We could watch a video." But his voice was unconvincing as his gaze locked with hers, his palm resting on her cheek.

Linda's heart pounded, hard enough that surely Armand felt it.

This is absolutely nuts. Completely the wrong time.

I don't care.

I want him. I need him.

She leaned forward to kiss Armand. Hard. His hand slid off her cheek, fingertips trailing along her neck before firmly resting against the back of her head. Linda managed to keep the contact as she shifted so that she straddled Armand's lap. He moaned and his other hand pressed against her lower back.

Their lips parted. Linda rested her forehead on his.

Armand.

Vanilla musk scent. Gray-blue eyes gazing into hers. His *presence*—already soothing, already a comfort.

"Take me to bed," she whispered. "Make love to me. Help me forget this mess."

"Are you sure this is the right time? With everything that is going on?"

"Probably not, but *I don't care*." She shivered, and began to gabble. "I'm scared and worried and you're here and you care and oh God, I want you and have wanted you—"

Armand stopped the jumble of words spilling out of her mouth with a kiss. He guided her down on the couch, lying half on top of her. His lips trailed along her jawbone to that spot between jaw and neck which sent prickles of desire through Linda and made her gasp.

He raised his head. "You are sure?"

"Yes. I'm afraid something's going to happen and—oh God. I don't want to wait. I want you, Armand Martiniere. I want you now, just in case—"

"Me too. Oh, me too," Armand murmured. And then he grinned. "However, we'll be more comfortable in the actual bed."

He slipped off of Linda, then swept her up in his arms.

AFTERWARD, WITH JUST THE ONE BEDSIDE LAMP ON, ARMAND leaned on one elbow as he traced the outline of her lips with an index finger. Linda smiled up at him, savoring the now heavy-lidded, satiated expression on her new lover's face, softer than his everyday look.

"Better?"

"Oh yes," she whispered. "I think I can sleep now. With you."

"Good." Armand turned off the light and wrapped his arms around Linda. She nestled into him.

Safe. Protected.

Perhaps even *loved*.

CHAPTER 10
NEXT STEPS
MAY, 2030

I'M NOT IN MY OWN BED. I'M NOT ALONE.

Linda startled awake, gasping, not certain of where she was.

Then she inhaled. Vanilla musk.

Armand. That's right, Armand and I—last night—

Armand's arms tightened around her. "Are you all right?"

She exhaled and relaxed back into him, nuzzling into his chest. "Just a moment of disorientation. Nothing major."

"Good." He stroked her brow. "Because you did have nightmares."

"I don't remember them."

"I'm glad you do not. You were moaning and thrashing a lot, but settled whenever I said something, or kissed you. I was hoping that meant you went back to a restful sleep."

"Mmm. With you here, of course it was restful." She took another deep inhale of that delightful scent which meant Armand. "Thank you. For everything. For being you."

"No regrets about last night?" His face tightened into blankness.

"Maybe that I should have done it sooner?"

Armand laughed. "How many weeks has it been that we have known each other? Not that long. We did not exactly *go slow.*"

She chuckled in response. "Ruby warned me that *go slow* means something different in the Family's world. On the other hand, you and I have been through a lot in a short period of time. More than most couples experience in a lifetime."

A faint smile touched his lips. "Couples. I like how you are thinking. Alas, we need to be considering certain realities. There is a lot that we don't know about each other yet."

"You know that I prefer tomato juice to orange juice." She grinned at him.

His brows raised. "That is true. And that you like to sketch, and were on swim team."

"I suspect we had very similar childhoods. It sounds like you went to boarding school as well."

"A Martiniere tradition, at least for high school years. Northview Military Academy, same as Gabe and Serg. The girls go to Ms. Rushton's Academy. Both schools have a strong emphasis on learning fighting and self-defense skills on top of academics, and are pretty selective. We are not the only well-off family sending selected members to learn not just regular academics but organization, management, and defense."

"I wanted to go to Ms. Rushton's," Linda sighed. "But Sara and I were sent to a polite Lutheran girls' school that was heavy on marriage preparation. Grandmother Norma paid for it. I think if it had been up to Dad, he would have let me go to Rushton's. He just didn't want to raise a fuss with Grandmother."

And to be honest, he didn't want to spend the money.

"I was lucky," she continued. "Good science instructors, and I was able to participate on a robotics team. That's where I met Ruby—at robotics competitions back in high school. She was carrying the rest of her high school team with her designs."

"Mmm. Robotics team. I never did anything like that. Gabe did rodeo and skiing until he messed up his knee, and I was on the fencing team as well as swim team."

"A man of many talents."

"That is Gabriel, and why he is the Martiniere now, at a relatively young age."

"I was talking about you, silly." Linda kissed Armand. "You also have many talents."

"I am glad you think so. But I am not as skilled as Gabe. Yes, I can organize any messy situation, bring order to chaos. If you need something tracked, monitored, or researched, I am your man. However. If you need something creative—that is someone else's job. Gabe's strength."

"You have different skills from Gabe. You sketch. You paint. That's creative."

Who would have thought that Armand had a slight inferiority complex?

Then again, isn't that you and Sara? Sara's always been the best at what mattered to everyone else in the family, except Dad. And even then....

"Not the same," he sighed.

"*I* think that you shouldn't be comparing yourself to Gabe," she said firmly. "Yes, he's charismatic and powerful. But you know what? That's not something that appeals to me. Otherwise, I'd still be back in the US, listening to Clyde."

Armand chuckled. "I can't quite see you doing that." He rested his forehead against hers. "Oh Linda. You are so good for me."

"Well, the same back at you. I admire your organizational skills. The way you've been caring for me during all my family drama—you *are* a nice person. My family weirdness has sent several men running away as fast as they could—or, like my latest ex, they've bought into the worst aspects of it."

"The Martinieres have their own peculiarities. I had similar experiences with the women I have dated—everything Martiniere was just too much for them to tolerate. Not that there have been many women. I have just been too busy trying to build my credentials."

Linda stroked Armand's temple. He closed his eyes and smiled. "I think we fit," she said.

Armand smiled, then opened his eyes. "Which leads to—where do you see us going? Maybe this is rushed, but with everything going on—"

"I don't know. I like being around you. I'm open to exploring a relationship further, but I'm also kind of scared. I saw what happened with my parents after Grandma Jenni's death. But they were drifting apart even before then. I don't want to be like them. I want the love of my life to last. I want—" she gulped, swallowing hard. "I want someone who cares about *me*. About any kids we might have. Not disassociated like Dad was most of the time while I was growing up. In spite of everything, I think he was disappointed I wasn't a boy."

Armand stroked her cheek. "I know what you mean about drifting apart. That happened to my parents as well. I do not wish it on anyone. They were not each other's first choice."

"That's the situation with my parents as well." Linda closed her eyes, savoring Armand's touch. "I want to know you better —not just as a colleague, but as a lover. Part of a couple. There's so much about you that just—resonates with me."

"Me as well." He began pressing tiny kisses on her cheek, then engaged her lips.

Before long, they were making love.

The second time was as sweet as the first, if not better.

"GABRIEL MARTINIERE."

Armand's phone woke them from a light drowse. Armand held Linda tucked into his side as he picked up the phone. "Yes, Gabe?"

Linda heard Gabe's voice as she rested her head on Armand's chest, even though Armand didn't put the phone on speaker.

"Hope I'm not disturbing you—and Linda, if she's still at your place."

"No, not disturbing anyone." Armand pulled his phone away from his ear to check the time display and grimaced. "Though moving a bit slowly this morning."

"Understandable, given Justine's late-night call. We're somewhat in the same situation. Do you have breakfast plans? Can't call Justine or Linda's family to find out what's going on yet; middle of the night there. But I think we should meet to discuss potential options—*outside* of our regular working hours. Can you check with Linda to see if she can join us?"

Linda looked up as Armand arched a brow at her. She nodded.

"I do not think that will be a problem, Gabe. We will both be there. How soon?"

"Half an hour—mm, no, Ruby's scowling at me. Better make it an hour."

"See you then."

"All right. Oh—tell Linda that her family is fine. There was a scare about an intrusion, but by the time I talked to Justine last night, it had been resolved."

Linda exhaled.

"That will be a relief for her," Armand said.

Gabe hung up.

Armand put the phone down, sighing, and turned on his side. "Sounds like Gabe's going manic on us."

"Going manic? Like manic-depressive?"

"He is not manic-depressive. Just a past history of PTSD and trauma. But when something like this happens, it is all-hands-on-deck, ready to go because he starts sparking off ideas and plans. Doesn't matter if it is Corporate, a security threat like this, or brainstorming new bot ideas with Ruby. Gabe is notorious for pulling forty-eight-hour programming and design stints without rest." Armand ran his hand down Linda's side, to her hip, resting his hand on it.

"I suppose I'd better get up and go to my place, shower and get dressed."

"I suppose," he said, a wistful note in his voice. "Much as I would love to stay in bed with you, we have work to do."

"At least it's not a horrible commute."

"True." He kissed her. "Too early to make plans for tonight?"

"My place," Linda said firmly. "Bring a change of clothes. I'll make dinner. We'll watch some of my movies. Or read. Or something."

"I am sure we can find *something* to do, my darling!" Armand smirked at Linda. She gently punched his shoulder, laughing, before she rose and pulled on her discarded clothing from the night before.

—*Keyed the door to your ID,* she texted Armand before getting into the shower. —*Feel free to come on over. I want coffee before we join Ruby and Gabe.*

—*Then coffee you shall have,* was his response.

Linda grinned and started her coffee maker. —*Don't worry about it,* she sent back. —*Mine's already started.*

—*I feel guilty.*

—*Don't.* She added several heart emojis before she stepped into the shower. At one point, she thought she heard the bathroom door open and close, but the tint on the shower door kept her from seeing Armand clearly.

When she opened the shower door, a cup of coffee sat on the counter, in a Thelwell mug. Linda smiled at the image—a young girl blithely riding a snorting, bucking pony—and sipped from the cup before she dried off and dressed.

Armand sat on her couch, head thrown back, eyes closed as Linda exited the bathroom, cradling her coffee cup. She paused when he didn't stir. Was he asleep? He definitely looked tired— then again, she had taken a moment to put light makeup on to conceal the fatigue showing in her face, as much to make herself feel less tired as well as conceal some tell-tale sagging.

He startled awake and sat up as she walked toward him. "Just catching a quick nap." Armand picked up his cup—one of his, not hers, a big mug with Monet lilies on it. "Ready?"

"Let me top off my cup."

Armand followed her to the coffee maker and held his mug out, a half-pleading expression that transitioned to a real smile that crinkled his eyes and lips as she refilled his cup as well as hers.

"A woman who understands the importance of caffeine," he purred. "I love you."

"Thank you for delivering my cup to the bathroom."

"It is the least I could do, considering you brewed it." Armand exhaled. "All right. Ready to join Ruby and Gabe for breakfast?"

"I guess so. Is this considered a working breakfast?"

"I am bringing my tablet." Armand picked it up from her table. "My biggest regret is that it makes my hands full, so that I can't put my arm around you as we walk."

"Easily solved." Linda gathered her Hermès bag and slid her own tablet inside. "This bag can carry two tablets."

Armand chuckled and put his tablet inside the bag. "Then shall we go, my dear?"

Her stomach rumbled in response. Linda giggled. "Is that enough of an answer?"

"It is one I understand. I am hungry, too." He mimed a sad face. "And here I was hoping to cook breakfast for us this morning."

"Tomorrow. *We'll* cook breakfast," she said.

"I am holding you to that promise."

A quick kiss, then Linda slung her bag over her shoulder and they headed out the door.

It felt different walking down the hallway with Armand's free arm around her waist. The Residence was sufficiently private, especially after they crossed the grand foyer between their wing and Ruby and Gabe's, that their intimacy didn't seem out of place.

"Is this wise?" she murmured as Armand continued to hold her. "Walking in like this isn't going to be an issue?"

"With Gabe and Ruby? No. It *will* mean it's time for him and me to go through that personal relationship questionnaire." Armand eased his arm free to tap in his access code for Ruby and Gabe's quarters. When the door opened, he replaced his arm around Linda's waist.

"I suppose I'll need to go through something with HR."

"Has Gabe been talking to you about us?"

"Yes."

"Then that's been your HR interview."

"Oh."

Linda contemplated that information as they went toward the kitchen. It made sense, but all the same, it was so very different from what she would have otherwise expected.

Then again, everything Martiniere is different.

Ruby and Gabe had a formal dining area separated from the living room by a half-wall, different from the greenhouse space where they had gathered for breakfast on Linda's first day. Linda and Armand passed through the formal area to reach the kitchen. A nook containing a cozy booth that looked out on the Residence's gardens was part of the kitchen. Ruby and Gabe used that for smaller, less formal meals.

Ruby raised her brows as they entered, turning away from the small stove next to the massive commercial one. "Oho. I see you two come bearing coffee cups."

"And they still have coffee in them." Armand tipped his cup up and took a big swallow. "Less coffee now."

Gabe smirked as he looked up from setting the nook table. "Appears that you and I need to have that talk, Armand."

Armand hugged Linda before releasing her so that she could slide into the nook's bench seat. "Yes, Gabe. After breakfast. I need the fortification first."

"Good thing I'm making pancakes, then." Ruby flipped the ones currently cooking.

"You owe me." Gabe hobbled over to Ruby, kissing her neck. "I plan to extract payment for you losing the bet."

"You only beat me by twelve hours! I *said* they would be together by tonight."

"Bet's a bet. I won, you lost."

Ruby rolled her eyes. "As if we aren't doing it anyway, bet or no bet. Check the sausages, will you, Gabe? Linda, Armand, breakfast is pancakes and ring sausage chunks baked in canned peaches and apricots. Not super-fancy but I remember that it's one of Linda's favorites. Figured you might appreciate something familiar with everything going on."

"Thanks, Ruby." How many times had she or Ruby consoled the other with just this breakfast during their college years? Heartbreak, difficult classes, family troubles? One or the other of them made pancakes and ring sausage baked in canned peaches and apricots. Definitely an old favorite.

Linda set her bag at the end of the table and leaned against Armand. He wrapped his arm around her shoulders.

Gabe pulled the baking dish out of the oven. "You have excellent taste, Linda. This is one of my favorite Ruby dishes, too." He placed the dish on a hot pad in the center of the table and turned back to grab the coffee carafe. "More coffee?"

Linda gulped about half her cup and extended it for a refill. Gabe topped off both her cup and Armand's, then Ruby's and his. He eased into the bench seat on the other side of the nook's table, turning so that he could rest his bad leg on the seat.

"Won't be able to get updates on what condition your father's in until this afternoon, unfortunately." Gabe tapped his fingers on the table. "Linda, I'm really concerned about what we've heard so far. I suggest that your family leave the United

States, as quickly as possible. Justine and Donald have the means to help them do that without a lot of complications, while preserving your family's property and financial holdings."

"Dad's been very adamant about not leaving until he knows who killed Grandma Jenni—and brings them to justice."

"I know." Gabe waved his hand. "You've told me that already. I don't think he needs to be there to make justice happen. He needs to talk to Justine and Donald. And Piotr."

"I'll try talking to him."

Ruby brought the plate with pancakes over. "The Double R could be a decent short-term option for your parents."

"At the very least, we need to get Linda's sister Sara and her daughters out of the US, if she's serious about not going back to Newsome." Gabe eased his leg off of the bench so that Ruby could sit. "But Linda, I also want to ensure that your parents are secure, whether that means bringing them here, Canada, or Mexico." He took the lid off of the baking dish and put the serving fork and spoon in it. "Dish up. So here are some things we should investigate and get lined up should we need them…."

EVACUATING HER FAMILY AND LOOKING FURTHER INTO GRANDMA Jenni's death weren't the only topics over breakfast. They discussed the performance of the biobots—had that field test only been just yesterday morning?

It seemed like it had been forever.

By the time breakfast was finished, Linda had a full "to-do" list that required her attention. Once again, she chose to work in the main offices rather than go back to her private one.

Can't call until afternoon, Gabe had said. *Let's get together about three in the afternoon our time; eight in the morning Roseburg time, and contact your family first, then Justine. Let me do the talking.*

Plenty of time to get in a full day's work.

The test bots were still sending back data—they had gotten

through the first twenty-four hours with less disruption than Linda had expected. She reviewed her work on the proximity issue from the day before, then began running sims based on her programming changes.

She also had Armand's interview with Gabe to fret about. Both of them were solemn when they retreated to Gabe's office, and even Ruby seemed subdued.

At least work kept her somewhat focused.

All the same, it was a relief when Armand appeared in the doorway. He grinned as she put aside her 3D sim goggles, waiting until she secured them and was oriented before he strode across the room and took her into his arms.

"All clear now," he said, after kissing her thoroughly.

"I was worried—it's been—" she checked the time. "—An hour since the two of you went into that meeting."

"We had some other things to talk about as well." He pushed a stray strand of hair out of her eyes. "Gabe and I wanted to ensure that there are official records of our relationship, that you are on record as being more than just a Martiniere employee. It gives us more influence should Newsome try another abduction. That is not the usual state of affairs with the intimate contact questionnaire."

"Wait. Those kidnappers were definitely tied to Clyde? Not just based on what Sara said?"

"Over the weekend, McNeil resigned as the ambassador's press secretary and resurfaced back in the US." Armand's face went solemn. "Ruby was finally able to talk to the embassy twenty minutes ago. McNeil left a mess, and there are weird ties not just with the Electric Born, but with old corporate Martiniere Group foes tied to Zingter Enterprises and the Braun family. Major infiltration of the US Embassy. The Ambassador called Ruby, because *their* investigation revealed that you were not the only target. Gabe and Ruby are as well. It is further fuel for finding a means to waive the usual five-year residency requirement for Ruby so that she is a dual US/French citizen. Gabe is already a dual citizen."

"Oh dear."

He nodded. "Gabe and I were talking to Legal when Ruby found out. She told us, and asked me to tell you, because she is still digging into the information from the embassy. She may have more to tell you later."

Harriet McNeil. Electric Born. Clyde. Braun—

Suddenly Linda knew what the answer was to that niggling question that had bothered her on Saturday night.

"Armand. I haven't said anything because I couldn't recall for certain, but there's been something nagging at me. I wasn't sure until now that I wasn't just straining to create a further connection between Harriet McNeil and Clyde, above and beyond her role in the Real Truthers. But now I remember the details. McNeil used to work for the Brauns."

He frowned. "It is not in her bio."

"It wouldn't be. She was the Real Truther courier between the Braun family and Philip Martiniere." Linda shivered. "I over-heard Clyde talking to someone on the phone several years ago, shortly after he married Sara. I think it was Philip himself, at least someone that Clyde was calling Philip. Telling him that the new Real Truther leader was legit because she had worked for Walter Braun. That she had personal connections to his daughter-in-law Vera. I'm pretty sure that was McNeal."

Armand tensed. "Vera Braun and Philip tried to kill Gabe and Ruby. Ruby killed them instead. If that is the case—do we ever have a tangle to unwind."

"I'm sorry I didn't make the connection until now. Clyde talked about her occasionally, but not very much."

"Oh my darling, I am so glad you told me about this." His arms tightened around her. "And this news makes me very, *very* glad that Gabe and I have set up protective structures for you."

"Oh?"

"You are enrolled in the Martiniere Family Trust as a close

relation which—will help your progress toward dual citizenship. Normally, given my level in the Family and that we are dating, not engaged or married, that Trust status is provisional and temporary, dependent upon the duration of our relationship. Gabe—made your rank permanent."

"What does that mean?"

He kissed her brow. "For all intents and purposes, you *are* a Martiniere now, with all the privileges that go along with being part of the Family. That status extends beyond you to your parents, your sister, your nieces. Gabe can call what happens to you and your family a matter of concern for the Family, and bring its full weight down on Newsome. This role makes it easier for us to get your family out of the United States, because they are now considered to be Martiniere Family members."

"Oh my God, Armand. Really?"

He nodded. "A situation like this has not arisen since the nineteenth century. Gabe married Ruby promptly when things blew up for them. But they were also living with Ruby's family, and they had the Double R as a defensible refuge. You do not have that possibility, and while Gabe and Ruby married after a short relationship, they had been together before their marriage for longer than we have." He gulped. "I would marry you right now if that is what it takes to keep you and your family safe. Still may need to do that. But we thought this might be a better choice."

Linda stared at him, overwhelmed. "You'd do that for me? For my family?"

"We have. And I will. You are precious to me, and keeping your family safe—I hear the love in your voice when you talk about them."

"Thank you." She buried her head in his chest.

After Armand left, Linda switched tasks and typed up what she could remember Clyde saying about the ties between Harriet McNeil, the Real Truthers, the Braun family, and Philip Martiniere. When she was finished, she was appalled by just how much information she had managed to overhear.

Linda shivered.

I never realized it was this bad.

She sent copies to Armand, Ruby, and Gabe.

Gabe was first to respond. —*This is incredibly useful, Linda. Thank you.*

—*The Ambassador and I are having serious words right now,* Ruby answered. —*Thank you for this information.*

Last of all was Armand. —*Oh my darling. I am even more worried about you. I did not realize you knew so much. Please stay safe. Forwarding this information to Piotr for Gabe.* Several heart emojis followed.

—*I'm not going anywhere other than the Residence today,* she texted Armand. —*I promise to stay safe.* She added heart emojis.

—*Good,* he replied.

"Lunchtime," Armand announced, waving a couple of cardboard food boxes at her. "I ordered in—now that I know what you usually like."

"I can't—"

"It used to be against the law to eat lunch at your desk here in Paris," he said. "I am invoking that law now. Come on. You need a break. Save your work."

Linda saved her work, accepted one of the boxes and let Armand take her free hand. He guided her outside, into the Residence's gardens. They followed a graveled pathway until they reached a shaded wrought-iron bench surrounded by roses; the warm air laden with a heady fragrance.

"One of my favorite places." Armand produced a small

Thermos from a pocket, and shook out two travel cups. He poured tea into the cups and offered one to Linda.

"Thank you."

Even though Armand had gotten her favorite ham sandwich, Linda picked at it, barely eating half. When she finally put it aside in its box—hopefully for later—and started to rise, Armand gently restrained her.

"You need to take your full lunch hour."

"But there's so much to do—"

"Especially today."

An odd note in his voice made her frown at him.

"What's happening?"

He rested his arm on her shoulders. "Hopefully, nothing major or problematic. But that could easily change soon. The information you gave us makes me even more glad that Gabe and I took those steps to integrate you into the Family structures."

Linda exhaled. It was oh-so-tempting to lean into Armand. To just set everything aside, close her eyes, and take a brief nap.

But what about Dad? Mom? Sara?

Her muscles tightened and she straightened up.

"Shh," Armand murmured. "You can't go full-tilt all the time, dearest. Relax. Lean back. This is a perfect, quiet place to settle for a brief respite from the day. I have set an alarm for when it is time to go back to work."

"I feel guilty taking it easy." But she leaned against him again. It *was* soothing to be sitting here with Armand, inhaling the scent of the roses, savoring the warmth.

"Don't. Because things can change very quickly." His lips brushed her forehead. "Catch your breath. Be here with me. We will know more in a few hours. But until then—"

She raised her head and their lips met in a long, slow, lingering kiss. "Tempter," she finally said, resting her head on his chest.

He ran his hand up and down her back. "Rest, Linda. Save

your energy. We may need to move quickly once we know what we're doing with your family."

"You know something?" She sat back up.

"Nothing yet. But knowing what I do about Newsome, the Electric Born, and some of the others involved as a result of the information you provided—things will happen soon. Rest."

She settled back down into the crook of his arm. He held her tight and rested his head against hers. They drowsed together in the quiet peace of the rose garden, snatching this brief moment of serenity.

CHAPTER 11
FAMILY, FAMILY, AND MORE FAMILY
MAY, 2030

ARMAND SPENT THE REST OF THE AFTERNOON WORKING IN HER office. Linda appreciated his presence, because otherwise her skittering thoughts took her down a pathway of constant worry. Even if he didn't smile when she looked up, just gazing at her new love—the way his blond hair fell into his eyes occasionally, the various expressions he made as he worked—all kept her from fretting. He was a soothing, steadying presence—something she hadn't experienced since Grandma Jenni died.

They had both set alarms for 2:50 PM. When they went off— her chimes, his jazzy notes—Armand stretched, grinning sheepishly.

"Another way we are similar. You use your alarms a lot, don't you?"

"I try to maintain both electronic and paper calendars. Working plans out on paper helps me stay organized."

Armand nodded. "I am wholly electronic, but I have known people who needed all sorts of visual cues." He stood. "Gabe wants us to join him in his formal office."

"All right."

This time they held hands as they walked to Gabe's office. Ruby and Serg waited for them, along with Gabe.

"My phone or yours?" Gabe asked Linda once she was settled into her chair.

"Let's do mine. Less of a shock for them."

"I think video is best," Gabe added.

Linda nodded. She wanted to see what her father looked like after his abduction. Reassure herself that he was *all right*.

"The other thing?" Gabe paused, obviously uneasy. "I—want to tell your parents about the attempt to kidnap *you*. I hope that will provide further incentive for them to leave the country. It's overstepping, but I'm going to be speaking as Gabriel Martiniere, the Head of the Martiniere Family, not the Head of the Martiniere Group. They need to know that you're part of the Family—and that they are, as well."

"Which means they'll know about me and Armand."

Gabe nodded. "I apologize in advance for being the one to break the news about your relationship, because it is so new. Unless you want to tell them first—I'm doing it in the context that you're in danger, so are they, and—" his face tightened.

Ruby raised her brows. "Gabe, remember, I told my grandparents about us before you talked to Gramps, back when we first got together. I think it's fair that Linda gets to tell her parents first about her and Armand. If it's really necessary."

He scowled at her. "Do *you* think I'm overstepping, Rubes?"

"Throwing your weight around as the Martiniere, yes." Ruby waved a hand. "Sure, sure, it's expedient and all that, but you *are not* a Royal Personage."

Gabe rubbed his face. "I'm just afraid that excitement and congratulations might overwhelm the necessary part of the talk. Dilute the impact."

"*Gabriel*." Ruby's lips tightened. "You're capable of presenting important information effectively without overstepping boundaries. Give Linda her space."

"Linda?" Gabe focused on her.

She swallowed hard. "I *would* like to be the one to tell Dad and Mom about me and Armand. But if you think it's better for you to do it—"

Ruby grimaced. "Don't give him that excuse, Linda."

"I'm sorry." Gabe pinched the bridge of his nose and leaned back. "It's just—this is personal to me. My fucking father was responsible for the rise of politicians like Clyde Newsome and the power of both the Electric Born and the Real Truthers. I feel the need to make amends. Especially since I suspect that he might have been somewhat responsible for your grandmother's death."

"You're—sure of that?" Linda's voice quavered.

Gabe nodded. "That's why I think I should be the one telling them. Speaking as the Martiniere, the Head of the Family, taking responsibility for my damned sperm donor's actions. It's entirely possible that we can access records here, using Martiniere accesses, that will provide your father with the information he needs."

"There's still the bringing them to justice piece." Linda looked down at her hands.

"We can only do so much." Gabe's voice softened. "But we can try—and they'll be safer here than there while he works toward that goal."

Armand's hand closed on hers. She looked at him. He gazed at her steadily, unwavering. "Whatever you choose, Linda. I will support your decision."

She drew a deep breath and turned back to Gabe. "I want to be the one to tell them about Armand. The abduction—that part doesn't matter as much. But for me and Armand? I want to tell them."

"Then that is what we will do," Gabe said.

Linda took a deep breath. She released Armand's hand and tried her mother's number first, since she had no idea where her father's phone might be. Her mother appeared, still in night-gown and robe—unusual for Mary Coates, given that she was otherwise a stickler for appearances.

I hope that doesn't mean that Dad's worse off than I thought.

"Oh, Linda. So glad to see you, not just hear you." Her mother frowned at the screen. "Not the clearest projection—is that your office?

"No. I'm not alone," Linda cautioned. "I'm with Gabe, Ruby, Armand, and Serg."

"Oh!" Her mother frowned. "I need to get dressed!"

"Don't worry about it," Gabe said, projecting a reassuring tone in his voice. "Mrs. Coates, we need to talk to all of you. You, your husband, and Sara. If you're more comfortable with wearing something else, go ahead and have them come on screen while you get dressed."

"Thomas doesn't want anyone to see him like he is—"

"Mom, I need to see him. To make certain that he's all right."

Her mother turned her head. "Thomas? It's Linda—and some other people. Linda really wants to see you. Sara, can you come here as well?"

"Let me get Charity's breakfast and settle Prue." Sara's voice was faint, far away, punctuated by baby wails and toddler cries. "Faith! Hope! Stop teasing your little sister!"

"Don't want to be on display for everyone," her father muttered.

"Dad, please."

"Mr. Coates, it's hardly our first go-round with seeing people after they've been roughed up," Ruby added. "Gabe and I are coming off of serious injuries that nearly killed us. I need to have a replacement knee surgery—my second one. You're not going to scare or shock us." She glanced at Linda. *Sorry,* she mouthed. "Not even Linda. Brace yourself—she was attacked this weekend as well."

"What? Lin, are you all right?" Her father popped into view as her mother moved away, peering closely at her. "I don't *see* any marks on you."

"Knockout drugs only, Dad. Felt like a bad hangover without the fun. Luckily, I'm wearing a security tracker and Armand was

with me. I'm under the highest level of security now. But you—"
Linda bit her lip at the sight of her father.

Left arm in a sling. Face covered with bruises. Bandage over his nose and another on his forehead. Strands of hair disheveled and poking out from under a third covering his head.

"I know. I look awful," Thomas Coates said bitterly. "And my head hurts like hell."

Gabe grimaced. "I've had my fair share of times looking just like you do now, sir. No judgment."

"You must be Gabriel Martiniere."

"Yes." Gabe gestured to Armand. "This is my executive assistant, Armand, who is Linda's counterpart. He was with Linda when she was attacked. And next to him is Serg Vygotsky, of Vygotsky Security. Both Armand and Serg are my cousins, so this is all Family."

"Except for us." Her father frowned. Sara appeared in the background, her latest baby, Prudence, resting on her shoulder.

"Oh, you're included in the Family as well." Gabe's tone was light but not flippant, coupled with an enigmatic smile.

"Because Linda works for your wife?"

"Partially." Gabe gestured to Linda and Armand. "Your turn, Linda."

Another deep breath. Armand took Linda's hand again.

"Sara, Dad—I'd wait for Mom, but—"

"Here I am," her mother said, reappearing in dressier slacks and blouse than she would normally wear around the house. "What is it?"

"I'm dating Armand Martiniere."

"What?" Sara exclaimed. "Really? Linda, congratulations."

Her father peered at Armand. "That's fast. But what does your relationship have to do with anything? You two can't have been together for very long. How does dating this man make us included in the family?"

"Because *I* say so." Gabe's voice bore the full weight of his *The-Martiniere-Has-Spoken* presence. "As the Martiniere, I'm the head not just of the Martiniere Group but the Martiniere Family. If I say that something is so when it comes to the Group and the Family, then it is."

"Quite the autocrat." Her father raised his brows. "Confirms what I've heard about you Martinieres."

Gabe shrugged. "We're an aristocratic family association that has kept our Family structures going for several centuries. I take my responsibilities seriously, and that includes protecting my own."

"Which now includes Linda and us."

"Exactly." A thin smile that didn't move beyond his lips flitted across Gabe's face. "Specifically. Linda is Ruby's right-hand woman, which means she's already pretty much close family, as I see it."

"Interesting."

"But there's more to it. Armand's position both within the Family and the Group means that any person he chooses to become significantly involved with is entitled to certain rights within the Family. That includes a share in the Martiniere Family Trust. Now, as you observed, Linda and Armand haven't been dating for very long. But given Linda's work with Ruby, your abduction, the attempt on Linda, and your connections to Clyde Newsome—these are extraordinary circumstances that demand an unusual response."

"Wait." Her father grimaced and shook his head. "Am I hearing you right? Linda has a share in the Martiniere Family Trust, just from her job and dating—this man?" He waved at Armand.

"Yes," Armand said firmly. "Sir, I have fallen in love with your wonderful daughter. To that end—" he raised Linda's hand to his lips, kissing it, then squeezing it gently. "I have sworn to Gabriel that my intentions toward her are honorable. Should something happen to me, the Family will treat Linda as if we *were* married. An extraordinary response for extraordinary circumstances. Something the Martiniere Family is far too familiar with."

"I see." Her father leaned back, lacing his fingers together. "So—for us—"

"You, your wife, your other daughter, and your granddaughters are explicitly included in the Family's protection, along with Linda." Gabe's posture mirrored her father's, except for Gabe's piercing look. "This status makes it easier for us to evacuate you and your family from the United States."

"And you think this is a necessary action."

"Yes. Mr. Coates—may I call you Thomas? Feel free to call me Gabe. These—" Gabe waved a hand. "—fanatics aren't going to stop with just this one abduction—intervention—whatever you want to call it. They'll keep it up until they get what they want. My family is very familiar with the antics of the Electric Born and the Real Truthers."

Her father exhaled, swallowing hard. "Mary—Sara—the grandkids—they need to be safe. They can go. I'll stay."

"I won't leave you," her mother said.

"Mary!" Her father sighed. "All right, then. Sara and the girls. I suppose we won't know where they go?"

"You'll know because *all* of you need to leave, as soon as possible," Gabe said firmly.

Her father scowled. "I'm getting close to finding out more about what happened to my mother. I *won't* leave the US until I'm certain."

Damn it, Dad! This is no time to be stubborn! I want all of you to be safe!

Linda started to open her mouth but Armand clenched her hand. She glared at him and he shook his head, then nodded toward Gabe.

"I am ninety percent certain that I already possess the answers you seek, Thomas," Gabe said softly. "Here. In Paris."

"What are you saying?" Her father's voice quavered.

"Martiniere Group records available here. Archived data from Philip Martiniere."

"You're saying that your father was responsible for my mother's death?"

Gabe winced. "Yes, I'm pretty damn sure that my *sperm donor* played a major role. I don't claim Philip, by the way. Saul Martiniere is and always has been my father. In any case, Philip's records are archived here, where you can dig into them to your heart's content. I've done just enough investigation on my own to confirm that Jenni Coates was just one of a number of activists that Philip Martiniere played a role in silencing."

"I—see."

"How is this going to work?" Sara came forward, still cradling Prudence. "I don't have passports for the girls—and Clyde can object to me taking them out of the country. How am I supposed to get them past Customs? Plane tickets? Airport security? I'm not leaving without my girls!"

"I wouldn't ask you to do that, Sara. We have a private jet. My sister Justine and her mother-in-law are managing the legal paperwork," Gabe said. "While getting you to Canada or Mexico would be easier than bringing you directly to France, Justine's mother-in-law has a lot of experience with helping women in situations like yours."

"How? Who is she?"

"Barbie Atwood. She's the financing and power behind Real Lives for Women. My sister Justine spends quite a bit of time helping her."

Sara's eyes widened. "Oh. *Oh.* Clyde *really* doesn't like her. *Now* I understand."

"Yes. How soon can all of you be ready?" Gabe pulled up a message on his phone, frowning at it. "Justine can have everything prepared in three hours. I'd like to see all seven of you on that plane."

"I don't know." Her father hesitated. "I hate to run—"

"Thomas, I'd feel better. And I want to meet Linda's

boyfriend," her mother said. "Haven't we been subjected to this hellish situation long enough?"

What?

That was the *last* thing Linda expected to hear from her mother.

It seemed to surprise her father as well. He raised his brows and cocked his head. "Mary, I thought you didn't want to leave your mother?"

Her mother gulped. "Thomas, she said some very hateful things to me about your abduction yesterday, as well as about Linda and her work. I—between that and what Sara's been telling me, it's opened my eyes."

"Grandmother Norma is raging about me not returning to Clyde's house," Sara said softly. "She has turned completely irrational about Clyde—it's almost as if she worships him. Dad, she was just plain *awful* to both me and Mom." Sara shivered. "These last twenty-four hours have been like a roller-coaster ride. I don't know who or what to believe anymore—I just want to be safe. And after everything I've heard Clyde say, safety for me is nowhere around him."

Wow. This is—wow. Unexpected. What on earth has been going on?

"We should probably avoid further details until you are in a secure location." Gabe glanced at his phone again. "You will hear from Justine shortly. No specifics from me."

Her father sighed. "All right. I can't fight all of you. And after what those Electric Borners said to *me*—Lin, honey, please. Do your best to be safe."

"I will."

"We'll see you soon," Gabe said. "Thank you. If you don't hear from my sister within a couple of hours—call back. Please."

"I will," her father said. "And Gabe—Gabriel. I'm more comfortable with that usage. Thank you."

"It's nothing." Gabe shrugged. "If I had a daughter like Linda, I would hope that *someone* would move heaven and earth to keep her safe should she fall into difficult circumstances. And I see no reason not to include her family when it comes to keeping her safe. We Martinieres believe in family, and protecting family."

"I look forward to seeing you here," Linda said.

"Oh honey. After what I went through—" her father blinked. "I am so, so glad that you are not within the Electric Born's reach. We'll be seeing you—and meeting your love."

He hung up. Linda exhaled.

"I hope that worked for you, Linda." Gabe sank back in his chair, pinching the bridge of his nose.

"It went better than I thought." Linda looked down, at her hand entwined with Armand's. "There's something more going on. Something they aren't talking about."

"Most likely threats from the Electric Born," Armand said. "But at least they are on their way here."

"At least," Linda echoed.

All the same, she wouldn't feel relieved until she could see her family again.

Too much could go wrong.

Somehow, Linda managed to finish the day's work. Gabe sent a confirmation from Justine that a plane would meet Linda's family at seven that evening, Paris time. Armand lured her into the pool for their regular workout, and afterward, they went to her suite. Linda kept checking her phone for possible updates as she cooked.

"You are going to burn the sauce," Armand said finally, easing her away from the stove.

"I'm just—until I know for sure they're on the plane—"

He took her into his arms. "I know, dear. The waiting is hard." He rubbed her back and she leaned against him. "It will work out." Then he let her go and took over the cooking.

But she noticed that he also became fidgety after they had eaten and cleaned up and seven o'clock Paris time drew closer. They ended up sitting in her office, staring out at the late afternoon/early evening garden shadows, holding hands as they waited.

Seven.

Nothing.

Seven-fifteen.

Linda started pacing. Armand scowled at his phone.

Seven-twenty.

Still nothing.

"Maybe it's just taking a while for everyone to get settled in the plane," Linda said finally, staring out at the garden.

It shouldn't take this long.

Even with little children who might slow hurried adults.

Armand came up behind her and wrapped his arms around Linda. She turned and clung to him, dread tightening throughout her.

"Gabriel Martiniere." Armand's phone.

Linda's gut clenched.

Something went wrong.

Armand snatched the phone out of his pocket, putting it on speaker, no video, holding Linda tight with his free arm. "Yes, Gabe?"

"We have a problem," Gabe said grimly. "No one showed up for the plane. And, somehow, a Vygotsky operative alert was blocked until just now. The message is garbled. Piotr's working on it, but it's clear something unexpected happened. And—" he sighed. "Justine has just gone into labor. From what Donald tells me, it's a hard one. He can't leave her. So they aren't available to help."

"No," Linda moaned.

My worst fear. Now what?

Armand kissed her forehead. "What are we going to do?"

"The pilot had to leave the airport because she was getting

hassled. There's an alternative exit strategy involving Canada. Sending in the special team you've been training with. I need you to lead it because you know the principals, have the connections. You and Linda—come on over. After you're packed."

"We will be there shortly." Armand hung up. He continued to hold Linda. "My love. I am so sorry this came up. I had hopes that this would go smoothly, but these extraction operations always have a high potential for problems. I hope that this is a simple glitch, and it will just be a little longer than expected until you see your family again."

"Do you think they're all right?" She fought back a sniffle. "And why do *you* need to go?"

Armand slipped a finger under her chin, raising it so her eyes met his. "Canadian passport, my darling. And training. That special team is one I have worked with for contingencies like this. There are situations where Family members need to take direct action to rescue people of importance to the Family."

"I want to go."

"You've not had enough training time. You will be assigned to a team soon enough." He tugged at her. "Come on. Be with me while I pack. I—" his voice broke. "Every second is precious right now."

Linda let Armand guide her to his suite. She dropped onto the bed as Armand went to the second armoire in his bedroom—this one secured with a heavy-duty electronic lock. She had wondered about that—just this morning?

Armand tapped the lock open and brought out a backpack mounted on a frame. "If you could hold this steady for me?"

"Sure." Linda held it upright, surprised at how light it felt.

He retrieved several items from the pack, then began to rummage through the armoire, sorting through several drawers and piling his selections next to Linda and the pack.

Medic kit. Protective masks. A second medic kit that carried vials—Armand flipped it open to check each vial. Taser. Pistol. Several items she didn't recognize. Makeup kit. Knives. Several boxed minidrones that resembled some of the base models that Linda and Ruby worked with. Dronecams. Field ration kit. Water containers, as yet unfilled.

After Armand finished retrieving what he wanted from the armoire, he methodically loaded the items into the pack—each secured with internal Velcro or straps. Space remained when he was done. Armand nodded to himself, and turned back to the armoire. This time he selected socks, two pairs of camouflage slacks and matching shirts. Then he exhaled.

"That is it for the pack."

Armand pulled out a set of form-fitting body armor—knee-length pants and short-sleeved top. He tried and failed to smile, the corners of his lips barely moving.

"Need to strip down for this—" He shook his head. "I can't make that joke. Not—"

"Would it be better if I stepped out?"

"*No*. I just wanted to make a crack about *do not get too excited,* but—" he sighed.

"I'm glad you're wearing it. But it looks like it could be uncomfortable in hot weather."

Armand took off his slacks and boxers. "It is lighter than it looks, and vented. I end up needing to go commando—let's hope I do not have any accidents because this outfit is difficult to clean."

"Only one set?" Linda wrinkled her nose. "That could get stinky."

"Uh-huh. It is because I don't need to wear it that often." Armand carefully adjusted the bottoms before pulling on the top. Then he reached back in the armoire and pulled on a third set of camouflage slacks and shirt. He sighed. "Ready to go now."

"Just a second." Linda carefully leaned the pack against the bed and went to Armand. She wrapped her arms around him. The faint vanilla musk scent was there, but the body armor between them—

It will protect him. It has to protect him.

"I still wish I were going with you."

"Next time," he murmured. "Because there will be other times." Armand took her face in his hands, kissing Linda slowly at first, then more urgently. Then his hands slid to her back as he hugged her, as hard as he could.

At last he pulled away. With a sigh, he started to put on the pack. Linda helped him.

Then, hand-in-hand, they walked to Ruby and Gabe's suite.

BITS AND PIECES.

Linda focused on Armand's *presence*, holding his hand as he and Gabe spoke, not paying attention to anything other than Armand.

"Pictures," Ruby insisted when Gabe was done. "Give me your phones."

"Might not be safe for Armand." Gabe's voice was soft, even though it held a cautionary note.

"He has the same level of security on his phone that you have," Ruby countered. "And remember our photo exchange when we got together."

"True. But if Newsome gets his hands on it—"

"I will *gladly* endure any complications that might arise from Newsome's finding pictures of me and Linda together," Armand said.

"Besides, you can show them to my family," Linda said, trying to keep her voice light.

"True."

So. Pictures. Armand hugging her. Them kissing. An individual shot of Armand for her phone; an individual shot of her for his.

Then another urgent kiss. Walking with Armand to the waiting SUV. One last hug.

"I will bring your family back safely," he whispered. "Text you before landing."

"You stay safe."

"You as well."

Another kiss.

Watching his vehicle drive off, with Ruby and Gabe resting their hands gently on her shoulders.

Going back to Ruby and Gabe's suite. Staring at a forgettable video until it was time for her to return to her suite, escorted by both Ruby and Gabe.

The slow routine of bedtime prep. Flashes of memory from the previous night, making love to Armand.

Trying to settle in bed. Staring at her tablet, falling asleep over the book she was trying to read, snapping awake suddenly. Checking the clock.

Finally—Armand's message.

—*Preparing to land. High security from now on. Love you, darling. Wish you were with me. Stay safe.*

She sent heart emojis in return.

But she didn't sleep any better.

CHAPTER 12

LOVE AND SAFETY

MAY, 2030

SILENCE.

No messages in the morning, either from Armand or her family.

Justine still in labor, and no response from Gabe's inquiries *there*.

"You're hanging out with us," Ruby insisted, when Linda appeared in her office. "It doesn't look like you've slept worth a damn, and this way you'll know right away when we hear anything."

Not that they learned anything new throughout the morning. Linda and Ruby worked in Gabe's official office. That seemed to help her focus a little bit.

Piotr Vygotsky sounded increasingly frustrated with each check-in call, audio only due to security settings. "I do not understand what is happening, Gabriel," he said during the pre-lunchtime call.

"How so?" Gabe rubbed his chin, frowning.

"People do not *just disappear* without a trace in this day and age, especially my Vygotsky operatives. Our internal messages—especially that operator alert—do not *just get buried*. Not unless there is government-level collusion going on."

"Which there is." Gabe scowled. "We know that. I also

suspect that it is entirely possible that Philip managed to get at least one infiltrator into Vygotsky. A sleeper, someone you wouldn't suspect at all."

"That should not be happening either."

Gabe rolled his eyes. "Piotr. Really. Keep in mind the Braun and the Russian mafiya ties to those damned Electric Born and Real Truther groups. We *know* that they are involved—and that significantly affects the situation. We probably *are* up against the Feds. Newsome has no reason to love any of us, and given his level of influence—"

Piotr snarled something in Russian. Gabe answered, also in Russian. From the tone, plus Gabe's expressions and hand gestures as he growled responses, Linda suspected that the conversation had taken a significantly obscene turn.

"I can understand about one word in five," Ruby muttered to Linda as she stood. "And most of those—" She shook her head. "Let's leave them to yell at each other. Since there's clearly no news, and it's lunchtime—want me to order in for you? Who knows how long they'll be bickering? Gabe has the Board meeting in here after lunch, so I'm ordering for us anyway."

"No, I have something to eat. I'll get it."

"Meet me in the atrium." Ruby scowled. "I'll work on extracting Gabe. Who knows how long he and Piotr are going to swear at each other about this situation if I don't? As if yelling and swearing will make any sort of difference. *Maybe* I'll get him out of there by the time you get back."

Relief washed over Linda. She had been afraid that Ruby might suggest eating outside. Perhaps even the rose garden.

Please, Armand. Stay safe. For me. For us.

GABE WASN'T IN THE ATRIUM WHEN LINDA ARRIVED WITH HER leftovers.

"Artie dragged him off to the cafeteria. Something about

meeting a new lab team of his, before going into the Board meeting at one." Ruby said.

Linda nodded. Neither of them said much during lunch. Linda picked morosely at the leftovers of yesterday's ham sandwich, not wanting to talk, and Ruby seemed to read her mood, pulling out her tablet to tune into a horse show channel.

After forcing herself to finish, Linda sighed. "Where do we want to work? Your office or mine? Or should we plan to be at that Board meeting? I didn't get a notice."

Ruby paused her tablet and took out her ear buds, scowling. "Lunch hour isn't over yet, and I don't think the Board meeting involves us. I'll check with Gabe."

"I—"

"My private office, at one. I won't unlock the door before then. Take a *break*, Linda." Ruby's expression softened. "I will be *so* glad when Armand is back, for both your sakes." She pressed her lips together, then sighed. "I'm worried, too. I'm afraid that Gabe might be tempted to do something if things dangle too long with Armand and your family."

"What do you mean? Something like lead a rescue mission?"

Ruby nodded solemnly. "That is exactly the sort of thing Gabe would try if he thought it necessary. I don't know what Gabe's discovered about your grandmother's death. He said when I asked that he felt that your father should be the first to know, so he wouldn't tell me anything. Because he knew damn good and well that I would tell you."

"That doesn't sound good."

"No. It doesn't. I just wish—" Ruby bit her lip. "I had hoped that Philip's death would put an end to all our problems. That we could focus on climate change rather than politics. Instead, it's like we chopped the head off of a hydra and it keeps sprouting quadruples of new heads every time I turn around. And for people I care about to be affected is just—damn it, I can't feel sorry about killing Philip. I just can't. I know I should but— it's because of my late father-in-law that your family is in danger. Clyde Newsome wouldn't have gotten this far without Philip's support." She reached for Linda's hand and gave it a quick squeeze. "I'd walk with you, but my knee is worse today. For you to just get started in a relationship with Armand, and to have *this* happen, so soon, so right away—"

"Our relationship would probably have taken longer to unfold if it hadn't. Or it might not even have happened. And that would have been a loss. Armand is—" Linda fumbled for words. "He's not Tony. Or Ollie. Or Perry. He's special."

"True." Ruby closed her eyes tightly for a moment. "Armand is also one of my favorite Martiniere cousins. Same for Gabe. But it just plain sucks that you two have to go through this, so early in your relationship. You didn't have the amount of time together that Gabe and I did before the Martiniere madness kicked in. That just isn't right, Linda. It sucks. I *know* how that feels, all too well." She drew a deep breath. "And I'm fretting because I'm worried about Gabe, the time it's taking for Justine to have her baby, and my knee hurts like a son-of-a-bitch, so I'm snappy. Sorry. Please. Do something that will make you relax. Even though it's a shitty situation we're in. Otherwise, I'll get sucked into the vortex of worry along with you and Gabe. Please."

"All right," Linda conceded. "Maybe I'll go for a walk. You'll let me know if you hear anything?"

"You'll be the first to hear from me."

"Thanks." Linda hugged Ruby.

SHE WENT FOR A WALK IN THE GARDENS, CIRCLING AROUND THE Residence. When she reached the path leading to the section where she and Armand had eaten lunch yesterday, she turned around and walked back.

There was no comfort amongst those lovely, lovely flowers. It seemed as if an eternity had passed since she had leaned on Armand's shoulder in the rose garden.

Twenty-four hours ago.

Twenty-four years, decades—longer than mere *hours*.

Her return route brought her into the Residence's back door, close to the entrance to Ruby and Gabe's quarters. Linda tapped in her code and headed for Ruby's office. It was exactly one o'clock—Ruby came down the hallway and they met at the door.

"What about the Board meeting? Aren't we supposed to be there?" Linda asked as Ruby pressed her palm against the door lock.

Ruby grimaced. "We *should* attend on general principles, as part of asserting my right to attend these functions. I don't feel like fighting for general principles today. I don't imagine you're in the mood for Martiniere wrangling right now, either."

Linda followed her in. "Not really, but—are you sure it's all right? That we're not missing something important?"

Ruby shook her head. "I glanced at the agenda. Nothing that needs our input. It's a quarterly organizational meeting. National division heads. Piotr isn't attending because he's still tracking down his missing operatives and your family. Gabe would prefer that we keep on chugging with the bots rather than fret in the meeting. I'm good with that."

"All right. Any—news?"

"No. Justine still hasn't had her baby. That worries me, but I suppose this is typical for a first child."

"Sara was in hard labor for thirty-six hours with Faith. She didn't want a Caesarian unless it was necessary, and since the baby was doing all right, the doctor went with her wishes."

Ruby rolled her eyes. "That sounds like Justine. All right then. But Armand's overdue with his report, and there hasn't been any further word about your family, either. I grabbed Gabe's phone when he came back from lunch. He won't need it during the meeting, and someone needs to answer calls since

Armand isn't here to do it. So we'll be the first to know —anything."

"Good. I guess."

"Better than nothing. Lance is filling in for Armand in the Board meeting, and I'll page him if we learn anything. He will let us know if Gabe needs us to do something."

They settled in. But neither of them could focus.

"Wish the horses were here and I was cleared to ride," Ruby muttered at one point.

"I'd suggest swimming, but I'm afraid we'd miss a call."

"Nah, I have a waterproof link and I wouldn't be swimming, anyway. Gabe and I usually do our pool exercises together. But if you want to swim to blow off steam, I'll keep you company."

Linda thought about swimming, without Armand.

No.

"I'll have my scheduled security practice in an hour, anyway. I need to salvage *something* from this day." Linda frowned at her 3D sim.

So many mistakes.

Absolutely frustrating. But she doggedly scrolled through her programming, scowling at the code, editing her mistakes, *finally* falling into the flow and being able to concentrate.

Gabe's phone chimed, startling Linda. *"Donald Atwood."*

"All right! At least one concern settling, at least I hope this is good news." Ruby snatched the phone. "Hi Don. Gabe's in a Board meeting. Should be out soon—they've been at it for several hours."

"Baby's here, *finally*," Donald said. "Long little girl—twenty-two inches, seven pounds, fourteen ounces. Justine and little Marguerite Gabrielle are doing just fine."

Ruby winced. "Gabe wasn't particularly fond of the idea of naming any kid after him. Something about ill-wishing the poor child. I thought you were naming her Marguerite Marie. Or Marie Marguerite."

"Justine insisted. Something along the lines of *this baby is already as stubborn as my big brother. Gabriel can just take a flying leap if he doesn't like it."*

Linda stifled a smile. "How can a newborn be stubborn?"

"She was born face up and got stuck behind Tine's pelvic bone," Donald said. "Irregular contractions. Thought it was going to be a c-section for a little bit, but they got her loose. Little Margie wasn't in distress, thankfully. And does she ever have a set of lungs! She was screaming her head off once she was born."

Both Linda and Ruby cringed.

"I'm glad Justine and Marguerite came through labor and delivery just fine. Congratulations, and I look forward to meeting my niece. But *that* image of the baby getting stuck behind the pelvic bone makes me want to run right out and reproduce. NOT." Ruby shivered.

"Eh, not that bad. Sara went through that with Prudence," Linda said. "All the same, it's no fun. And Prue was her fourth baby, not her first."

"I was sure getting cussed out during the whole delivery process." Donald exhaled. "But mother and daughter are healthy and doing well. Any news about your family, Linda?"

"Nothing." Linda tightened her lips.

"Someone or something blocked Piotr's operatives," Ruby added. "No news from that front, either. Last I heard, Piotr was pulling his hair because he couldn't figure out how it happened."

"That *is* a concern." Donald paused. "All right. Need to be back with Justine and Ms. Margie. It sounds like we may be cleared to check out fairly quickly, since we have medical staff at home capable of supervising us. Ms. Margie aspirated some fecal matter during delivery, so there's a wee bit of concern, though given her screaming...I think everything will be all right. Once I know what's happening with the family, then I'll take a nap. After that, I'll see what I can find out."

"Your family comes first. Don't run yourself ragged," Ruby cautioned. "We can handle this situation."

"We both feel bad about the timing. Absolutely the worst moment of all, Linda. So sorry."

"Can't be helped. Babies come when babies come," Linda said. "I know that from Sara's pregnancies."

Ruby's voice softened. "Take care of yourselves, all right?"

"We will. Got to make other calls now." Donald hung up.

Ruby sighed. "All right, so *that* worry is out of the way."

Linda's alarm chimed. Time for security training.

Maybe there would be news of her family by the time she finished.

And Armand. The last report was that he and his team had shut off their trackers and—that worried her.

SHE TOOK THE TIME TO SHOWER AND CHANGE AFTER HER SECURITY training. Her trainer had pushed Linda hard, schooling her in 3D run and shoot sims. Linda visualized each target as wearing Clyde's face. It was effective, but left her sufficiently stinky and sweaty that she didn't want to wait on cleaning up until it was time to swim.

When she returned to the office, Gabe hobbled back and forth, the length of the office, while Ruby leaned against her desk, her arms crossed, lips set in a thin line.

Gabe pulled up short when Linda entered. "Glad to see you're back. We have news."

"Good news, I hope?" Though she doubted it, from the grim expressions on both Ruby and Gabe's faces.

"A missing Vygotsky operative has surfaced," Gabe said. "One of Armand's team, carrying a demand note."

"How much ransom do they want?" Maybe this wasn't tied into everything else, maybe this was just someone who thought they could make some money off of Linda because of her new Martiniere connections.

"You," Gabe said solemnly. "They want you. Escorted by me. In return, they'll release your whole family."

"Nothing about Armand?"

Gabe shook his head. "But since the operative comes from Armand's team—the situation does not look good."

"It's a fucking trap," Ruby growled.

"*Of course* it's a fucking trap!" Gabe snapped. "Otherwise they'd be asking for money instead of me and Linda! The authorities want us to sit tight and do nothing. I'm—not inclined to follow that damn advice. Jenni Coates died because no one in authority took her situation seriously. It would be awfully fucking convenient to have her son's family die as well."

"Gabe, what were you going to say to my father about my grandmother's death?"

Gabe pulled up short, glaring first at Ruby, then Linda. "You told her, didn't you, Rubes?"

"She has as much a right to know as her father. Especially in this circumstance." Ruby set her jaw, facing Gabe's glower.

"Ruby, I—" Gabe rubbed his face. He exhaled. "Damn it. All right. Linda, your grandmother discovered information about Philip's dark money funding of the Real Truther Party, in order to buy himself a Presidential nomination. Complete with a blueprint for assassination of his foes using toxins and poisons. A detailed plan for establishing an autocracy once he got himself into office. Jenni Coates was killed on her way to talk to Federal authorities about what she had learned. It's entirely possible that the authorities she talked to may have betrayed her. That's the piece we don't know yet."

Linda nodded. "Dad has suspected this all along."

"He was right to do so. I've seen the proof in Philip's records, now that I finally got my hands on them. But this adds an additional layer of complexity to your family being kidnapped. I don't know how much of this information Clyde Newsome is privy to. Or to what degree he supported it. I suspect he's heavily involved. I will be interested in hearing what your sister has to say about things she's overheard as Newsome's wife. The Reals and the Borns tend to be careless around their women."

"Oh God. That means my sister and family know too much, then." Linda bit her lip. "We have to cooperate with the ransom demand."

Gabe raised a brow. "Not *we*. *I* will do it, along with a Vygotsky operative wearing bioplastics to mimic your biometrics."

"I'm going, too." Linda crossed her arms. "It's my family."

"I promised Armand that I would keep you safe." Gabe glowered at her.

"And where is he?"

"*I don't know.*" Gabe shook his head. "I don't know if his team is maintaining cover before they act, or if they've been intercepted. Armand usually doesn't surface when he's out on a mission like this, not until he's good and ready. I understand his reasoning, but damn it—Linda, I promised him I'd keep you safe. On my honor as the Martiniere."

"Well, then, it's a damn good thing that I'll be with the two of you, because *I* didn't promise *anyone* anything," Ruby said tartly.

Gabe whirled. "Rubes. Not you too? This is rapidly becoming a very bad idea."

"I'm not letting *you* do this alone," Ruby said firmly. "If that's a bad idea, then so be it. And if I'm going, then Linda should be able to as well, because I want my assistant with me."

Gabe rolled his eyes. "Ruby—"

"Logistics, Gabriel. Neither of us are in one hundred percent condition for this kind of action. We're going to be dependent on the support of others when we do this. Realistically, neither you nor I should be doing *anything* beyond staying here, waiting for surgery, and monitoring the situation. But—we won't do the logical and realistic thing. If you weren't going, then I would be."

"But to risk both of you, my love—" Gabe's voice cracked. "I can't—I have to—"

"I *can't* sit here in Paris while you walk into that den of vipers." Ruby gulped. "I just *can't*, Gabriel. Not knowing if you're dead or alive, not knowing what's happening—I'd much rather be sitting with the rescue force monitoring the two of you going in. And if I'm going, then Linda deserves to be there as well."

They stared at each other for a few moments.

Then Gabe sighed. "All right, Rubes. You win. Both of you are going with me. But—" he raised an index finger. "I plan to talk to Linda's security trainers about her progress. See if they recommend if it's actually her, or a surrogate, who shows up at that meeting site. Then, and *only* then, will I make my decision on that front. Period."

Ruby met Linda's eyes, raising her brows in question.

Linda exhaled. "All right. But I'm going."

"*We're* going," Ruby said.

THE REST OF THE DAY PASSED IN A BLUR OF ACTIVITY.

First came a meeting with Gabe's cousin David, the Martiniere-in-waiting.

"Are you *sure* you should be doing this, Gabriel?" David asked. "This feels like a very bad idea."

"By all reason, I shouldn't be," Gabe sighed. "But David, I feel responsible for settling this situation. Linda's family is in danger because her grandmother learned too much about my damned sperm donor's schemes. I need to be the one to put things right, as best as I can."

David winced. "Understood. Family honor."

"Yes. Family honor."

They proceeded to a discussion of scenarios and resources. Linda wondered at first why she and Ruby were present—and then the discussion shifted to team recruitment and logistics.

"Since it's an issue of Family honor, I'll make a few calls,"

David said. "I'd feel better if we had solid Family backup for the three of you, especially given your suspicions about Vygotsky possibly being infiltrated."

"I will happily take any and all support from the Family," Gabe said. "Reliable members, of course. Kendra and Scott. Jamie. Maureen. Caroline."

Ruby beamed as Gabe listed the names.

That must mean they're good. Reassuring.

"The Scots kin, hmm?" David raised a brow.

"Who better?" Gabe smirked at David. "More than that. Charles has hinted that he wouldn't mind joining in."

"My brother Vincent. Let's see—who else—" David rubbed his chin.

By the time they finished discussing the possibilities, Gabe and David had created a list of ten candidates to accompany them. Ruby and Linda focused on the itinerary while Gabe and David spoke to Family. Ruby murmured locations to Linda as each Family member accepted, so that Linda could plan their travels.

"We'll spend the night at Mist Knoll," Ruby said finally. "I hate to impose on Justine and Donald since they have a newborn, but we could sure benefit from Knowles and Atwood support as well as Martiniere. Seven Family members isn't going to be enough, I'm afraid."

"We'll need that Knowles and Atwood support to bail us out if we run into any complications," Gabe said.

"I'm just amazed that everyone is ready to step in," Linda said.

"We aren't the top aristocrats," Gabe said. "Just the ones who have needed to fight to survive. Some—like my damned sperm donor, who put us into this position—consider themselves to be nobility. The rest of us have needed to pull our weight and keep supporting the Family. That's how we have survived as the Family and the Group for as long as we have."

"But for me? My family?"

"You are Armand's love and Ruby's friend. That's good enough." Gabe's words were slow, heavy, and weighted.

The last three words resonated, sending a chill through Linda.

The Martiniere has spoken.

For the first time, Linda thought she glimpsed what that might *really* mean.

It's a really good thing that Gabe apparently doesn't share Philip's political ambitions. He would be scary.

And yet—someone like Gabe might be the only possible political counter to Clyde and his supporters.

THEN IT WAS OFF TO ARMORY AND GETTING WEAPONS PLUS DISCREET body armor that was heavier than what Linda had already been issued.

"Good thing you have a small bust," Ruby grumbled as she adjusted her top under the supervision of Vygotsky's female fitter.

Even at that, Ruby was done long before Linda, and had time to help Linda adjust her settings.

Weapons. Not just several types of handguns, in varying sizes and configurations, depending on circumstances, but knives, poison and antidotes, toxins and antidotes. A small compliance baton that could be carried in a pocket. Taser.

"Are we going to need all these weapons?" Linda asked Ruby.

She shrugged. "Better to be prepared than not."

AND THEN THERE WAS REGULAR PACKING.

"Five-day supply of underwear," Ruby advised. "Several changes of shoes. One dress pair, the others should be ones you can comfortably move in. Bring period supplies even if you're not due. While your last knockout gas exposure wasn't one that can trigger a menstrual cycle, I wouldn't put it past Newsome's people to try to set one off, either to cause a miscarriage or muck around with your hormones."

"They've used knockout gases with that effect?"

Ruby nodded, scowling. "Justine and Donald have encountered women escaping from the Electric Born who have experienced periods and miscarriages after knockout gas was used on them. Plus it's been used at protests. We have been taking a *lot* of precautions to keep Justine safe during this pregnancy."

Then the specific clothing Linda needed to pack.

A formal outfit. Camouflage, forest and desert both. Slacks and pullover crew shirts for business casual. One set with the Martiniere logo on them; the rest unmarked.

By the time Linda collapsed into a seat on the jet taking them back to Oregon, she was exhausted. But she had trouble napping as they flew, contrary to how she usually behaved when traveling.

It's happening. Now.

Armand, are you safe? Where are you?

SEVERAL STOPS LATER, AFTER PICKING UP THE OTHER MARTINIERES who were part of their team, they finally flew to Mist Knoll. Ruby and Gabe were tense going through the abbreviated Customs and Immigration intake in Portland.

"If they wanted to grab us, this would be the perfect spot," Gabe muttered before they landed in Portland.

Luckily, the intake was uneventful. Soon enough they were back in the air and flying to the airstrip at Mist Knoll—Justine and Donald had just finished installing it.

They piled into crawlers and rode up to the house. Donald met them at the door.

"Welcome to newborn chaos."

Cousin Kendra rolled her eyes. "I should know, after two kids of my own—is Justine up for visitors?"

Donald shook his head. "Just Ruby, Gabe, and Linda right now."

"I want to have words with my sister," Gabe said. "I didn't think she was going to name her daughter what she did."

Donald rolled his eyes. "Do you seriously think you're going to win *that* argument with your sister?"

"You're probably right."

They followed Donald down the hallway to his and Justine's suite.

"Same suite as before," Ruby murmured to Linda.

And then they were in the bedroom. Justine cradled her daughter. She grinned at Gabe.

"Our little Margie is *definitely* strong-willed, Gabriel. Of course I'm going to name her after you."

"You're ill-wishing her," he said.

"Perhaps. Or perhaps she'll soar higher than any of us would expect."

Gabe snorted. "Let's hope so, because she is likely to become the Martiniere after me, unless something happens and David becomes the Martiniere. But he isn't about to put Juliette up for the leadership. So surprise, surprise, your daughter is in line to become the Martiniere-in-waiting, once she's old enough."

Justine froze. "What about yours and Ruby's kids, Gabie?"

"There won't be any," Ruby said flatly.

"Gabriel—"

"We've agreed on that," Gabe said in the same dead tone as Ruby. "No hostages to fortune. And since both you and David have daughters—well, let's hope that little Ms. Marguerite Gabrielle lives up to her name. It's about damn time this Family accepted the notion of a woman as the Martiniere."

"Wow. That's—a lot." Justine gazed down at her daughter. "You hear that, little girl? Your uncle is determined to catapult you to infamy." She looked back up. "All right, Gabriel. We'll do our best to ensure she's up to the job."

"I have absolute confidence in you and Donald."

"Well, it is about time this happened." Justine exhaled. "Want to hold her? Who goes first?"

To her surprise, Linda was the first to hold Margie. She studied the little girl's features, experience born of being an aunt helping her to soothe Margie when she started to fuss.

Ruby, then Gabe, held Margie next. Ruby passed the baby off quickly, but Gabe studied her for a while.

"I think this little girl is going to go far indeed," he said softly. Then he handed her back to Justine.

———

LINDA SLIPPED DOWN TO THE POOL AT MIST KNOLL. IN ALL THE bustle to get organized and out of Paris, she hadn't had time to swim. Her muscles ached. A short set of laps should relax her enough to nap before they needed to prepare for their meeting with her family's abductors.

But she couldn't swim.

Tears overwhelmed Linda as she stood on the pool deck, remembering that first glimpse of Armand the swimmer, just a few short weeks ago. No matter how hard she pushed herself, she just couldn't get into the water.

She ended up fleeing to her suite, and soaking in the tub instead.

Swimming had always been her refuge—until now.

For it to fail her like this—

Armand. Beloved. Please stay safe. Please.

CHAPTER 13
THE MARTINIERE WAY
MAY, 2030

Fortunately, Linda didn't need to meet with Gabe and the team until after an extremely early breakfast at two in the morning, Corvallis time. It was tough enough to choke down anything more substantial than a cup of coffee because of her nerves, not just about Armand but her family. What would it take to get everyone back safely? It didn't sound like Gabe was going to tamely cooperate with the kidnappers' demands.

Which meant—what? While other billionaire families had kidnappings that made the news, the Martinieres never seemed to be one of them, in spite of the Family's size.

Security protocols, not being identified as targets yet, or something about the way that the Family handled these threats?

She still wasn't certain which of those options was the case, but she suspected that if this was a common Martiniere reaction to a kidnapping threat, then they were probably not frequent kidnapping targets.

Linda ended up eating a biscotti, dipping it bite-by-bite into her coffee. A couple of fake cheeze chunks finished off breakfast —the thought of consuming more than that, even fruit, roiled the butterflies in her stomach. At last, she gave up trying to force herself to eat anything more and got dressed.

Wear clothes you can move easily in, Gabe had said last night, in the preliminary briefing while they were in flight to Portland. *We still don't have a confirmed place and time, but should when we meet in the morning. If we can get a location early enough, we'll move before daylight. Make sure you're wearing something you'll be comfortable in should we need to spend some time in confinement. We'll get into additional details once we know more.*

Linda hadn't liked the sound of *that*, but Gabe didn't seem overly concerned about the notion. Neither did Serg.

So *capture* must be one of the contingency plans they were devising on the fly, with options for freedom. Which meant that Gabe was confident they could escape, even if caught. An argument that the Martinieres frequently managed these situations on their own, without resorting to authorities. Which made sense, given the security training Linda had already received, and the fact that Armand was already part of a *special team*.

The Martiniere way.

As it was, in so many instances.

The prospect still made Linda nervous as she dressed. First came her body armor, with the oh-so-convenient hidden pockets to hide her Taser, spray, and knife. She wore her lightest pistol. Then she pulled on chinos, one of the plain polos, and running shoes. She brought not just her Hermès handbag but another of her security kits.

Keep the weapons simple, Gabe had also said. *But have several handy.*

Linda took a deep breath before leaving her suite.

If I'm to be part of Armand's life, then I suppose circumstances like this are going to be more common. I guess I'd better be ready for it.

But am I?

Linda wavered for a moment, then thought of Armand.

Yes.

They gathered in Mist Knoll's basement conference room.

"Completely secure," Donald said, after running a scan. "Part of the design of this office. I always check, however. Never say never, because there can be an exception to the rule."

"Thank you. I can always count on you to be paranoid, Don." Gabe wore jeans and a plain dark blue long-sleeved snap-button Western shirt, along with trainers. Ruby was in almost identical attire, except for her beloved boots.

Donald smirked. "That's why your sister and I get along so well. Like minds."

That elicited a faint chuckle that quickly faded away.

Linda glanced around. She knew ten of the twenty people in the room. The others wore Atwood security insignia on dark-colored uniforms, and were not introduced until it was necessary.

"We've identified the location near Mt. Hood where the demand message was sent from," one of the unknown Atwood security people, a Black woman, said, snapping up a projection that showed a forested area. A nondescript, twentieth-century-era metal-covered trailer house, sat on the property, along with several decrepit outbuildings. "Scans show a nearby underground facility with ten heat signatures. Four small." She tapped one of the outbuildings near the trailer house.

Linda caught her breath. Could it be just this easy?

"Sure it's not a trap, Shanice?" Kendra—one of the Scottish Martinieres—asked.

"Oh, it's quite possible." Shanice grinned. "However, they aren't very good at setting it up."

"They're likely to have secondary forces, don't you think?" Gabe said. "Held in reserve somewhere close by."

"The other option is that they're hoping to distract us with a focus on the hostages, hoping that we'll commit most of our forces to rescue while they attack here," Shanice said. "Which isn't going to happen. I have reserves stationed at Mist Knoll. If they attack here, the fight will be big enough to attract more attention than someone like Clyde Newsome will want."

"Maybe we should move to another base, to keep Justine and the baby from getting caught up in this," Gabe said. "The Double R is further away, but—"

"That is not going to be an issue," Donald said firmly. "Mist Knoll has defenses, just like the Double R. And baby or not, Justine and I are more capable of scrambling to bug out if needed than either your parents or Ruby's grandfather are at the Double R." He bared his teeth in a fleeting grin. "I guarantee that Mist Knoll has some nice little surprises waiting for anything that Clyde Newsome or the Real Truthers want to spring on us. And if they don't like it, they can just argue with the Knowles family and my British passport."

"You're certain about that, Don?" Gabe raised a brow.

"The risk is to *my* wife and child—I'm positive. You would not be here otherwise, Gabriel."

Gabe nodded. "I wanted to make certain. This situation has the potential to get ugly very quickly. The timing sucks."

Another brief smile touched Donald's lips. "If anyone's experienced in dealing with these situations, it is me and Justine. I'll have the lawyers ready and waiting should you need them, Gabe."

"Perfect. All right, then." Gabe glanced around the room. "We're going in. Linda and I will stay back with Ruby, in case this is an attempt to capture us as well. Be careful, everyone."

Silence ruled as they headed for the jet that would take them to waiting backup closer to Mt. Hood.

"Stay in the rig unless we hear otherwise," Gabe muttered over his shoulder to Linda from the front seat. Their team's SUVs halted near a grove of tall Douglas firs in a short, narrow gorge between cultivated fields. The property where they thought Linda's family was being held was adjacent to the gorge.

Their SUV eased into a pullout while the others idled,

waiting for directions. Serg shut off their rig and darkness surrounded them.

Nursery stock fields lined the western end of the gorge—Linda had seen both Colorado Blue Spruce and assorted deciduous trees in the headlights of their vehicle as they approached it. According to the drone pictures taken yesterday near sunset, the eastern end of the gorge, near the property where they hoped to find Linda's family, opened into a thicker stand of Douglas fir that shaded a long, gated driveway leading to that trailer house.

Ruby brought up the comm as Serg and their security slipped out to stand guard. Its pale green flicker illuminated the front seat. Gabe eased over Ruby and slid behind the wheel, tense, ready to drive away if needed. Linda listened to the comm as the rescue team led by Kendra and Scott went over the final plan.

Getting through those fields was going to be a major challenge, but apparently was a specialty for Kendra and Scott.

Then Kendra and her people were off, on foot, working their way to the edge of the blue spruce field. The other SUVs left, taking up stations at intersections near both ends of the gorge to watch for any unwanted activity—*including law enforcement in this particular area*, Gabe had said tersely, during the briefing as they flew from Corvallis to the nearest airport, in Troutdale. *This is the worst damn place to deal with the cops, but can't be helped.*

Nothing happened for what seemed to be forever.

Then the comm crackled, making Linda jump.

"About time," Gabe muttered. "Scott. What's your status?"

"We've got them," Scott said tersely. "Safe. Mr. and Mrs. Coates, Sara Newsome, and her four daughters. One surviving kidnapper, who has a message you need to hear, Gabriel. Bring the SUVs in."

"Doing so now," Gabe confirmed.

He slid to the side, yielding the wheel to Serg. The rest of their security team piled in, giving Linda space in the second seat row but cramming themselves tightly.

Linda bit her lip. No reference to Armand. Did the lack of

mention mean he was all right, or had something else had gone wrong?

But at least her family was safe—at least she hoped they were in good shape. Linda clenched her hands tightly together as they drove the short distance to the trailer house. An automated livestock gate secured by a code lock box barred the driveway.

Gabe raised his brows at Ruby. "Rubes? Looks like we have a job for you to do after all. This is something you're good at doing."

Ruby snorted, and clambered out to deal with the code lock. A few quick passes with a scanner, and the gate swung wide.

"Still have the touch with those security locks," Ruby cackled as she climbed back in. "Easily beaten code."

Gabe shook his head and tried to look severe, furrowing his brows at Ruby. But he couldn't stop the grin that spread across his face. "Surprised you never turned into a hacker, Rubes."

Linda snorted. "Ruby? You didn't tell him?"

Gabe laughed outright as they bumped along the potholed driveway, echoed by Serg. "Oh, she's shared her infamous history of breaking into labs for various reasons."

"Just living up to the Barkley name." Ruby rolled her eyes. "Some would say it's in the blood."

The brief moment of levity faded as they pulled up in front of the trailer.

Kendra and Shanice met them. "No sign of Armand." Kendra's face was tight. "Scott's been interrogating the remaining kidnapper. The others killed themselves—or were conditioned to kill themselves—the moment we broke into the underground holding area—really nothing more than a glorified root cellar. The survivor raised his hands and dropped his weapon." She took a deep breath. "We found the bodies of Armand's task force. He's not among them—and there's one other task force member missing. Cody."

"And my family?" Linda clenched her hands.

Please let them be all right. Please.

She refused to let herself think about what this might mean for Armand's fate.

"They've been roughhoused, but no permanent injury. The children were sedated." Shanice shook her head. "Your sister argued with her captors, and got slapped around for it. I think she's the worst injured."

"Where are they?"

Kendra jerked her head toward the trailer—metal-sided, dingy yellow with a couple of exterior panels missing, insulation bulging out. The wooden deck lacked a railing and didn't appear to be all that solid.

"Your family is in there, Linda. Gabe, we're holding the kidnapper in the garage." She pointed toward a half-collapsed ruin that reminded Linda far too much of similar places around Roseburg.

"I'm seeing my family." Linda hurried to the trailer.

The stairs were wobbly, a couple of boards felt suspiciously soft under Linda's feet, and the doorknob twisted in her hand like it would come off at any moment. Linda swung the door open, wrinkling her nose at the whiff of mold. Then she saw her family huddled around a scarred old wooden table, and forgot about how trashy the trailer was.

"Dad, Mom, Sara!"

Her father looked up from burying his head in his hands as her mother crouched close, her arms around him. Bruises mottled his face, mostly old but a couple looked new. Fortunately, her mother only looked disheveled and dirty, not like she had been slapped around.

He looks awful. Even worse than in the call.

And then there was Sara—

Sara cuddled Prue as the other girls clustered close. Caked, dried blood from one nostril trailed across Sara's cheek. Several bruises marked her face and her eyes were red and swollen. Faith buried her head in Sara's side, trembling, while Hope and

Charity held each other, their eyes widening as they spotted Linda.

Linda went to her parents first, hugging her father gently, then her mother. Her parents held her tight for a moment, then returned to clutching each other.

More affection than I've seen between them in years.

Then she went to Sara and the girls. Linda brushed off the strands of hair covering Sara's forehead, biting her lip as she saw yet another bruise. Hope and Charity flinched away from Linda, but Faith gave her a tiny smile.

"I've been so scared for all of you," Linda said. "So worried."

Sara grabbed at Linda with her free arm, pulling both Linda and Faith close. "Are you sure you're safe? Being here?"

"If I'm not safe with the Martinieres, I'm not safe with anyone."

"Why *did* you return?" Her father exhaled.

"Armand came to help you. And Gabe decided it was time to get involved. Since Ruby won't let him come alone, and she wants me by her side, well—"

"You were safe in France." Her father sat up.

"Armand is missing," Linda blurted. "He was leading a team from Canada to help evacuate you. His tracker is turned off so we don't know where he is. He has a Canadian passport so it's supposed to be easier for him. I'm not going to sit on my rear in France while he's at risk."

Sara pursed her lips. "What does he look like? I don't remember much from your call."

"Here's a picture." Linda pulled out her phone, brought up the pictures of her and Armand, and showed them to Sara.

"Oh no," Sara groaned. "Linda, he's with Clyde."

"What? So Clyde is involved for sure?"

Sara nodded. "Mom and Dad didn't see Clyde and your Armand, but I did. Pretty certain he was the one I saw Clyde shoving into a beat-up truck. Clyde and the church elders were talking in codes, but I know Clyde's codes. They're taking him to the river camp."

"The one next to Grandma Jenni's old cabin?"

"Yes."

Before Sara could say more, Gabe and Ruby came in.

"We have coordinates for Armand's location," Gabe said. "Way up in the back of beyond on Mt. Hood."

"I know exactly where it is," Linda said. "So does Sara. She overheard Clyde's codes."

"Oh *really*?" Gabe raised his brows.

"It's tied to an old wilderness camp on the river," Linda said.

Gabe kept his gaze on Sara, his glower amping up. "Just how do you know where they were taking my cousin, Sara?"

Sara didn't flinch away from Gabe's glare. "Clyde kept Mom and Dad locked up pretty tight but not me and the kids. He said that if I played along and didn't try to run off, then I could still be his first wife." Outrage filled her voice. "After four children, he's ready to get rid of me just because he can't manage to sire a boy! I thought he cared—" She shook her head. "But it wasn't just me. Faith overheard Clyde saying that it was time to pick some huckleberries. She whispered it to me after Clyde and the others took off. She was confused because it's nowhere near huckleberry season."

"She's leaving things out," Thomas Coates said, his voice trembling with exhaustion. "Sara tried to escape, and fought back until Clyde damn near knocked her out cold. Faith almost got away."

"Daddy's *mean*." Faith scowled. "I hate him. I hate him!"

"*Faith*," Sara sighed. "Oh what the heck. She's right. I hoped to keep Clyde distracted by arguing with him, so that Faith could go for help."

"Faith was *stupid*," Hope said.

"Was not! You're Daddy's pet!"

"*Girls*." Linda intervened as Faith and Hope bristled at each other while Charity shrank away from her sisters. "This isn't the time or the place."

Linda turned to Faith, checking her niece. No bruises on her face, but Faith held her left arm stiffly. From the way she flinched when Linda touched her shoulder, it didn't look good.

Gabe joined her. Ruby was right behind.

"Manhandling kids," Ruby growled. "Did Clyde do this?"

"No, it was one of his men," Sara said. "They went with him. The ones left behind were all sworn Electric Born, and—" she gulped. "I thought I knew what was coming when your people —with Linda's Armand—broke in. I was sure we were dead, especially after they killed our rescuers. I tried to hide the girls' eyes so they wouldn't see their death coming…." She swallowed hard.

Linda set her jaw. "I know where Armand is. I'm going to rescue him."

"No you won't," Gabe said. "I promised him—"

"*I'm getting him.*"

Gabe's phone rang. He pulled it out, a quizzical expression crossing his face as he looked at the ID, before he answered. "Newsome. You're on speaker."

"I suppose my *dear wife* and her family are with you."

Linda couldn't help but shiver at the malignant, sarcastic note in Clyde's voice. Her eyes met Sara's.

Her sister bit her lip. "He left us as bait," she whispered. "I know that tone. He's not at all serious."

"Is that really your business?" Gabe's tone was playful, but his brows furrowed and he glared into the distance.

"She's my wife. And those are my kids. I have a right to know, because it *is* my business. They're mine!"

"Real men don't batter their wives. Or allow their children to get hit by their subordinates." Gabe's scowl deepened. "And don't give me that Electric Born bullshit about them being yours. You don't own them. They are their own people."

Clyde laughed bitterly. "I forgot, Martiniere. You're one of *those* pussy-whipped men. Given your history with your father and Walter Braun, it's not surprising."

Ruby bristled but Gabe held up a hand, soundlessly forming the words *no, don't*. She scowled at Gabe and crossed her arms, turning away from him.

"Newsome, let's knock off the posturing. You aren't calling me to play insult games. What do you want?"

"I believe I have one of your prized *Family* members here. Someone who's been playing around with my sister-in-law and future wife."

"What do you want?" Gabe repeated, voice sharper.

"Gabriel." Armand's voice was weak. "I fucked up. They had a mole in my team. Led us right into an ambush."

Gabe exhaled. "You were spotted by a member of Linda's family, so we knew that Newsome had you. Don't worry, cousin. The Family will do what is needed."

"Thank you." Armand's voice trailed off.

"My understanding is that this cousin is rather special to you, Martiniere," Clyde continued. "I've sent some pictures."

Gabe's phone chimed. His lips thinned and his glower intensified as he looked at them.

"So what the hell do you want, Newsome? Enough of these fucking word games and dodging the subject. You haven't bothered to tell me what you want."

"I'm doing more to your cousin unless you give me my wife."

"I'm not going!" Sara yelled.

"Not you, *bitch*. Traitor. Cursed woman with a cursed womb that only spits out girls. No. I want Linda. The sister I should have married."

Thomas Coates went pale. Mary Coates clung to him, eyes widening.

Linda thought she heard Armand faintly protesting. Then a loud, shrieking cry.

"I'll do it. For Armand's sake." She stood up, facing Gabe,

expecting a glower. Instead, his lips tightened into an even thinner line and he nodded curtly at her.

"You hear that, Newsome?"

"Glad to hear that at least *one* Coates woman knows her place. I'll send you the coordinates and time for a meeting place. You bring her yourself. We'll exchange Linda for your cousin. And this time, there *won't* be any Martiniere tricks. If there are any, all of you die." Clyde hung up.

Gabe bared his teeth at the phone once the line was clear. "Oh, Newsome. You do not have any idea of the depth of my wrath right now. No Martiniere tricks? Oh, just you wait. *The Martiniere tricks have only started to happen to you.* Fuck with my cousin? Oh, I am so, so not done with you. I *am* Philip Martiniere's son, after all, and sometimes I can channel my biofather *quite* well."

"Gabe!" Ruby whirled back to face him. "You are *not* going down that pathway."

He shook his head. "Sorry. Just had to get that out of my system."

The phone chimed. Gabe studied it.

"Newsome's a damn fool, to give me the location this much in advance. Unless he thinks he's setting me up for a trap. Damn fool." He spun, surprisingly quick for how much he had been hobbling the past few days. "Ruby. Serg. Implement Option C." He thrust the phone toward Linda. "Do you know this location?"

Linda took it, raising her brows as she recognized the address. "Definitely where we thought it was. By the river. That wilderness camp where Sara and Mom and Grandmother Norma used to spend the summers." She showed the address on the phone to Sara. "Isn't it?"

Sara nodded. "Grandma Jenni's old place is right next to it. Clyde bought it from the developers, through me. I'm surprised he's using the camp and not my property."

"What?" Their father started to struggle up.

Sara and Linda grinned at each other.

"Grandma Jenni's place is in my name," Sara said. "Clyde was trying to avoid taxes. He's not done very much to the property. I've had to keep up the maintenance myself. The girls and I go there every summer, to pick blackberries, huckleberries, and hit the local u-pick farms for canning and preserving purposes." She wrinkled her nose. "Clyde doesn't like me canning in our house. He says it smells. Even though he likes showing off the results."

"So the old trail is still there—probably?" Linda pursed her lips, thinking.

"The girls would know. Faith. Is there still a pathway by the river?"

"Yes, Mama."

"Pathway?" Thomas Coates frowned at his daughters.

"Just because I went to camp with Mom and Grandmother doesn't mean I stayed there all the time," Sara said. "There's a back way into that camp from Grandma Jenni's place. It involves a trail that goes into the river in several places, to keep it from being too obvious. If you didn't know, you'd just think it was a trail between beaches. I'd sneak out to meet up with Linda when she was staying with Grandma Jenni. No one else knew about it."

"Can you pick it out on a map?" Gabe asked.

"If the map is detailed enough," Linda said.

"Then let's make it happen." He bared his teeth again. "Clyde Newsome is about to learn that you don't challenge a Martiniere like he just did. Especially when he brings up *my* past as an insult."

After discussion, they decided the best route was to launch river rafts from Sara's property, and float to a beach just below the camp. Security would meet them at a park further down the river that was close to the airport. Linda's family would wait for them there. Then they would fly to Gabe's grandmother Donna's place in Quebec, unless Armand's injuries were too severe for security's medical team to manage.

To Linda's relief, most of their team already had river rafting experience.

"It's early enough in the year that the river is running high and cold," her father said. "Your defensive suits won't look out of place. And it's the only time of year that river is high enough to be floated."

Lance Helgessen procured river rafts from—somewhere. All the Martinieres came along as part of the team, including Ruby.

"Someone has to stay with the rafts," she said. "And since you won't listen to sense and be that person, Gabe, that's my job."

Gabe tightened his lips, but didn't respond to Ruby as he stood while Lance fitted a brace Linda hadn't seen before to Gabe's bad leg. He had already accepted a shot of something that made Ruby's scowl deepen. The shot seemed to give Gabe more energy and help him move better, but his eyes glittered with a feverish glow that suggested the cost of that injection might be—problematic, and beads of sweat dotted his forehead.

Soon enough, they were in the rafts and floating downriver. Linda opted for one of the kayaks, as a more experienced river runner. Kendra also took a kayak, as did Charles.

First daylight on the river—any river—was usually something to savor, with creatures stirring and the light on the water. This morning, Linda's worry and the need to be as silent as possible interfered with any enjoyment of being on the water, even though misty mornings like this were usually her favorite when rafting. She remained focused on the rafts ahead of her.

Once they landed and equipped themselves, Gabe kissed Ruby. Then he nodded to their force. Mostly Martinieres this time, with a handful of security.

"Linda, do you have any idea where they might be keeping

Armand?" he murmured. "Given the pictures they sent, it's close to an industrial kitchen. Is there a main lodge in the camp?"

"Can I see the pictures?"

Gabe's lips tightened. "They're graphic." But he pulled out his phone, scrolled through it, then handed it to her. "That's the best of the lot."

Armand was naked, tied to a chair, slumping against restraints that included a blindfold and gag. Welts and cuts marked his torso, and there was so much blood—Linda covered her mouth to hide her cry.

Don't think about that now. Figure out the location.

Yellow checkered vinyl under his feet, that had been *old* years ago. Old pine cabinets—yes.

"The main lodge's kitchen," she whispered. Then, before Gabe could take the phone back, she thumbed through the other pictures quickly—all shots of Armand being actively tortured.

"I wanted to spare you that," Gabe groaned.

Linda blinked back tears. "That fucker Clyde will pay for this."

Gabe met her gaze, his eyes hard. "Yes. If not today, then soon. I can wait for vengeance. Armand's safety comes first, for today. Don't get reckless."

"Agreed."

"Lead us to the lodge." Gabe rested a hand on her shoulder. "And Linda, don't get captured, all right? It's pretty damn clear what they'll do to you." He winced. "Bad enough what they did to Armand. Don't let it happen to both of you. Don't be like me and Ruby, where we both got hurt, okay? Stay strong and safe for him, if it's at all possible. Please."

She nodded.

WHAT HAPPENED NEXT PASSED IN A BLUR. SLIPPING THROUGH THE old camp, darker than it was on the river thanks to the heavy tree canopy. The camp was falling into disrepair, brush obscuring pathways. A few cabins looked to be well-maintained, unlike the rest of the camp.

It was weird seeing people Linda had previously known in a business or family setting attacking the guards around the main lodge, deftly subduing them without raising a fuss.

Martiniere training in action.

Grim though the situation was, Linda *was* thrilled to know that the hours spent training could pay off.

The Martiniere way.

Gabe and Linda held back, waiting for the others to give them the all-clear.

"Don't rush when you see him," Gabe muttered into Linda's ear as they waited for Scott and Kendra's signal. "Let Maureen and Charles check to make sure he isn't hooked up to a bomb or something. I wouldn't put it past Newsome."

"Got it."

Once they got the signal to go inside, she pointed to the kitchen, doing her best to ignore the cuffed bodies on the floor, not wanting to look close in case she recognized someone. Maureen and Charles scanned for bombs, followed by Vincent, checking for chemical or biological agents. Linda and Gabe were only allowed inside once they had cleared the main dining area.

And then they were in the kitchen, where Armand—and no one else—was.

"This feels like a trap," Gabe muttered.

Linda clenched her fists, using them to block her mouth so she wouldn't start screaming at Armand's condition.

"Agreed." Maureen pointed to thin filaments leading from Armand's legs and hands. "The sons-of-bitches. Hooked up to his restraints. They thought we'd react without thinking."

"All the same, I don't like this." Gabe frowned. "Lance, check with Shanice. Have her send backup. My guess is that they're waiting for us to remove Armand before they attack."

"Backup's waiting next door," Lance said. "Have them move to cover our escape route?"

"I think that's a very good idea."

Linda kept jamming her fists in her mouth to keep from screaming as Lance and Gabe continued to discuss their next steps.

Armand looked worse than in the pictures Clyde had sent to Gabe. Naked, slumped against his restraints, head lolling, caked blood on his body, long wounds carved into his torso and arms, gagged and blindfolded. Blood covered the floor around him. He raised his head and groaned, doing his best to make out words.

"We see the hookups to the explosives, Armand," Gabe said, keeping his voice calm and steady. "Maureen and Charles are here to disconnect you. Understand?"

Something sounding vaguely like *uh-huh* came from Armand.

"Linda's here."

Distressed moan.

"Talk to him, Linda. So he doesn't move wrong while Maureen and Charles are working." An edge crept into Gabe's voice as the two Martinieres started tracing the lines from Armand.

"I'm here, my love," Linda said, doing her best to keep her voice from quavering. "My parents, Sara, and her girls are safe." At least she hoped they still were. "Don't move. We'll get you loose soon." She continued to talk, not knowing what she said, just repeating words over and over as Maureen and Charles followed the filaments, trying not to listen as they muttered and swore.

"All right," Maureen said finally, straightening up. "It's done."

Gabe held Linda back when she would have run to Armand. "Wait. Let Maureen and Charles release him. It's possible there may still be more."

It seemed to take excruciatingly forever as Maureen and Charles slowly freed Armand, starting with his blindfold.

"Missed one!" Charles snapped as they worked on Armand's wrist restraints.

Gabe grabbed Linda and swung her behind him.

"Clear!" Maureen announced, finally.

Armand swayed and would have fallen out of the chair, except that Maureen and Charles steadied him before Linda could reach him.

"Stay—back—covered—in—blood," Armand gasped, trying to stand up.

"Don't be silly. Blood washes out." Linda wrapped her arms around him carefully. He slumped against her. "I'm here, darling. I'm here."

"And we're getting you out of here. Now," Gabe said.

"Thank you," Armand whispered.

Linda dared to hope they could get Armand safely moved without further incident. He held onto her as Gabe and Charles managed to get soft clothing on him, then eased him onto a foldable stretcher. She clutched Armand's hand, running alongside the stretcher as they hurried toward the rafts. Just get past the big meadow, tree line obscured by fog, then into the trees and the careful descent to the river—

The clicking of weapon bolts as they reached the big meadow told her it wasn't going to be so easy. A group of armed people wearing the uniforms and insignia of the Electric Born's militia arm stepped out of the trees, aiming their weapons at the Martiniere forces.

"Damn it," Gabe growled. "We aren't surrendering. Lance, where the hell is our backup?"

"Right behind them."

"Good. Kendra, call Donald, to alert legal support. This could end up getting nasty."

Their security and the other Martinieres fanned out around

Gabe, Armand and Linda, aiming their weapons at the Electric Born militia.

At least it's not the cops.

Surprising, given how friendly Clyde was with the metro-area politicians.

"Donald has the lawyers ready," Kendra muttered to Gabe. "Just push the button if we need them."

A chuckle, and Clyde stepped forward. "Thought you were gonna get away with it, eh, *Martiniere*?"

Gabe shrugged. "Always worth a try."

"Well, it's not gonna work this time." He pointed at Linda with his index finger, crooking it in a *come-here* motion. "Time for you to know what a *real* man is like, Linda, not one of these Martiniere pussies."

Armand growled and tried to sit up. Linda patted his shoulder. "Stay down, darling. I've got this." She straightened her shoulders and glared at Clyde. "You're married to my sister, and as far as I know, you Electric Borns don't believe in divorce."

"I can put her away for only giving me girls."

Linda put her hands on her hips. "So what's to say you wouldn't do the same to me?"

Clyde burst into laughter.

Gabe swayed. His knees buckled, but he turned as he straightened back up.

Stall, his lips formed. *Keep him distracted.*

Linda nodded sharply as Gabe faced forward again. She spotted movement in the trees behind the Electric Born.

What can I do to keep Clyde's attention? Insult him. Get him worked up so that he'll be so mad that he'll want to hit me.

Clyde stopped laughing. "Your sister was a decent starter wife. But she's not worthy of being a governor's wife, much less a President's wife. She can cook and clean for us."

"And you think I'd go for that? On what planet are you living, Clyde?"

Atwood security forces eased out of the trees, silently

creeping up on the Electric Born militia, who were focused on Clyde and Linda, not watching their backs.

"You're an ambitious woman. Not like your sister. Here's the deal. Give me sons and you'll be my first wife." Clyde puffed up. "I'll make you First Lady of the land. Gonna win the governor's race, then the Presidency. A smart woman like you isn't gonna turn down a winner like me."

"Ha! You, President, much less Governor? I don't think so, Clyde."

"Just you wait and see!" His face started to flush.

One of the Electric Born militia members let out a yelp. Clyde started to turn toward them.

Do something. Fast.

Linda laughed, unable to keep her voice from quavering slightly. "You honestly think I'd get involved with a loser like you?"

Clyde turned back to her. "You'll learn to keep your mouth shut, woman!"

"No way in hell will I ever get involved with you, Clyde Newsome! I'll die first."

"That can be arranged." Clyde aimed his rifle at her. "If I can't have you, then no one else will! Now get your butt over here, woman, or I'll shoot your darling and then you."

"I'd think twice about that threat," Gabe said.

Clyde spun toward him. "I think not. Maybe I should take you out first—"

Security tackled him.

"Get going *now*," one of the Atwood security said. "We'll take care of things. Boss says get out of here, get on the plane, get clear. He'll be able to hold the law off for a little bit longer, but you shouldn't dawdle."

Gabe nodded. "Thank you."

And then they were moving again.

Ruby raised her weapon as they crashed down the slope toward the rafts. She lowered it when she identified them. Gabe headed for her, growing wobblier as he walked, until he staggered into her.

"Damn it, *Gabriel*, you would do this to yourself!" she scolded as she eased him into a raft.

Linda slipped into the raft with Armand. He gave her a weak smile, clenching her hand. She kissed it, and did her best to stroke his forehead gently.

It seemed like forever before they met the others, and were rushed into the plane. She held Armand in her arms as they occupied one of the two beds on the jet, Ruby and Gabe in the other bed. Armand clutched Linda, burying his head in her chest, whimpering until the painkillers kicked in.

Her turn to comfort him.

CHAPTER 14

NOW. ALWAYS. FOREVER.

JULY, 2030

"Turn, please," the atelier said, tapping her lower lip with the pencil she had been using as a pointer as she and her fitters added the final touches to Linda's wedding dress.

Linda obliged. Her office had been turned upside down, it seemed, with her mother, Sara, Ruby, and the Martiniere aunts working together on wedding preparations. And ever since Gabe's Aunt Jeannette had spent an hour with Sara and pointed out to Ruby that Sara was superb at managing social arrangements—Sara, too, was on the Martiniere payroll, as Ruby and Gabe's social coordinator. One less duty for Linda and Armand to manage. Jeannette took Sara under her wing, introducing Sara to her social circle.

The job of my dreams, Sara had said, just last night, after the pre-wedding dinner. *Clyde didn't like me socializing because I was better at schmoozing and flattering his allies than he was. He got jealous of other men quite frequently. What a hypocrite.*

Ruby and Sara returned from hanging up their dresses in Linda's bedroom. Sara was going to be Linda's matron of honor, and Ruby the other attendant. Aunt Jeannette, Justine and baby Margie, and Mary Coates supervised these final fittings for tomorrow's ceremony, with Jeannette occasionally checking in with the men—Armand, his brother Julian, and Gabe—to see how their fittings were proceeding.

Her mother sighed happily. "You are going to be *such* a beautiful bride. But not just you, Linda. All three of you will be just gorgeous."

"It'll be a prettier wedding than mine, for sure," Sara said, wrinkling her nose. "All that brown that Clyde wanted me to wear, and that plain dark church. *So* glad to be done with that."

"I imagine so," Linda said.

Over the past seven weeks, she had seen a side of her sister emerge that was part-old, part-new. Sara had always been secretly rebellious while outwardly compliant to the measures required by their Grandmother Norma. And when she had wanted to resist, before marrying Clyde—the deal to keep their father free from charges related to a false accusation of assault required that Sara marry Clyde.

Those revelations from Sara and their father on their flight from Quebec to France, after Gabe and Armand had recovered enough to travel the rest of the way, made Gabe tighten his lips even more at any mention of Clyde. Linda knew just enough to be aware that there were significant ties between Clyde and Philip Martiniere.

But after a few sessions where Gabe and her father met alone, neither man talked about their discussions. However, Thomas Coates made the pilgrimage from the Hôtel Martiniere to the Residence several times a week, working in an office near Gabe's in the main Residence complex. He had some project going in conjunction with Gabe—just what, she wasn't sure.

The independent spark that Sara had kept hidden from Clyde revealed itself in more detail as the days passed.

"Let's hope the girls cooperate," Sara muttered. Faith and Charity were excited to be part of Linda's wedding, as flower attendant and ring-bearer. Hope, on the other hand, sneered at her sisters and absolutely refused to participate. She had been in a protracted sulk ever since their arrival in France.

"Oh, I'm sure they will," Linda said. "Charity and Faith are excited."

"Yeah, but Hope—" Sara's voice trailed off. She coughed, then continued. "I won't send her back to Clyde. No matter what. Right now, she idolizes her father. But what happens when she discovers what he truly is?"

"Not much you can do about that," Ruby said. "Unfortunately, some folks have to learn the hard way. Just keep working with her. I know this syndrome far too well, from the Barkleys."

"I don't want to talk about anything related to Clyde," Mary Coates said. "Tomorrow's a happy occasion. Let's focus on that instead."

"I'm all for that," Ruby said.

Linda smiled down at the ring on her left hand. Armand had put it there just this morning, during their civil ceremony at the town hall this morning. *She* certainly wasn't in the mood for talking about Clyde Newsome. They would have to deal with the problems he posed soon enough. But for the next ten days—

So much had been done, but there was so much more to do. Establishing political refugee status for her family and herself. Forty days residence in France before she could legally marry Armand. Thirty days of posting the banns for their marriage. Tomorrow's ceremony was exclusively for the family, since the legal ceremony had happened today, in accordance with French law.

We'll treat tomorrow like the real date, they had decided. *For family's sake.*

No church. No priest. David Martiniere would preside, as the Martiniere-in-waiting, since Gabe was already a groomsman. The ceremony would be in the Residence gardens, with Armand and Linda reciting vows they had written. The guest list was small but prominent—mostly Martinieres, but Dr. Green had managed to make the trip.

And I get to see the Martiniere labs, he had chortled when Linda called to invite him. *Two of my best former students have inside connections.*

The other two contenders for the Martiniere Grant last year, Ollie and Perry, had also found a way to attend, along with their wives. Linda suspected that either Armand's family or Donna Martiniere had provided transportation from Canada to France.

No Grandmother Norma, of course. She had repeatedly called and pleaded with Sara to return to Clyde, until Sara blocked her number. When the rest of the family wouldn't let her talk to Sara, Grandmother Norma's pleas became threats. They hadn't heard anything further from Norma after blocking her number, not until last week when a letter dripping with vitriol informed them that Norma Mitchell had disinherited her *unnatural daughter Mary and her twisted offspring.*

That led to one of their mother's now-rare drinking sessions.

Linda couldn't blame Mary Coates for that. As for herself, *she* didn't need anything from Grandmother Norma, and now that Sara was safely within the Martiniere world, she wouldn't need anything from their toxic grandmother, either.

"Done," the atelier pronounced, after circling Linda, studying every aspect of the dress. "Now be careful! I am on call tomorrow, if you need me, but best that you don't."

Linda retreated to the bedroom, Sara and Ruby following, to help her out of the dress.

"How are you going to keep Armand from seeing the dress?" Sara asked. "Or *are* you two spending the night together? After all, tonight *is* your official wedding night."

"We haven't really decided," Linda said. "Today's been awfully busy."

There had been the legal ceremony. Then rushing back to work, in time to meet with Dr. Green and Ruby about the programming glitches in the RubyBot, before Gabe took Dr. Green to talk to the administration at the University of Paris about possible relocation. The afternoon fittings. She hadn't seen Armand since they got back from being married.

They had tentatively planned to swim together this evening. But after that—

"Maybe I need to schedule time for you to be together." Sara rolled her eyes.

"Oh, they'll figure it out," Ruby said. "Besides, they'll have that honeymoon. Starting in Amsterdam—still not sure why the two of you think that's so exciting, unless it's about the coffeeshops."

"It's the light," Linda said. "Armand tells me that I'll understand Rembrandt and the Dutch Masters better after I've been to Amsterdam. And the Rijksmuseum, and—"

"Not my thing." But Ruby grinned. "Just let me and Gabe know if the two of you decide to retire to a life of creating art, all right?"

"No danger of that." Linda laughed. "Neither of us are that good, nor are we likely to be. Hobbyists at best."

"Vienna," Sara sighed. "That's what I really want to see, once I can."

"Doable soon enough," Ruby said. "Once we get your asylum finalized."

Justine joined them, baby Margie on her shoulder. "Wish I could be part of all this, but—" she shrugged. "You would think I'm a prime dairy cow with all the milk I'm producing. Too bad Weeza can't be here."

Silence hung in the bedroom. Justine and Donald had appeared at the Residence three weeks ago. Nothing had been said that Linda knew about, but from the way that they settled into their suite in Ruby and Gabe's wing, it appeared that they were here to stay for a while—at least Justine and baby Margie. Horses had accompanied them, not just Ruby and Gabe's Sunshine and Midnight but Justine's Glory and Donald's Strider.

Louisa had begged off attending Linda and Armand's wedding with the simple statement that *I can't leave Remy or our parents.* Coupled with Justine's unexpected arrival, and Donald's grim demeanor, it didn't bode well for developing events in the United States.

Ruby coughed. "Well, Ms. Margie is certainly thriving."

"Yeah, she's a big little girl." Justine smiled down at Margie.

Jeannette stuck her head inside the bedroom door. "Linda, Armand's here."

Linda bolted from the bedroom, grateful for the excuse to leave the difficult conversation—though difficult conversations seemed to have dominated the past few weeks.

Armand smiled as she came into the room. It wasn't the same slow smile that Gabe frequently gave Ruby—Armand's joy at seeing Linda was immediate, a huge beaming grin that transformed his normally solemn expression into one resembling a child contemplating holiday presents. A goofy grin revealing the part of Armand Martiniere that few saw.

"Are your fittings completed? Ours are, and I think the two of us should take the rest of the day off—*together*." He opened his arms.

"I agree." Linda went into his embrace. They kissed, Linda losing herself in Armand—that lovely vanilla scent, the delicate brush of his lips that became firmer as she responded, his arms around her.

The time spent together during his recovery had confirmed her love for this man. Even though several times she had been tempted to deck him because, like Gabe, like apparently so many other Martinieres, Armand tended to push himself harder than he should while recovering from injury.

Noblesse oblige, Ruby had said about the Martinieres. And it was true.

"Come on." Armand pulled gently at her. "I know just the place for dinner. Let's swim, then eat."

"All right." She turned to go back to her bedroom to retrieve a fresh swimsuit. When Armand would have followed, Linda shook her index finger at him. "Ah-ah-ah. No peeking at my gown before the ceremony."

"I suppose that means you can't see my suit, either." Armand mock-pouted. "And I had so many plans for tonight—"

"No such restrictions for the men," Jeannette said. "Though perhaps there should be."

Laughter filled Linda's ears as she ducked into the bedroom.

SPECIAL DINNER TURNED OUT TO BE A PRIVATE, CATERED MEAL IN Armand's apartment after they swam. Last one, since after their honeymoon they would take up residence in the largest suite in this wing of the Residence. Linda and Armand had gone through the moving details with Sara, Mary, and Justine.

But for tonight—

Candlelight. Champagne. Table decorated with a single, exotic-shaded yellow-bordered purple day lily in a delicate green and blue vase featuring a winged nymph that embraced a tree. A flavorful cold fruit soup, salad with balsamic dressing, fish on sushi rice with a ginger sauce. Ending with strawberries in champagne.

This is where everything began, really.

Armand smiled at Linda as she savored the strawberries. "You look deep in thought."

"Just thinking that this is where it all began for us. Your suite, after I was attacked. You holding me in your arms because I had vertigo and wasn't sure which way was up."

"And you returning the favor after I was hurt."

"During rescuing my family from Clyde's machinations."

Armand sighed and shook his head. "Clyde Newsome. A problem we will spend the next few years handling. Gabe is determined to do something about the man. Both will be eligible to run for the Presidency in a few years. Gabe keeps talking about that possibility." He shook his head again. "I hope it does not come to that."

"A lot can happen in a few years."

"Indeed."

They fell silent. Armand reached across the table and took her hand. "Meanwhile. We can deal with these problems later. For tonight—" he rubbed his thumb across her palm. "We are newlyweds."

She grinned at him. "That we are."

An impish expression came across his face. "There are more strawberries in the bedroom. With whipped cream. I thought we might want to get creative with them, especially since it is our last night in this suite."

"Create memorable moments."

"Absolutely." He eased her up and away from the table. "Because, my dear, given everything ahead of us—I want to keep those moments. Now. Always. Forever."

"Now. Always. Forever," she murmured back to him.

Words that were part of their vows, to be recited tomorrow.

Words that she had whispered to Armand during that nightmarish flight to Quebec.

I am yours now, always, and forever, Armand.

He had whispered those words back to her.

Now. Always. Forever.

Words she intended to be true to—now. Always. And forever.

THE END

NEWSLETTER

Like what you've read? Want to follow Joyce either through her monthly newsletter or through an email feed of her irregular blog posts?

Sign up for Joyce's newsletter here:

https://tinyletter.com/JoyceReynolds-Ward

Or follow Joyce's irregular blog posts on her Substack, here:

https://joycereynoldsward.substack.com/

Interested in a different one of Joyce's universes? Check out Martiniere Stories on Substack.

https://joycef1d.substack.com/p/an-introduction-to-martiniere-stories

BOOKS AND PUBLICATIONS

The Martiniere Legacy

First Meetings: A Martiniere Legacy Short Story
Inheritance: The Martiniere Legacy Book One
Ascendant: The Martiniere Legacy Book Two
Realization: The Martiniere Legacy Book Three
A Belated Christmas Honeymoon: A Martiniere Legacy Short Story
The Enduring Legacy: The Martiniere Legacy Book Four

The People of the Martiniere Legacy

The Heritage of Michael Martiniere: An Agripunk Thriller
Broken Angel: The Lost Years of Gabriel Martiniere: An Agripunk Thriller
Justine Fixes Everything: Reflections on Mortality: An Agripunk Thriller

The Martiniere Multiverse Books

A Different Life—What If?
A Different Life—Now. Always. Forever.
Dreamwalker: Gabriel (to be determined)
The Cost of Power (to be determined)

Goddess's Honor titles currently available (chronological order):

The Goddess's Choice: A Goddess's Honor Short Story
Beyond Honor: A Goddess's Honor Novella
Exile's Honor: A Goddess's Honor Novelette
Birth of Sorrow: A Goddess's Honor Short Story
Pledges of Honor: Goddess's Honor Book One
Return to Wickmasa: A Goddess's Honor Short Story
Crown Anniversary: A Goddess's Honor Short Story
Challenges of Honor: Goddess's Honor Book Two
Cleaning House: A Goddess's Honor Outtake Story
Unexpected Alliances: A Goddess's Honor Rough Draft Outtake Story
Choices of Honor: Goddess's Honor Book Three
Judgment of Honor: Goddess's Honor Book Four

Netwalk Sequence Author Preferred 2022 Editions

Life in the Shadows: Book One
Netwalk: Book Two
Netwalker Uprising: Book Three
Netwalk's Children: Book Four
Learning in Space: Book Five
Netwalking Space: Book Six

Bright Star Fair Witches

Becoming Solo: A Bright Star Fair Witches Novella

Non-Series Titles currently available:

Alien Savvy: A Western SF Novella
Klone's Stronghold
Beating the Apocalypse

Vella Titles:

Falcon of the Martinieres (part of *Justine Fixes Everything*)
Bearing Witness

Beating the Apocalypse

A Different Life—What If? An Alternative Martiniere Legacy Novel

Becoming Solo

A Different Life—Linda's Story: An Alternative Martiniere Legacy Novel

Audiobooks Available:

Alien Savvy: A Western SF Novella

Released from other publishers:

"Queen of the Snows," in *Once Upon A Winter: A Folk and Fairy Tale Anthology*, edited by H. L. Macfarlane

"My Man Left Me, My Dog Hates Me, and There Goes My Truck," in *Black-Eyed Peas on New Year's Day: An Anthology of Hope*, edited by Shannon Page

"Lost Loves," in *All Worlds Wayfarer*

"The Wisdom of Robins," in *Whimsical Beasts: A Campcon Anthology*, edited by Joyce Reynolds-Ward

"The Cow at the End of the World," in *Well…It's Your Cow*, edited by Frog Jones

"To Plant or Pull Up Stakes," in *Pulling Up Stakes: A Campcon Anthology*, edited by Joyce Reynolds-Ward

"The Notice," in *Children of a Different Sky*, edited by Alma Alexander

ABOUT THE AUTHOR

Joyce Reynolds-Ward has been called "the best writer I've never heard of" by one reviewer. Her work includes themes of high-stakes family and political conflict, digital sentience, personal agency and control, realistic strong women, and (whenever possible) horses. She is the author of *The Netwalk Sequence* series, the *Goddess's Honor* series, and the recently released *The Martiniere Legacy* series as well as standalones *Klone's Stronghold*, *Alien Savvy*, and *Beating the Apocalypse*. Samples of her Martiniere short stories/novel in progress and her nonfiction can be found on Substack at either Speculations from the Wide Open Spaces (general, writing) or Martiniere Stories (fiction). Joyce is a Self-Published Fantasy BlogOff Semifinalist, a Writers of the Future SemiFinalist, and an Anthology Builder Finalist. She is the Secretary of the Northwest Independent Writers Association, a member of the Science Fiction and Fantasy Writers Association, and a member of Soroptimists International.

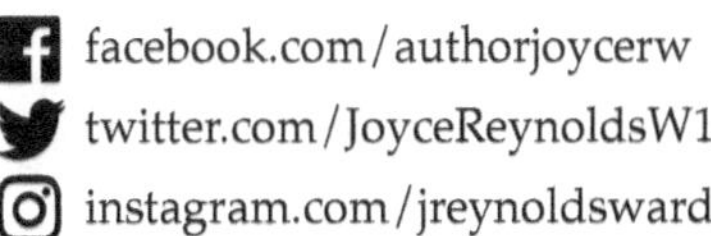

facebook.com/authorjoycerw

twitter.com/JoyceReynoldsW1

instagram.com/jreynoldsward

www.ingramcontent.com/pod-product-compliance
Lightning Source LLC
Chambersburg PA
CBHW030816210726
48290CB00002B/624